THE LION OF DELOS

THE LION OF DELOS

ANNE WORBOYS

DELACORTE PRESS / NEW YORK

Designed by Ann Spinelli

Library of Congress Cataloging in Publication Data

Worboys, Anne.
The lion of Delos.

I. Title.
PZ4.W92Li3   [PR6073.O667]   823'.9'14   74-4196
ISBN: 0-440-04814-1

FOR

WAL

THE LION OF DELOS

CHAPTER 1

The stairs were steeped in gloom but they opened onto a landing lit by a skylight. Spiro unlocked a door and the full flood of a Piraeus morning met us. A blazing sun; the scents and cries of the market below; the tang of the sea. Local color, I told myself with humility, is not found at the Hilton. This is on the spot, and cheap. My room was small with a narrow, board-flat bed covered by a gray blanket. Board-hard, I guessed, too. There was a chest of drawers with mirror, and the bare tiled floor that one finds everywhere in Greece.

"Nice," said Spiro, striking an attitude, head on one side, black eyes gleaming. He had the sexiest hips I had ever seen and he moved them with flippant panache. A sportive flick of the left leg, a flexing of the right. I was enchanted with him. "And cheap," he went on, looking lovingly round the room with an implied astonishment at my luck. "I will charge you only fifty drachmas."

"Fifty!" Where did one get even such a bare little room as this for the price of a couple of packets of cigarettes?

He must have misunderstood me for he said swiftly, "Forty, because my cousin brought you."

Spiro's smile from beneath those heavy, black-lashed lids was a miracle of Eastern guile. I could not help smiling back. He had a smooth olive skin, magnificent flashing teeth, and a minuscule waist. I reckoned him to be about twenty-three years old. I thanked him. "It will do very well." I hesitated. "There is only one thing. It is—er—noisy. Will the streets be quieter tonight?"

"Very quiet, for the market will be closed. Very, very quiet," Spiro assured me, but I was unconvinced. "Very nice. And now," he extended a slim-fingered hand, "you will have this key. You will leave your luggage here. You will go sightseeing? The Acropolis? Or shopping?" For a nervous moment I thought he was going to offer to escort me. But: "I will tell you how to get to Athens. You will go by rail," Spiro said. "Two and a half drachmas to Omonia."

"Omonia Square. Yes, that's the center, isn't it?" I might as well go sightseeing, now. There was nothing else to do. And nothing to be gained by sitting here worrying . . . and wondering. I said briskly, "Is there any chance of my having a shower or a bath? I have been traveling for some time."

It seemed Spiro's hospitality extended to every eventuality. There was a shower room across the landing and plenty of warm water. He was accustomed to travel-stained guests, and I was travel-stained indeed. Four days in a mini-bus, the cheapest mode of travel I could find, sandwiched between a fat Greek mamma with a baby and an unwashed student, had left me with an overall feeling of gray. The calamity from which Spiro's cousin, the taxi driver, had extricated me was really the final straw.

"I think you have missed the boat for Mykonos," he had warned me back in the city of Athens, "but I will do my best." His English was well-nigh perfect and perhaps it was that filled me with misplaced confidence, for had I known the electrifying extent of a Greek taxi driver's "best" I would have given up on the spot.

I am not a nervous passenger. Hadn't I come through Belgium, Germany, Austria, Yugoslavia and the full length of Greece at high speed and miraculously without incident? Nonetheless, as Spiro's flashing-eyed, black-haired devil of a cousin bolted through the gray streets of the city raving at fellow drivers, hurling insults, waving threatening hands that ought to have been clutching the wheel, I found myself wedged in a corner of the car using my suitcase as ballast, and praying to all the Greek gods that I might live to tell the tale.

And we did miss the white ship for Mykonos. Perhaps I should have done my Greek homework better, but before setting out I had omitted to pray to Hermes, son of the great god Zeus and guardian of wayfarers. We missed the *Opollon* by the depth of a rung of a ladder. Two dockers, standing by to cast off, had done nothing to help. Apparently they found it extremely amusing to see a distraught English blonde tearing down the wharf as fast as the impediment of a case and a clutched jacket would allow. Leaning over the rail on the aft deck, two men, one in shirt sleeves and with a villainous moustache, the other a Greek priest in long robes, discussed my predicament with dramatic gestures and blackhearted enthusiasm. The dockers below, grinning, cast off the lines.

"Imbeciles!" My taxi driver, leaping from behind his wheel and dashing up behind me, flung down the gauntlet; the travelers on deck took it up with alacrity, and they proceeded to forget me in a colorful exchange of insults.

I turned my frantic attention to two seamen at the head of the rising gangway but they, bent double over ropes, seemed oblivious to the show below.

A tall man who could have been English was leaning on the rail, a quizzical expression on his face. "Make them let the gangway down again," I cried, reaching out to him in my despair. "There isn't another boat until tomorrow. Please make them stop for me!"

He moved forward, obediently it seemed, speaking to the two men with what I took to be plea on my behalf. But I was mistaken. Perhaps he had not even noticed me, for to my surprise he picked up his bag and, as agile as an ibex in spite of his size, ran down the lifting gangway, the end of which hung now five or six feet above the wharf. The Greeks on deck bit off their argument to shout warnings at him. Ignoring them, the man flung his suitcase down and jumped after it, landing on his feet. He looked up then and our eyes met. His were a curious, tawny lion color—penetrating and hard. And his lean face was hard, too, or perhaps it was just that I had seen him in that frozen moment between danger and release.

"Oh Lord! Oh heavens! Oh damn!" Suddenly I was weak-kneed and shaky; the false hope, the disappointment, the terrifying race to the port had taken their toll. I collapsed onto my suitcase, close to tears. The man walked past me going toward the town, giving me a stare as he went by, and I wondered if he was after all a German, or even a Greek. He may not have understood my request.

The steamer began to move away from the wharf, brown oily waters boiling around the propellers. The scent of port refuse drifted in, acrid and decayed. The game the Greeks love so dearly—the discussion and argument—was over, and the villain with the moustache shrugged carelessly as he walked away along the deck. My taxi driver spat and produced a tiny string of amber beads from his pocket. He shook them, frowning. Clickity click. Clickity click.

"It was terribly kind of you," I said. "I really am most grateful. But there you are, we've missed the boat after all and I shall have to put in a day and a night here."

Worrying about Lee.

Perhaps I, too, should buy myself some worry beads. I eyed them skeptically. They were very beautiful, flashing gold in the sunlight. "Do they work?" I asked, trying to make myself laugh.

The driver grinned, slipping them between his fingers. Click. Click. Clickity click. "They are good," he replied obscurely. "Yes. Good."

I hoisted myself up from the suitcase, smoothing my dusty jeans, thumbing my sticky blouse away from my back. "Do you always drive like that?"

He was immediately outraged. His sooty eyebrows shot up with savage alacrity. Then those coal-black eyes softened. "It was for you," he said innocently. "Only for you, lady."

Perhaps Hermes had after all been watching over me, for at least I was alive and in one piece.

And now, here I was in the rooming house of the taxi driver's cousin who also, opportunely, spoke English. Tourist English, anyway, and that was sufficient. I was close enough to the wharf to be certain I would not miss tomorrow's sailing. I went to the window and looked down, listening to the squabble of noise. This was not a market place as I knew it from my sojourns in France and Italy. Rather, it was a collection of narrow, busy streets full of provision shops, packed with a noisy throng of plump, black-clad women wearing black head scarves and carrying bright plastic bags. Full, too, of burly, busy, heavy-browed men in shirt sleeves, arguing, laughing, demanding, gesturing in their Hellenic way.

Directly below, a small donkey in a pretty hat stood serenely between the shafts of a tiny cart loaded with oranges; huge melons shaded a soft river green; apricots, cucumbers and those wonderful purple eggplants fatter, shinier, grander, more lush by far than any eggplant one saw in English shops. A plump man carrying long, crusty loaves pushed into Spiro's store below and for a moment there was the fragrant scent of hot bread lingering on the air. The babel here was a dozen decibels higher, the pace faster than in any market I had seen before.

I leaned on the sill, forgetting for the moment my urgent need to wash. My attention was taken across the narrow street to a glowing mattress of wool spilling from a shop doorway in skeins of pink, gold, orange, primrose, brown, blue like the Grecian sky and green like Irish grass. Next door a butcher in a white-tiled cave bustled between raw stalactites of carcasses. A tabby, the only well-fed cat I ever saw in Greece, leaned smugly against a giant mincing machine, and in the street a man standing between the shafts of a handcart advertised his wares in strident voice. With a crash and clatter a van, labeled mysteriously δσμη, jerked around the corner. The driver leaped out and began unloading flagons of Pepsi-Cola with the fervor and speed of an actor in a film run at high speed. A little truck with motorcycle engine and klaxon horn came racing into the driveway and blocked the truck. The inevitable furor began.

I smiled to myself and straightened up. I had not visited this lively, sunlit land before, but I had been told life here was lived in a high key. Already, after such a short time, I had been struck by the superabundance of talk, the magnitude of arguments, the crazy gestures the Greeks used. Had not someone said that two Greeks together constituted an argument; three, a revolution? One could see where the notion had come from.

I was turning away from the window when my eyes met a pair of amber ones beneath a broad brow and brown hair that caught the sun, glinting chestnut. It was the man who had so precipitously left the steamer. He had been staring up at my window, watching me. Now he swung away quickly and crossed the street. A flood of anguish poured through me. I could have got aboard, I thought uselessly, now that it was too late, if that man had cooperated. If he had stopped halfway, held the gangplank, forced it down. If I had run forward . . .

It was so terribly important for me to reach Mykonos quickly. I had not the money to fly. I had been expecting to visit my sister in midsummer when my bank account would have been in a healthier state. Two major disasters, a fire in my London flat and the loss of an uninsured suitcase containing nearly all my clothes, had left me temporarily short of funds. It was when I was in this predicament that the cry for help had come from Lee.

No, nothing had changed since the split between my twin and me. Dressed alike as children, educated at the same school following the same curriculum, going on school trips together and generally living in each other's pockets, we were bound close. And indeed, we were happy enough with this way of life, foisted on us as it was by Fate, and an admiring parent who enjoyed the novelty of owning two where others owned one. We found, to our chagrin, however, as we grew older, that male escorts did not seem particularly to care which one of us was available. The pay-off came when Lee began to fall in love with a young doctor who seemed, outrageously, to be enamored of both of us. Maddened by his "If you can't make it, perhaps Virginia can," my sister, in a *cri de coeur*, declared it was time to consider parting.

It was I who was the independent twin; I who had always wanted to visit Greece; I who had read Homer (not, I hasten to add, in the original Greek, but in English in Penguin Classics, for I am not a scholar). I had gone on from there to a small love affair with Greek mythology and a fascination with their vengeful gods. I

still had my schoolgirl photographic memory. I knew
Byron's *Siege of Corinth* by heart.

In my third year at school I had the luck to play
Deianeira in Sophocles' *Women of Trachis* and in my
fourth, when we put on *Antigone*, I had been given a
beard and the magnificent challenge of the harsh King
Creon:

> *You crawling viper! Lurking in my house*
> *To suck my blood! Two traitors unbeknown*
> *Plotting against my throne.*

"Not quite my thing," Lee had said distastefully and
gone on to win the needlework prize.

"Pallas Athena, virgin patron of the household crafts,"
I told her affectionately, "presided at our christening on
your behalf." She shrugged. The Greek myths left her
cold. One day, I said to myself time and again, when
Lee and I are earning, we two will travel in Keats'
Realms of Gold. When I talked to Lee about it she said
indifferently, "It's just a lot of old stones, though, isn't it?
The grandeur that *was* Greece! I'd really rather try
New York." So I was startled indeed when my sister cut
the cord. Clutching the address of an Athenian business-
man who had advertised in the *Times* for an *au pair*, she
took off precipitately for my own Land of Lost Gods and
godlike men.

Lee is artistic and has the temperament that goes with
her gifts. Nobody thought at the time that our young
doctor was the answer to a really discerning maiden's
prayer, but I was willing to concede Lee may have felt
more strongly about him than any of us guessed. I never
knew whether the flight to Greece was her way of slash-
ing out at me, or if in the unweeded garden of her mind
there lay some thought of drawing closer to me by separating us.

Early in the new year, Lee wrote to say someone she

met in Athens had offered her another job, working in a gift shop on the Cycladian island of Mykonos. A little later, when her original employer made a pass at her, Lee, who had always been easily frightened, fled and took the offer up. The man's name was Kriton Fileas. Because he lived in or near Athens, I understood Lee was to run the shop alone.

My sister's letters from Mykonos had been ecstatic. There were lovely white windmills, she wrote, with thatched cones and canvas sails; white, cube-shaped houses; streets of white-ringed stones. A glaring white island inhabited by kindly, hospitable people, and boasting magnificent beaches. She begged me to visit her in midsummer, and I had planned to. Until that recent letter came . . .

I am getting a little worried about my situation, Lee wrote. *I had not realized how isolated I am on this island, living totally among foreigners and not speaking the language very well. It's all right when everything is swinging.* And then there was a phrase that had been crossed out. Perhaps an older or younger sister might not have done it. Perhaps it takes a twin to find a magnifying glass and worry her way through the scratchy lines until the words, which were to send me hot-footing through five countries, became clear. *When something goes wrong . . .*

Under a generous waterfall of hard, limey water that broke all the rules of cheap accommodation by emerging warm, I washed my hair and by ten o'clock was out once more in the streets of Piraeus. It was hotter here than I had expected. Summer instead of spring. Greek women, whose blood was clearly thinner than mine, were wearing cover-up blouses and even cardigans, with heavy shoes. I was barely cool in my sleeveless cotton dress with its open neck and short skirt, my bare feet in thonged sandals. Over my shoulder I had slung my perennial traveler's aide, a suede hold-all containing tickets, passport, money, guidebooks.

A man with a bunch of huge black-and-white feather dusters perched on his shoulder, like indignant turkey cocks, brushed carelessly past. The men here, I had been forewarned, were rough and uninhibited, and I had better watch my P's and Q's. I turned left, uncertain which way I should go, and passed a shop with huge plastic sacks of sweets leaning drunkenly together on the pavement like blowsy, overfed women. Next door were shirts, skirts, blouses and piles of sunset-bright socks spilling out of open stalls onto the pavement. I hesitated. Was I going in the right direction? I did not remember this taverna. It was full of men sitting at marble-topped tables and I could smell the pungent scent of coffee and hear a roar of talk. I also felt I hadn't passed these coils of shining nylon rope—apricot and pearl-white—strung from an overhead bar.

I turned about. Yes, I had come the wrong way, for there was the fruit stall I remembered, lying farther back with its cherries black as a night sky, and some blood red; its bunches of curly-bearded garlic; peaches, soft pink and gold; unrecognizable greens; and its two salesmen shouting their wares in strident Greek voices. Yes, of course, the railway station had to lie in the opposite direction. I passed the doorway of my lodgings and the shop.

"Good-bye, Miss," called Spiro, rushing out from behind his mountain of packaged display goods and striking a pose on his Pentelic marble step.

"Good-bye," I called, "and thanks." I swung away, then found myself doing a double take. A man had emerged from the passage that led to my room. A man with square shoulders and brown hair that glinted in the sun. And he was walking in the same direction as I. Walking with purpose and intent.

Momentarily I felt faintly chilled, and then I thought:

why not? Spiro lets rooms. I mingled with the jostling market crowd and forgot him in the excitement of a day's sightseeing in the violet-crowned city of Pericles. I could see the station now, looming beyond an opening in the narrow streets. With my eyes momentarily diverted I bumped into a priest thoughtfully admiring a bundle of fat chickens, their pink, headless necks drooping over yellow plastic baskets. "Sorry," I gasped, extricating myself from his robes and his not inconsiderable bulk. He said something apologetic in Greek, steadied me, and I went on my way more slowly and certainly with more care. I paused to look again. This market fascinated me, for I had never been in such a close-packed, lusty, brilliant, noisy and, yes, friendly scene. A thin fishmonger in dark-blue apron approached me. "You wish some—" and then his English ran out. He gestured across the width of his shop; sardines, their metallic glitter undimmed by the awning's shade; red mullet; pink squid, their tentacles drooping like soggy ribbons; pale prawns on a marble slab.

I smiled at him and shook my head.

It was on the Acropolis that I saw the man again. I was standing between Ictinus' untrue but optically even Doric columns on the Parthenon, measuring them with my outstretched arms. My gaze was on the gray ruins backed by a white-hot sky when I caught sight of him standing with one foot braced against a marble segment that once, before the holocaust of that accursed Venetian shell, had been a section of this lovely temple. He was watching me, a faintly puzzled smile playing about his rather hard mouth. My arms dropped and I felt my muscles tighten with fright. Then I said firmly to myself: *Everyone comes to the Acropolis.* And yet my heart beat faster for I knew instinctively that this man was following me. He had jumped off the boat because I was left behind. He had followed me to Spiro's, from

the port of Piraeus to Omonia Square, and thence to the
Acropolis. I did not stop to ask myself why, but only
where I could lose him. Below, and a little to the north,
ancient Athens and the flea market lay huddled.
Though I had not yet been there, I had studied the
map and knew how to find it. At this hour just before
midday, the narrow, tortuous streets would be teeming
with shopkeepers and tourists. From what I had heard it
would take a tracker dog to find a girl there. Of course,
if the man had taken a room at my lodgings I was going
to come up against him on my return if that was what he
had determined. But I did have a friend of sorts in
Spiro, the taxi driver's cousin; someone who spoke English and to whom I might turn in an emergency. For the
rest, it was a strange city where hiding places could
be discovered only accidentally and where there was one
thing of which I could be absolutely certain: no one
cared.

I took a flying leap from the base of the goddess
Athena's temple, landing on rough ground among a scat-
tering of collapsed marble blocks and pieces. Brushing
the limestone dust from my knees, I turned and fled toward the majestic Doric and Ionic columns that marked
the Propylaea. A party of slow-moving Americans with
their guide stood gazing in silent awe upon the steps.
Breathlessly, I skirted them, lost my balance and came
skidding up against the base of the Temple of Nike
which I had passed before. I saw it now through a fuzz
of fear, and behind it the Mycenaean fortifications.

More steps, and blessedly, camouflage in the guise of
another guided party. I slipped through them and out
by the Beule Gate, then swung right, down the hill. There
was a stationary row of giant tourist buses and a rabble
of tourists, cameras at the ready. I melted thankfully
among them, casting an anxious look behind. There was
no tall, broad figure with sun-bright hair. I stayed a
moment to get my breath and wipe the perspiration

from my brow. The heat enveloped me like a white-hot cloak. Away below to my left lay the Doric Theseion I had intended to view. Instead, I ran on and took those marble steps two at a time, leaving the limestone plateau as speedily as any Athenian fleeing from the mighty Persian armies of the past.

"Watch it in Omonia Square," a well-traveled friend had warned me. "You've got to go there because it's the center, but there are always a million men gathered on a corner outside a bar, arguing. It's hell for a girl on her own. I was propositioned four times before I got past."

It seemed likely that the whole of Greece was hell for a girl on her own, I thought, as I melted into the pushing, swaying, lively crowds. Perhaps it was only something like this teeming activity that bothered Lee? She had never been very good at looking after herself.

Perhaps . . .

And yet, I knew in my heart the problem had to be more serious than that.

CHAPTER 2

Even at seven o'clock in the evening it was still hot. I had found a square called, on my map, Victorias Place, but, on a sign, I read: ΠΛΑΤΕΙΑ ΚΥΡΙΑΚΟΥ. Colored awnings spread themselves like the decor of a dozen country weddings beneath a shower of acacia trees. I sat down thankfully in a metal chair with orange plastic cushions and surreptitiously slid my dusty, swollen feet from their sandals. A waiter came and carefully wiped my small blue table. I ordered one of those tiny Greek coffees that arrive inevitably with a glass of water. Water like wine, the guidebooks said, and showed pictures of people drinking down long draughts of it on the slopes of Mount Olympus, home of the gods. Here in dusty Athens perhaps the gods did not care, for it tasted a little of iodine.

All around me the talk bubbled, swelled, exploded. Young men, old men, young women and a few older women sat closely packed around the tables, saying what they had to say with an energy and verve that bewildered and amazed me. The volume of noise rose, thickened, died away a little, lifted and swelled to fill the square. One could actually feel this noise beating against the senses. One could almost see the talk. A nation of talkers who had to use worry beads when there was no one to talk to, in order to ward off unwelcome tranquility. Entering an Athenian square was like entering a cocktail party of extroverts in a small, packed room at home.

There was an underground exit in front of me, prettily disguised by iron railings, and a mushrooming of striped umbrellas attached to chairs where shoeshines were doing a brisk trade. Over on my right a battling centaur streaked in pigeon white rose above the low trees on a marble plinth. I gazed at it musing. One of the lamps in the awning above my head was angled to shine across a corner of my table so that people sauntering past were lit alternately in gold and gloom. Someone paused beside me. I glanced up and found myself looking square into a pair of familiar eyes. For one moment my mind must have gone blank with shock for I only remember the aftermath of the violence of my reaction. I had risen and taken a leap backward, yet I was still holding the chair for support, and it had begun to fall.

"Hello," my pursuer greeted me disarmingly. "Aren't you the girl who missed the *Opollon* this morning?" The chair fell and he grabbed it. He grabbed me, too. I had been seated on the outskirts of the crowd next to a scalloped iron fence that cordoned off the grass. I had caught my foot in the fence and would have fallen but for his ready hand. He smiled, inexplicably incurious. I managed a faintly apologetic, if panicky, smile in return. We were after all, I told myself breathlessly, surrounded by people who had nothing else to do but watch. And a man cannot murder, abduct or rape a girl in full view of several hundred pairs of eyes. Or can he?

My heart was pumping with the strength and speed of a pile driver. I'll swear I heard it over the roar of the chatter round us.

"Do sit down," the man said. And then: "Do you mind if I join you?" He was English, if one could judge by a casually correct enunciation that few foreigners achieve. My heartbeats steadied. I lowered myself warily back into the orange chair.

A wave of new arrivals erupted from the underground, claiming the man's casual attention, and I had a moment's respite to think. Surely this meeting must be accidental! Is chance so quixotic, though? How many times had I checked as I spun around the snaking bends of the Acropolis this morning? If he had been following me when I launched myself into the teeming sea of loiterers in the Plaka he would certainly have lost sight of me within seconds. The careful looks I cast behind me during the afternoon had all reassured me I was alone.

He turned his attention back to me and I tried an old shock tactic that had been known to work. I asked him bluntly, "Were you following me?"

He smiled. "One doesn't often see such a beautiful girl on her own."

It was the classic politesse of his reply that told me the truth. He had been on my trail and evidently, now that the day was over, it was of no great importance whether I knew. "It's nice to have run up against you again," he said, settling himself comfortably. He had long legs. He looked beneath the table, finding a place for them. I eyed him warily. At close range he was very attractive. Those rather exceptional eyes were fringed with short, very thick, dark lashes. He had a thin face with jutting cheekbones and although he seemed English he had the Greek profile, the classical one of the pediments; forehead to nose in a straightish line; a mouth that was not so hard after all, but firm and precisely rounded. If he was indeed English, then he was English with a difference. I could not make up my mind whether or not to get up and go.

"I see you're drinking the Greek coffee," he commented. "You've accustomed yourself to it. Some people never learn to cope with the grains." He spoke as though he took me for an expatriate.

I said, "Actually, although this is the first time I've ever tasted it, I rather think I like it."

He gave me a long, cool look of appraisal with a touch of cynicism in it. A look such as my twin gives me when she is going to say, "Come off it, Virginia." I wondered why. The waiter appeared and the man ordered German beer. Chatter that had seemed to cease throughout the preceding strained moments pounded once more against my ears. Young people rose, still talking; others moved in, arguing and gesticulating. On the pavement there was a yellow kiosk hung with picture postcards. A running stream of people made use of its telephone. Two boys on motor bikes sailed confidently in to the curb, revved their engines into a final devilish roar, then silenced them, and parking, strutted peacock-like into the square, thumbs down in pockets, jeans tight against their slim bellies.

"What did you do this afternoon?" the man inquired, not quite casually enough to mask the fact that he was probing with intention.

"The sights," I told him, watching his face. "The normal tourist places. I went as far as I could—the Archeological Museum, the Stadium, the Royal Palace, Hadrian's Arch, the Temple of Olympian Zeus. Oh, and one or two Byzantine churches that I found in the area."

He leaned back in his chair, surveying me with an expression of such cool disbelief that I became a little unnerved. He made no comment, and that was a gesture of insolence in itself. At least he had not followed me all afternoon, and that was a relief. I had to take it our meeting here was an accident, then, but I was baffled by his manner. "Are you English?" I asked warily, groping for a guide. In spite of his enunciation, there was that profile. It seemed to belong here.

He nodded, brushing my question aside as of no importance. "Allow me to introduce myself. I am Nat Ross." And then, with the cool deliberation that marks a man who is not easily crossed: "You're—?"

I had a queer feeling he knew. "Virginia Sandersen," I said compulsively. "With an 'e' in the 'sen,' which is Swedish."

"Virginia!" He repeated the name, turning it over on his tongue, staring at me. And then he said it again, "Virginia?" I thought, this time, it sounded like a question, at once confused and mistrustful, but half of it was drowned by the roar and splutter of a motor bike starting up nearby.

"I am not Swedish, if that's what you're thinking," I said, pretending a nonchalance I was far from feeling. I did not suppose for a moment my companion cared a fig whether I was Swedish or not, but when I am nervous I tend to gabble.

" 'Sen,' " he said, still staring at me. " 'Sen.' You must have Swedish ancestry." He didn't care about that, though. I could tell. His mind was whizzing round in circles, and the Swedish chat was obviously to divert me and give him time to think. He was running his eyes over me from head to toe, appraising the hair that is rather more blonde than it might have been were I purely English, and the level, rather square shoulders. I suppose one could say Lee and I have a typically Swedish build. I was feeling desperately uncomfortable beneath his scrutiny. "My father was a Swede," I said, carrying on compulsively with this idiotic and totally unrelated matter, "but he died when we were two and Mother brought us back to England to live."

"When 'we' were two?" As he repeated my words I saw what looked like dawning comprehension in those unusual eyes. Then: "*We!*" The word exploded like a pistol crack.

"My twin sister," I said, "and myself."

"Oh!" Mr. Ross was not a very good actor. The word "twin" hit him like one of Zeus' thunderbolts, and I realized with a feeling of shock that he must have taken me for Lee. I saw this in his sudden relaxation when the suspicion fell away, the involuntary jerk of one hand in what was palpably a gesture of irritation at his having wasted a day on the wrong quarry. Of course Lee, who had worked in Athens for a year, would hardly spend an afternoon visiting the places I had listed. I did not have to ask now why he had made that hazardous leap from the Mykonos steamer this morning. He had seen a girl whom he took to be my twin, and for some reason he wanted to follow her.

Lee had written last week that she was scared. Lee, who had never been very good at looking after herself . . .

I took a gulp of the coffee, forgetting what it was and filling my mouth with those vile sandy dregs I had tried so carefully to avoid.

"You'll have to have more practice with that brew," said Nat Ross, smiling in a relaxed and friendly way now that I was no longer important to him, now that I was Virginia, the other twin. "I didn't realize you were such a new arrival. You were doing rather well at first. Shall I get you something else? Most of these places serve Nescafé now. And by the way," he chuckled disarmingly, "I can escort you back to Piraeus. I've taken a room with Spiro, too. It's so handy to the wharf. I guessed the taxi driver was finding you somewhere to stay, so I followed. I thought you wouldn't mind . . ."

* * *

The steamer was easy enough to catch the second time around. Spiro of the lively air and flashing eyes, keeping his promise, wakened me at seven sharp. Nat Ross was waiting at the top of the stairs to carry my bag, looking so familiar in the sunbeam shafting down from the skylight that I had to remind myself of yesterday. "Why are you going to Mykonos, Mr. Ross?" I had asked him the night before and received the careless answer: "Do call me Nat, since we're going to be traveling companions. To have a look. The islands are all worth seeing." I could not ask him why he had jumped off the boat. The question stuck somewhere in my throat because I was afraid of the answer. If Lee was in some sort of trouble it was better that I hear about it from her rather than from him.

We settled down on the top deck beneath an early morning sky, blue as a robin's egg, scattered our belongings and sat on one of those curved and slatted seats that I have always found uncomfortable but which occupy the best positions. According to my timetable the trip took six or seven hours. There were not many people aboard. The usual sprinkling of long-haired, eager-faced students with ragged trousers, skimpy cotton vests and packs on their backs: the girls looking like boys with their small hips and tiny breasts, the boys looking like girls with their long hair and only the occasional fuzzy chin as a flag of masculinity. Two priests came up the companionway, their enveloping black robes stirring in the morning breeze. I looked at the two pairs of twinkling, kindly eyes; two large hooked noses peeping over their luxuriant, graying beards; their thin hair knotted into buns and tucked halfway beneath their kalimafkis. One of them carried a tiny radio slung over his shoulder and the sweet, lively strains of a bouzoukia lay momentarily on the air before it gave way to a woman announcer's voice. I turned to speak to Nat, then paused, not quite surprised, only intrigued. His head was set at a listening angle toward the radio, his eyes thoughtful and a little amused.

I said deliberately, and perhaps a bit accusingly, "You understand!" I had to know about him if he was coming after Lee.

"What?" He blinked.

"You understand Greek. You're listening to that radio."

I thought he looked faintly taken aback. Then: "A little," he admitted. "Don't you? I mean, from school?"

"No one learned Greek at our school. I wish now that I had studied it, though."

He smiled. His face was not hard. I wondered why I had thought so. And he really had exceedingly pleasant eyes. "You'll get on all right. Most of the people you will come across talk Tourist English, but I dare say you have some good guidebooks anyway."

I took up his red herring. What did it matter that he spoke Greek and wished to hide the fact? It did not help me in placing him.

"Yes. I have brought some books with me. I haven't read them all right through, though. You see, I was not intending to come until late summer. I had plenty of time. Then—"

He gave me a stabbing look and yes, there was that hardness around the mouth after all. I turned away, adding in as casual a voice as I could muster, though my heart had begun to beat rapidly, "I changed my mind. I really could not wait."

A sea gull wheeled overhead emitting its wild, abandoned cry. A young man in tight jeans threw a crust on the water and the bird dived, a white-winged rapier against the blue. "It's all so beautiful," I said, speaking in a covering rush, one arm encircling with real enthusiasm the sea, the birds, the ships. "My sister says

Mykonos has the most perfect specimens of cube-like houses in the Cyclades. She sent some pictures and I must say the island looks fantastic."

"The most perfect specimens," Nat corrected me lazily, "are actually to be found on Siphnos, but it is rather remote. The splendid thing about Mykonos is that it's easily accessible. You were wise to come in May. You'll still get the wild flowers and yet avoid the main body of tourists. As well as the meltemi which, I believe, is hell."

"Meltemi? What is that?"

"It's a hot and rather beastly wind that blows in August—according to my guidebook. Look, we're moving."

I was suddenly reminded that this time yesterday a girl with despair in her heart had watched a man taking a hazardous leap to the hard concrete below. I dragged my mind away from the important fact that Nat had been willing to put himself at considerable risk to follow the girl he thought he recognized as my sister.

"The Greek mistral?" I asked.

"Something like that," Nat replied. "Headaches and parricide, but I don't know if the Greek courts give special dispensation." His smile was disarming. "The French are so civilized."

The steamer began to pull away from the wharf. I jumped up to go to the rail. Nat followed, unfolding himself lazily with an exceptional sort of manly grace that I had never seen in an Englishman before. And yet he had the wiry toughness of a player on a professional athletics field. "You're half Greek, aren't you?" I asked bluntly.

He laughed, but I thought I saw a shadow cross his face.

"Well?"

"Look," he said, "you're all on edge. A man doesn't have to be half Greek to have a bit of information about these islands. It's all in the guidebooks. I am an ordinary tourist with a penchant for following blondes. Why won't you accept that?"

I didn't, and he knew it. I leaned back against the rail, eying him with a skepticism I did not trouble to hide. He did not seem to notice. He smiled at me in the friendliest way and in the end, irritated, I turned my back on him. I was worried about Lee. Was Nat using me to lead him to her? I hardly thought so, since the guidebooks said there were only four thousand people on the entire island. Finding an English girl running a boutique in the only town there could scarcely be counted a difficult feat.

Unless she had gone into hiding! Into hiding? The ultimate in cloak and dagger! *Pack it in, Virginia,* I said to myself firmly. *You're going out of your mind. Look at the scenery. You're in Greece for the first time, and is not this where you have been wanting to be since you were twelve years old?*

We moved swiftly out into the stream. Over the wharf buildings the dusty, close-packed dwellings of the port of Piraeus took shape; spindly gray apartment houses cheek by jowl, factory chimneys, a pall of smoke or dust and then, moving in behind, its glory muted by haze and distance, the wonderful Acropolis with its archaic ruins. Below the brown port water swirled and beat against the ship's white hull, clearing miraculously as we went ahead. It turned blue, then bluer, and bluer still, the gray foam changing to white snow, white lace, white pearls.

Nat was beside me. "Let's be friends," he said. "It's better that way."

"What do you mean?" I asked defensively. "What is better that way?"

He looked at me gravely for a moment and I'll swear he was going to say something important. Maybe it was what he saw in my expression that changed his mind, for change it he did. One did not have to be psychic to see. I went to lean against the forward railing, turning my attention to the lively scene around us, but as I turned my head to brush a strand of hair I accidentally caught his eye. I swung away pretending interest in the shipping. On our starboard side, clean, painted working boats lay at anchor behind their rusted anchor chains, and beyond them brick-colored cranes like gaunt statues stood here and there. Behind the wharf buildings a house-packed hill had risen, crested with cypress trees that butted darkly through the haze of heat and factory smoke. Busy little white boats, blue boats, gray boats were rushing at us, head-on as a joyous caller might come, white petticoats flying.

I did not hear Nat's light footsteps on the deck. I jumped as he spoke. "We are a couple of tourists alone," he said lightly. "I don't know anyone on Mykonos. I'd like some company. Your sister must have some local friends. It could be fun."

"It could be, it you were a little more straightforward," I said shortly. "You haven't told me why you jumped off the *Opollon* yesterday and followed me."

He laughed. "I never knew a pretty girl who was so modest. Don't spoil what I had hoped would be a very pleasant interlude for both of us."

"You picked me up. Is that what you're trying to say?"

He frowned, apparently offended by the bluntness of my words. "There are better ways of putting it," he replied. "What does one do when there is no one to make the introductions? Let what might be a chance of a lifetime pass by?"

I wanted desperately to believe him, but when he looked at me like that with canny eyes I knew I had to stay on my mettle.

We were steaming out into the bay. Passing over the fact that I had not replied, he remarked conversationally, "My guidebook says Delos is worth visiting. You have read up on Delos, I suppose?"

Our eyes met. I thought there was the light of laughter in his, but someone brushed past us at that moment and he turned his head. When I saw his face again it was solemn and innocent.

"The Sacred Isle," I remarked.

"Sacred, is it?"

"Don't you know? Don't you really know?"

He laughed. "We have clearly got different guidebooks. What makes it sacred?"

I could have told him a great deal, but I thought I might be making a fool of myself. "Artemis and Apollo were born there while Leto clutched the branches of a palm tree." If you know the language you've surely got to know that, I thought. For those who are not familiar with the pagan legend which has given Delos its fame and which in earlier days gave it its prosperity, I recount it here: Leto, a mortal, pregnant to the randy great god Zeus, was so hotly pursued by Zeus' jealous wife, Hera, and the serpent Python, whom Hera sent to persecute her, that she was unable to pause in order to give birth to Zeus' twins. Nor could she find sanctuary, for, terrified of Hera's wrath, no country would accommodate Leto. At last, when her hour was at hand, one legend says Zeus himself, using a diamond pin, fixed the floating islet Delos to the ocean floor. Another version is that Poseidon made Delos rise out of the sea. Leto came then to Delos and, clutching the branches of a palm tree in the Sacred Lake, gave birth to Apollo and his sister Artemis while Zeus crouched on Mount Cynthos, guarding them.

"I'll take you to see that palm tree," Nat said, giving himself away. He was not half-witted. No palm tree of antiquity could be surviving today, if indeed it had ever grown, outside of mythology, in the Sacred Lake. Nat knew about Delos, if he knew there was a palm tree growing once again. My guidebooks said the French archeologists had planted it. I wondered if he was an archeologist. He did not look like my idea of one. And if he was, that posed the question once again: what could his interest be in my sister? Anyway, I would eat my hat if he did not know these islands rather well. And I was certain he had not learned his Greek at school. Not all of it, anyway. I fiddled with the brass buckle on my belt, plotting a new tack. "My sister has been to Delos," I said. "She sent me a photo of herself standing beside one of the famous stone lions that guard—" Having dangled the bait, I looked up at him innocently. "But why am I going on like this? You probably know the lot. Your guidebooks have got to have the lions in. The lions that guard the Sacred Way to Apollo's Temple."

Nat leaned back, both arms spread across the rail, his eyes slitted against the sun. The thinking pose. "Marble lions," he corrected me casually. "They're made of marble from the quarries on Naxos . . . my guidebook says."

His guidebook! I said with undisguised asperity, "I expect you have read Homer in the original Greek."

A sharp breeze tossed his hair and he flattened it with one hand, turning to me with a lazy smile.

"Have you?" I asked.

"I may know more about Greece than you, for I have been here a few months, but I am no scholar," he said. Only that, but I was left with the irritated feeling that he could have answered my question better.

CHAPTER 3

We crept across the diamond-bright sea guarded by Cape Sounion which crouched like a huge gray beast against a pallid sky. A sea mist rose whitely round its feet. At midmorning the ruins of the Temple of Poseidon rose starkly, and behind, a pall of smoke curtained a hillside and lay still. We left the mainland to slide between gray islands touched with green like unloved rockeries where the sea gnawed with jagged teeth against their granite base. Tiny islands, large islands, middle-sized islands; islands that crept up and caught one unawares; islands that peeped shyly over the horizon, then slid away.

Nat and I had not talked very much. After his insistence that he needed company, he showed himself to be a very self-sufficient man, busy perhaps with problems, for he frowned a good deal, and it was not always because he was looking into the sun. At midday he brought two coffees up on deck and an unappetizing sandwich of hard bread enclosing a pale sliver of cheese. "It's all they have," he said apologetically, "unless you want biscuits. We should have asked Spiro for a packed lunch. I don't think you're going to like this."

"It's very kind of you. But I'll just take the coffee." I was not hungry. I never can eat when I have something on my mind. I had removed my shirt and trousers and was stretched out on the hard deck in the bikini I wore underneath. With my fair skin I don't tan easily and this was a heaven-sent opportunity to get a summer color going. Nat had taken his shirt off. He already had a tan, and when I looked at his skin, I could see he had the sort of start a bit of Greek blood could give him. He demolished that dry-looking bread, too, with a continental's enthusiasm. I reckoned a true, full-blooded Englishman would have commented on its unpalatability.

I decided, when we put in at Tinos with its neat, double-storied villas and air of faintly grand Victorian respectability, that Lee's descriptions of the neighboring island of Mykonos must have been a little wild. But Mykonos bore no relation to its neighbor. It was a toy town, a riot of brilliant building blocks so dazzling white they hurt the eyes. Surely, I thought with astonishment, some child had piled them neatly, one upon the other against a pale-green, rock-strewn hill, and set toy windmills upon some rocks behind! I stood at the ship's rail and held my breath at the beauty and unreality of Mykonos. Cinnamon doors and windows, green wooden balconies, a blue curtain stark against the frost-white of the walls; caïques in harsh Greek reds, orange and vermilion within a hyacinth bay. Lee's ecstatic letters had not prepared me for the reality. "It's a film set, isn't it?" I murmured in disbelief. "Or the eighth wonder!"

Nat smiled. "Glad you like it."

I knew then, incontrovertibly, for all his English name

that in some way he belonged to Greece. I have never heard anyone say "Glad you like it" except when he stood in the role of a host. I wondered why Nat did not want me to know.

A little fleet of launches came out to meet us. Short, dark men in black peaked caps bundled our luggage in, hurrying us roughly but good-naturedly after it. We jostled one against another while they packed more and more passengers behind us in the happy-go-lucky Greek way. Then without a word of warning they cast off and jerked away in a shower of spray and laughter.

"You will have to get used to this," Nat said wryly, regaining his balance. "They fill buses the same way and depart when they're full, with a happy disregard for timetables."

I clung to the handrail. We sped into the little harbor, gay with brightly painted caïques at anchor, and swung around toward the quay. The atmosphere was suddenly lighthearted. People who had ignored each other all morning on the steamer were smiling and exchanging joking warnings. I pushed my way over to the side, free of the heads, where I could have a better view. There was a crowd of people gathered on the quay, the same short, dark-haired men, the same sallow-faced peasant women in black with head scarves. And a queue of tourists waiting to embark for the return journey. I removed my dark glasses, exposing my eyes to the blinding glare of the sun as I looked for a blonde head set on slim shoulders in a pale, short dress.

Lee, I was certain now, was not there. The engine spluttered to a halt and we bounced up against the quay. I climbed out with the assistance of a strong, brown hand. Nat was following immediately behind. I was uncomfortably aware, even without turning, of his proximity. I moved a little distance away while the luggage was being unloaded, searching and re-searching the crowds beyond the barrier.

Nat, at my side, saw my apprehension. "It's stating the obvious, but no doubt she met yesterday's boat."

"Of course," I agreed, "but she knew we would have to run dead on time to catch even the second one. They left within half an hour of each other. She would expect me to come today if the bus ran late."

Nat said lightly, as though removing my problem, "Don't worry. I'll carry your bag."

"That's very kind, but—" I turned away, trying to pretend I had not seen the look. Of course, he must come face to face with my sister. But I had to see her first. I had been unsuccessful in finding out anything at all about Nat this morning, but if Lee needed warning of his presence, then I must warn her.

My bag had been tossed up onto the quay and the boat was shooting off for another load of disembarking passengers. I made a move to pick up the bag but Nat had already dived. He took his own in the other hand. "Right-o," he said breezily. "What is the name of the street?"

I did not know, and that was a fact, but it was not on this account I paused. I had made up my mind to get rid of Nat and I was desperate enough to do it without tact if I had to. We stood there while people brushed past us on either side, calling greetings. A child rushed in noisily, separating Nat and me, and I might have got away as she was enveloped in the warm arms of an ecstatic old woman in a black shawl who blocked Nat's path, but what was the point, I thought, since he had my bag? We became widely separated. A plump woman with a cluster of small children nearly unbalanced me as she rushed into the crowd to embrace an old man whose possessions were overflowing from an unzipped bag. All the passengers were suddenly in a hurry, pushing, sliding through gaps, jostling. I was swept forward toward the promenade beyond the quay. Then suddenly the crowd freed me, and with a creepy feeling, I realized I was walking side by side with Nat. "I shall have to find a place to stay," he remarked in a businesslike voice. "Somewhere in the middle of things. The chances are I'll get a room in the same street as you. Taking in guests is big business here. Almost any open door is a possibility. If the first householder you try can't take you, he is bound to have an uncle or a cousin who can. Boutique Cleopatra. Now what did you say was the name of the street?"

I remained silent, and not only because I had yet to master the pronunciation of that curious Greek street name. It was the shock of hearing the name of Lee's boutique from Nat's lips. I would stake my life I had not mentioned it to him. A thick-set, dark-eyed fisherman in denim jeans and a black cap wandered across our path absorbed in winding a coil of nylon line. In my brief moment of hesitation I was aware of Nat's close scrutiny, but I could not bring myself to look up and see whether he had dropped the name Boutique Cleopatra deliberately or not.

I said bleakly, "You have been very good, but I won't trouble you further. I've a rough idea where to find the place. That bag is quite light, really. You saw me running down the wharf with it yesterday. I don't want to sound ungrateful, but I can cope very well alone." Lee's nonappearance had shaken me and unformed fears were splintering my mind.

Nat gave me an enigmatic look. Then: "Okay," he said lightly and put my luggage down.

"Good-bye, and thanks for—er—well, everything. I expect I'll see you around," I said, not looking at him. I picked my bag up and set off along the waterfront. He should worry! He knew the name of the boutique, therefore he knew the name of the street, and the chances were he even knew how to pronounce it! A new thought had struck me. Lee might have been watching through a pair of binoculars for the steamer's arrival. That was a reasonable enough premise, I said to myself. I wended my embarrassed way through the loiterers on the promenade, leaving Nat searching in a pocket for his cigarettes, to think what he would about my clumsy brush-off. If my hunch was right, she would have seen us standing together at the rail. If she did not want to meet him, she would not appear.

I hurried on, sidestepping a pelican as he waddled confidently across my path, his feathers shimmering in the naked sun as I picked up the vital smell of fish and drying nets, of animal dung and of sea water against the gray-white stones upon the quay. He strutted on to meet a fishing boat, opening his great golden beak hopefully. A good-natured fisherman in a salt-stained cap called, "Petros!" The bird changed direction with alacrity and caught a silver fish that was flung to him.

A great many young people here: girls perched on a low stone wall with bright daisies embroidered on their jeans; young bearded men in unbuttoned shirts and bathing trunks on a pile of golden nets. I did not look behind to see if Nat was following. What did it matter? There was no keeping him away. But I needed time to say to Lee, "There is a man looking for you. Maybe a policeman, a detective, an investigator. What have you done? And now let us put our heads together and find a way . . ."

I passed tavernas emitting the sweet smell of coffee and packed to the doors with dark-eyed men playing cards and talking. They all, it seemed, wore those intriguing peaked black seamen's caps, weathered from many a day in the blazing sun and many a storm. Some of the caps sat straight and low on their wearers' heads, some were cocked at a rakish angle. It seemed each one adopted the personality of its owner. They must be a sort of Mykonian uniform, I surmised.

A little farther on, beneath some white awnings, holiday-makers lounged at tiny tables on the cobblestones.

They actually were small paving stones that were thickly outlined in white as Lee had described them. The people sipped drinks, chatting and watching our arrival with idle curiosity. Several thin and rather hideous cats slunk across my path. On my left was a small beach lined with dinghies and boats of various sizes, some of them laid up on supports that were made from piles of flat stones.

And then the tavernas gave way to tourist shops spilling over with embroidered blouses, heavy-knit jumpers, lacy shawls and those bright folk-weave mats in the colors of the caïques—dark greens, brick reds and blacks. There were jewelry shops, too, full of ornate gold rings and prettily worked bracelets set with colored stones. I passed a general store selling boxes of sponges the color of pale primroses, racks of glass beads, necklaces of shells, pretty metal belts; and here and there the sun glinted on some giant amber-colored worry beads with silken tassels.

Here, it seemed, the business section of the quay ended. On my right the close-packed town had split and intermittent wanderers came down side streets, to the waterfront. I looked up a narrow way where whitewashed houses crowded close. There was one tiny shop displaying a clutter of leather belts, their huge metal buckles glinting in the sun, and beyond that, white steps rose to the upper story of white houses.

Lee had said, "I am only half a minute from the quay, just off the main shopping street." I thought this looked like a possibility for the main shopping street.

I ventured in. There was the smallest of squares with a narrow lane leading off it to the right and a brick-red bridge joining two houses across the lane, balcony to balcony, with bedclothes airing in the sun. Beyond, a row of white arches, and geraniums pouring in a deluge from a verandah enclosed by ocher railings. Again, I had the impression of a toy town. My apprehension began to fall away in astonishment at the beauty of the town. On my left now was a chapel with a green bell, its bell rope draped across the closed doors.

The lane, little wider than an alleyway, was aflood with a rush of tourists looking hot and in a hurry, making no doubt for the quay to escape this airless trap for the midday sun. If it is like this in May, I said to myself, how will Lee stand it later? I put my bag down and wiped the damp hair from my brow. There was a passage turning off to the left and a Greek name, with those strangely shaped e's and dissected O's. I moved a step forward, examining the word carefully: ΘΗΣΕΩΣ. Was not that the street name on my sister's letter? I snatched a furtive look behind. There was no sign of Nat. I reached for my bag, dragging it, in my eager, apprehensive haste with a scrape and swish across the stone flagging. Unzipping a pocket in the lid I pulled out Lee's letter. Ah! Yes, it matched. My heart began to beat rapidly. I turned left and there was the sign I sought: Boutique Cleopatra. I picked up my bag and strode swiftly across the intervening distance.

The place was empty. I stood in the narrow doorway, looking in. There were two steps leading down to a cool tiled floor the color of ox's blood with the Greek key design marked here and there in aquamarine. The pale, painted walls were hung with a treasure trove: ships in bottles, stone pendants on leather thongs, a velvet pad of earrings made from shells, and everywhere that unnerving evil eye on whose good resources the Greeks set so much store, as an emblem on brooch, medallion, ring, thonged necklace and ornately studded belt.

I descended the steps hesitantly and put my bag down in the middle of the room. "Lee!" I called. "Lee!" I listened. The place seemed deserted. Apprehension curled my fingers tightly in my palms. "Lee!"

Some narrow, railless stairs led up through an open skylight or trap door in the ceiling. My sister had said her flat lay above the shop. I went to the rear wall and called again. "Lee!" My voice came back to me eerily from the four walls.

It was close in here. I pushed the heavy hair away from my damp neck. Suddenly I was shaky and upset. An empty shop. A missing girl. Where did one start? And anyway, was this Lee's boutique? The stock was oddly untypical. I could not even visualize her buying it. In the right-hand corner was a small counter on which lay a wide, flat basket containing a jumble of glass ashtrays and model boats and windmills, while hanging from the sides like curious pendulums were oyster shells packed quaintly with tiny painted flowers. Lee had not, admittedly, talked to me in her letters about her stock but I had expected ceramics, peasant embroidery, wrought iron, perhaps. This clutter of rubbish could surely never have been chosen by my discriminating and fastidious sister. I was baffled.

Against the wall close by the bottom stair lay a small couch with a goatskin slung across it. Above that and a little to the left was a sort of peephole, deeply recessed and set with glass through which one could see the light outside. There was a lamp nearby, made from an enormous wine bottle with a hideous shade shaped like a hat. I shook my head bewilderedly. And then suddenly I saw some pretty lanterns strung across the wall, intricately and tastefully intertwined with a strip of golden net, some seashells and a very pretty brass kettle. This arrangement, and only this in the boutique, bore Lee's stamp. My apprehension grew overwhelmingly and exploded in a feeling of shock and disappointment. *Lee has been here*, I said to myself with certainty, *but she is not here now! She has been gone long enough for the stock and most of the decor to change.*

My back was to the open doorway. I sensed rather than heard a soft footfall. I swung around. The woman—she must have been about twenty-five or thirty—who came down the steps had straw-colored, straw-textured hair

with a band of dark showing through at the part. She
was short, not more than five feet three, with wide but
fleshless hips, a flat bosom, small feet and spatulate
hands. Her dark eyes were brown-fringed with long,
rather beautiful lashes. She had a sallow complexion, a
thin red mouth and long nose. She looked at me as though
she were seeing a ghost.

"Lee!" It was less a word than a croak.

I am accustomed to being taken for my sister. It hap-
pens to identical twins all the time. But the way that
woman greeted me, as though the heavens had opened to
produce me, froze the blood in my veins. I found myself
uttering a silent, rather idiotic little prayer: *Artemis,
virgin goddess of the moon and guardian of women of all
ages, look to my sister Lee.*

CHAPTER 4

The woman was wearing a calf-length skirt of some heavy woven material striped with dark Greek colors. She wore sandals and a black blouse, fashionably skimpy and cut away at the neck. "My God!" she said. She blinked. Momentarily she looked punch-drunk. Then suspicion dawned in those dark eyes and her face closed.

"No," I told her, and my voice sounded blank and queer. "I am not Lee."

She was no fool. She knew she had to pull herself together. She cleared her throat, then slowly and deliberately crossed the shop to pick up something from the counter. She held out to me an air letter addressed in my own handwriting and unopened. "You're her sister? Your name is on the back of this."

"Yes," I said. "Lee didn't get it? Where is she then?"

"I understand she has gone on a buying trip." The woman spoke diffidently, as though it were not her business to talk about Lee's affairs. She had already half turned away.

"Buying trip?" I repeated incredulously, indicating the goods on display. "Surely this stuff is made on the island?"

The woman did not want to talk to me or have anything to do with me. I could tell by the way she kept her head averted, fingering one trinket after another, picking them up from the basket and dropping them again as though she hoped I would pick up her purposeful coldness and go away. I did not go, and finally she said to me:

"I really don't know anything about Lee's business. She asked me to help out. Heaven knows, I am busy enough. I've my own work to do. But Lee did me a favor once and I couldn't very well refuse." She looked down at her hands, at the short, useful fingers brown from the sun. She had given up fiddling with the stock and was pressing her hands so hard against the painted wood that her knuckles showed white. Perhaps she saw my eyes on them because, with a sudden jerk, she whipped her hands away and pulled a packet of cigarettes from under the counter. She took one out and lit it the way a man does, arm extended as she waved the match out, puffing hard to get the thing started, not touching it with her hand. She emerged from the time-consuming ritual totally in command.

I said blankly, "What am I to do? How do I get hold of my sister? When did she go?" I pushed the letter down into my hold-all.

"When? Oh, a few days ago." The cold expression had vanished, and was replaced by one of vivid interest that was so palpably false I felt chilled. "Why don't you get the boat back to Piraeus," she suggested. "I expect there is time, if you hurry. Leave an address so that Lee can get in touch if she returns. You can fly over in no time at all. And there are the steamers each morning. Eight and eight-thirty, I believe."

I did not absorb much of what she was saying for I was too taken up with the fact that this woman wanted very badly to get rid of me. Only the "if" hit me like a hammerblow. "What do you mean, 'if'?" I asked angrily. "You said Lee has gone on a buying trip. Presumably she *is* coming back."

"I meant if your sister returns tomorrow, or the next day. Or—whatever . . ." She raised those strange, flat, brown, totally unreadable eyes to mine. "It's no use getting annoyed with me. I am simply doing Lee a favor. I am not even responsible for the boutique."

"Who is?"

She took a long drag at her cigarette. Her skin had the dehydrated look of a heavy smoker. "I've really no idea."

"If you are working here," I said reasonably, keeping my fear and anger in check, "you must know who is in charge."

She said diffidently, "Your sister has friends. For my part, I offered to open the boutique when I felt I could spare the time. And by the way," she glanced at her watch, a small and expensive-looking gold one, "I was about to lock up. Everything shuts around here until five. If you want to catch the *Opollon* on its return trip . . ."

"I don't," I replied flatly. I think she knew, before I said the words, she had not got rid of me. She moved her shoulders in a way that, in a softer person, would have been a shrug. There was nothing soft about this woman. I had seen eyes like hers burning out of emaciated faces in war documentaries. Belsen and Auschwitz eyes, with a couple of thousand years of resentment built up behind them. They weren't burning at the moment. She did not give a tinker's damn about me as a person. But she most significantly wanted to get rid of me. Behind that uncommunicative façade I knew her brain was spinning like the sails of a Mykonos windmill in a whipping breeze.

Well, I can be cool, too, when the situation warrants it, at least on the surface. "Perhaps you could suggest a place where I might stay," I said decisively. "I think I'll hang around a while."

The address the woman gave me, that of the widow Georgidaes, was at the top, and therefore the back, of the town. I left my bag in the shop and hurried up a steep, narrow lane hemmed in by tubs of geraniums, pink oleanders, jutting wooden balconies in blue, brick, ocher, and that hard Greek green. Small brown lizards sunned themselves on the white-ringed paving stones and in tiny arid patches by pepper trees. Street cats eyed me wistfully, the mangy fur bristling over their protruding ribs.

Behind the flat-roofed, blindingly white houses, I saw a round white windmill with a thatched roof, its sails still, the base hidden by tightly packed dwellings. And now I could make out a light-blue door with a metal knocker. "You can't miss it," the woman in the boutique had said. "The windmill, and then there is an acacia tree in a tiny square of garden on the lower side." Beneath the tree a gray donkey dozed on stiff legs, a pair of empty pannier baskets slung across his back. The middle-aged widow, dressed in black, came out to view me with a slightly dazed air as though I had wakened her from her siesta.

"I am sorry to trouble you at this time," I greeted her apologetically, "but I am looking for a room."

She comprehended the word "room" and smiled, exposing gappy teeth and raising one brown finger from a work-roughened hand. Since the guidebooks said a great many people on the island spoke English, and Nat had assured me anyone with a spare room was willing to take in a guest, I thought bleakly that I could indeed have been better directed. The woman nodded. She took a key from the wall inside her blue door and indicating that I should follow, led me up a narrow and precipitous flight of unrailed outside steps to a pale-blue wooden balcony. There was a narrow wooden door, also painted blue. She unlocked it and led me into a small room containing a metal bed, a chest of drawers, and on the wall, an unframed mirror. One corner of the room had been curtained off as a wardrobe. She beckoned to me and I followed her through. Here was a toilet and small hand-basin. A little apologetically, for I am accustomed to inexpensive rooms, I tried the hot tap. There was no water at all.

I turned helplessly to the woman and she gave me her explanation in a flood of incomprehensible Greek. A moment passed uncomfortably while we both wondered what to do, then she patted my arm to indicate that I must wait, and hurried off as quickly as her stiff limbs and heavy boots would allow. I returned to the balcony to enjoy the incredible view. That torpid sickle bay, deep indigo in the midday sun, lay like some fantastic silken backcloth against the alabaster town.

There was a clatter of footsteps and I swung around to see the woman emerge from a narrow lane opposite and come down some whitewashed steps beside a chapel with a red dome and a green front door. She carried a large tin jug of water and was preceded by a handsome black-eyed boy. I went down the steps to meet them.

"Tomorrow," said the boy, smiling beatifically up at me. "Water tomorrow."

"Do you mean it is turned off for today?"

He nodded enthusiastically. "Water tomorrow. Water tomorrow."

My heart sank, for it seemed clear the boy had run through his English vocabulary. They waited, their eyes bright with hope, for my acceptance.

"Thank—you—very—much," I said slowly, loudly, and overpolitely in that idiotic way one has of talking to foreigners. "I do not think I will take it. It is too—er—far away." I had a strange sense, here, of being cut off. It struck me chill to think that woman in the boutique had sent me right up to the top of this hill to stay in the house of people with whom I could not communicate.

"Water tomorrow," repeated the child.

I smiled uncomfortably and left them. Going back down the lane I began to think of Nat. He wanted to find Lee. Well, so did I now. I looked back. The woman and child, with the jug of water on the paving stones between them, watched me silently.

With a little jolt of fear, I began to run.

A somnolence, a heavy torpor, had overtaken the town. The jewelers were closed and barred, the little boutiques locked tightly; souvenir shops were unattended and shuttered, their wares still displayed, with a touching faith in humanity, on the pavement. Barmen and fishermen drowsed on shaded chairs, and even the sad kittens seemed to have given up begging and were stretched across the shadowed stones.

But Boutique Cleopatra was open! I could see the gaping door. Yet the woman had been anxious half an hour ago to lock up! With my heart beating rapidly I turned sharply left and peered in cautiously.

There was a Greek sitting on the couch, frowning and looking down at the floor. In one hand he held a pair of dark glasses and in the other a string of worry beads. He wore his hair rather long like an Englishman. It was blue-black, very thick, and had been cut by some expert in a current style. The waves flowed generously across his low brow in shining abundance, and the hair along his cheeks extended slightly below his ears. A luxuriant, powerful head. In spite of the low forehead and too large a nose, this man conveyed an impression of florid good looks.

"Good afternoon," I said.

He was expecting me. His eyelids flickered up, exposing

pupils as blue as the Aegean but considerably less transparent. He jumped to his feet. He was tall for a Greek and powerful. Beneath a revealing thin cotton shirt was a muscular chest he displayed quite proudly.

"Good afternoon," his voice was deep and, in spite of the heavy accent, pleasant, even sexy. "I am Kriton Fileas." He tossed his dark glasses on the couch, pocketed the beads and advanced like a tomcat on the prowl to shake my hand. His hand, to my surprise, though large, was soft and rather damp. "I am a friend of Lee's. And I take it you're her sister. Well, it's obvious, isn't it?" He struck a pose, one leg straight, the other bent, surveying me with blatant insolence.

Kriton! Lee's employer! "Oh!" I exclaimed in a mixture of amazement and relief. "Oh! You're the man who owns the boutique!"

"Lee owns the boutique," he said, speaking thoughtfully, his head a little on one side as though pondering the absurdity of my remark.

"Lee?" I repeated in disbelief. My sister could not possibly own the Cleopatra. She had no money of her own. Living in Athens, sightseeing, making the most of her time abroad, she had several times commented lightly that she would have to hitchhike home because she would never be able to raise the return fare.

"I am just a friend," said Kriton Fileas in that smooth, rich voice. "I help her a bit. It's not easy for a foreigner to cope singlehanded. Lee is very efficient, though. She's a magnificent manager, very independent, and runs the place to a T." He seemed proud of that colloquialism. "To a T," he repeated, looking me up and down as though taking my measurements with those impertinent eyes. "I am so sorry she isn't here. She only left the other day. Such a pity your letter didn't arrive sooner. I'd get hold of her if I knew where she was. She has gone to Athens, I shouldn't wonder. Why don't you—"

"I thought I would stay and look around," I said, cutting off whatever he had to say about returning steamers and aircraft.

"Well, by all means. If there is anything I can do . . . Irene said you're staying at the Georgidaes' place. I'll take your bag up."

"Thanks, but don't bother," I replied. "It's not very suitable. They don't speak English, and there is no water until tomorrow. It's a bit off center, anyway."

"Off center?" He seemed amused, but those blue eyes were not exactly laughing. "I see what you mean, but I think you might find it very enclosed down here. And rather touristy. It's an opportunity to get the feel of the place, living with real locals like the Georgidaes. I do think the average tourist tends to cling too much to familiar things. If you stay with a Greek family you'll go home knowing much more about the place."

"I doubt it," I retorted crisply, "since we cannot communicate except by sign language."

He let that pass. "And there's a magnificent view," he went on in his smooth, electric way, "probably the best view in town. I expect that's why Irene sent you. And it is cooler. You English tend to feel the heat, even at this time of year."

"I will leave my bag here for a while," I said. "I'll think about it. I haven't had lunch yet. By the way, why are you open?" I gave him a straight look, knowing the answer. I knew the woman Irene had gone hot-foot to tell him of my arrival and he could not wait until five o'clock to size me up.

He swung back toward the counter, reaching casually beneath it. "You may well ask. I was just going to close. I'll be back about four or half past, or Irene will, if you want to collect your bag."

"Four or half past? I thought everyone opened at five."

Fileas shrugged. "Well-l-l, sometimes we stretch a point. And by the way, if you do change your mind, I believe there's a plane in the late afternoon, but of course, there's the steamer tomorrow. You'll have seen the island by midday," he told me confidently, swinging the key around a thick finger on his powerful-looking hand. Limp it may have been to the touch, but there was nothing limp about it to look at. "A few windmills, a chapel or two, and that's about it."

"Over three hundred, I understand." I did not take my eyes off his face.

"Pardon? Oh, chapels? Three hundred and sixty, actually." His eyes lifted, met mine, held, and it was I who in the end looked nervously away.

CHAPTER 5

Why in the name of sanity and reason had I brushed Nat off? Surely only my own guardian angel, or the Greek Hermes, guardian of wayfarers and messenger to mortals, could have given me a man who spoke English, was English . . . My jostling, disturbing problems meshed. *Careful, Virginia,* I warned myself. *Take it easy and think about this.* Compared to Kriton Fileas and that woman Irene, Nat might look wonderful; he might have God Save the Queen written on his face and Union Jacks hanging from his ears, but did that automatically make him a friend? No, it did not, and I must not allow panic and this desperate need of comfort to cloud my judgment.

Nevertheless, I found myself hurrying through the snow-white warren of streets, so narrow here and there that geraniums billowing over one balcony became entwined with those in the window boxes opposite. I paused in the shadow of one of those external staircases where another shower of red, pink and white flowers spilled in natural profusion out of a row of tin cans. A wandering dove with a glowing, shifting rainbow scarf around its neck came up to me and fixed me with a glittering eye. I stared back at it, thinking: *At least I can confront Nat, if only I can find him. I must find out whether he knows these two, Kriton and Irene.*

Dear God, this jumble of impossible streets! Why had I not asked Nat straightforwardly what he knew of Lee? Why he sought her? Did he in fact know she was missing? When he followed me from the steamer in Piraeus, was it on the assumption that he had found a missing girl? Why had it not occurred to me that Lee was missing?

The dove came high-stepping almost to my feet, then bounced stiff-leggedly away. I looked up and down the empty, silent, shuttered way. Everything was closed for the siesta. Nat had said he would look for a room near the boutique. Possibly he had already found one. What next? He would leave his bag and go to get some lunch. Where? To some restaurant where he could be served outside, to be sure. The English abroad seldom miss an opportunity to eat in the open. Right! I would set about looking for him.

There was a left-angled bend in front of me, and beyond that a magnificent hibiscus tree bursting joyously out of a tiny front garden. Beyond, a cluster of white-clothed tables set on stone flagging. There were perhaps a dozen tourists lunching. My eyes swept over them. No. Inside? The Greek family in charge were grouped together beyond an open glass door, but the rest of the dining room seemed to be empty. A white-coated waiter came into the lane to entice me in.

"You wish lunch? We have specialty—"

I hope I smiled at him and was courteous. I only know

I muttered something about looking for a friend, and made off.

Another corner, a crimson-roofed chapel, a larger square. Three restaurants within the shade of fringed awnings and an enormous eucalyptus tree. I drew back against the wall so as not to attract attention. A sucking pig and four chickens were turning on a spit only a few yards away. The heat was stifling. Nat was not here. Nor there. Nor . . . My view was blocked by a salmon-colored pelican, standing on a chair and scratching itself with a fantastic beak. Everything was larger than life here. More glamorous. More colorful. I moved out into the open and collided with another friendly waiter coming to greet me.

"You wish to eat here?"

"No, thank you." I hurried through the diners and swung away to the left. Again I was frustrated to see that the view was shut off by high balconies and double-storied, shuttered houses. A gap, and a glimpse of the sea, with one of those fish-food restaurants close against a sea wall where an old man in a Mykonian cap stood over a brazier. Hope was fading and fear closing in and slowing my limbs. If I did not find Nat before he finished lunching, the chances were I might not find him for hours, or possibly even all day.

I threaded my way agitatedly around those close-packed houses, never knowing where I was or where I had been unless I ran twice past the same restaurant, and at last, perhaps half an hour later, I found Nat sitting alone at one of a cluster of tables on a slope facing the sea. The relief was like a breath from heaven. His burnished head was bent over a fan of photographs and so he did not see me approach, but he must have heard me, for he lifted his eyes, spun the pictures together and thrust them back into his wallet.

"Well met in lovely Mykonos," he said lightheartedly,

jumping to his feet. "If there is one thing I dislike, it is eating alone. I hope you've come to join me."

I flopped down in a rush-bottomed chair opposite him. My shirt was sticking to me and my face was beaded with perspiration. I wiped it with a grubby handkerchief. "I don't want any lunch," I said. "Nat, listen to me—"

"No lunch!" Nat, who obviously had the healthy male's instinctive need for a meal at mealtime, broke in with a shocked protest. "Of course you must have lunch. You're thin—sorry, slim—as a peastick and if you don't mind my saying so, there is quite a length of limb to keep covered. I can recommend this giouvetsi. It's basically roast lamb, but with a difference."

I looked down at the remains of meat and pasta on his plate. "My sister is not here," I said.

Nat did not answer immediately. He leaned on the table, looking at his hands like a doctor who has listened to the symptoms and now sets about diagnosing the complaint. He did not seem very surprised. Several moments passed. There was a quality of insistence about his silence that spoke to me as clearly as if he had said, "Okay, let's have it." Often, as I recalled later, I had to ask myself if my flood of confidences to him were prompted by a question he had asked that opened the gates. Often his leads were unspoken, but very persuasive. Now he merely looked up at me.

"They say she has gone on a buying trip."

"They?" He spoke cautiously.

The waiter came at the moment. Nat gave a gesture with one hand and the man receded, his soft shoes noiseless on the stones.

"A woman called Irene who says Lee asked her to help out, and a man called Kriton Fileas who is Greek, I suppose, only . . ."

"Only?"

"I mean, he doesn't look quite like a Greek. Well, he

does. They can't all have short hair and short legs, I suppose," I said. "He looks after the shop, too, I think. Listen, Nat, there is something—" I brushed a hand across my forehead, momentarily covering my eyes. The sun was blinding. As it moved to the west it had lost none of its force. It battered relentlessly down on the flat stones that formed a sort of dais on which the tables stood. I had slung my hold-all over the back of the chair. I rummaged in it for sunglasses and could not find them. "Damn! Now I've lost my specs." I sat back, feeling shaky. Feeling, absurdly, that the loss of my sunglasses was almost more than I could bear. Nat put a hand over mine. It was cool, dry and comforting, reminding me, that Kriton Fileas' fingers had been soft and damp. I shivered at the memory.

"What you need," said Nat, "is a stiff drink. Have you tackled ouzo yet?"

"Ouzo!" I did need something to pull me together, but I already knew ouzo, that colorless spirit all the Greeks imbibe, had the kick of a mule. "Anything strong in the middle of the day either sends me to sleep or makes me aggressive."

Nat laughed, and it was hard to think of him as an enemy. "I cannot imagine your becoming aggressive. You've been scared most of the time since I've known you."

And I was scared now. "They both tried to make me catch the returning boat," I said, watching him closely.

He rose and stood looking down at me, his face impassive. He was not ignoring me or my troubles. His expression told me that. The eyes had narrowed, the mouth had hardened. His reaction did nothing to smooth away my fears. I could not tell what he was thinking, but I had an unpleasant feeling he was interested in Lee's disappearance for its own sake and not on my behalf. I had a nasty sensation, now that I had found him, of being on my own.

"Shall we make it brandy?" he asked. "Perhaps it's a brandy situation. I'll get it from the bar. Self-service is the speedy answer." He disappeared inside and emerged almost immediately carrying two glasses that struck gold, red and amber in the sun. "There you are," he said, handing one of them to me. "Put yourself around that. You will be a new woman."

"Thank you." I took a good-sized mouthful and then another. The harsh, biting liquid closed my throat convulsively and brought tears to my eyes, but it also pulverized some of the fear and set me thinking again. I would treat him as a friend. I had to treat him as a friend. There was no one else.

"All right," said Nat in a businesslike voice. "Start at the beginning. You went to the Boutique Cleopatra. What happened?"

He could have been offering me a chance to ask him how he knew the name, but for the moment that did not seem important, and I let it go. "There was a woman there," I said. "I would think she is Jewish. Her name is Irene. She said she is a friend of Lee's, but if she is, I'll eat my hat. My nonexistent hat. You know, that's exactly what I need in this torrid town."

"I'll buy you one."

"No, really. Look, I've put you off your lunch. Do finish. It will be cold."

"There isn't a hot plate in the length and breadth of Greece," Nat replied dryly. "Haven't you learned that yet? Worry not about me. Why isn't this Irene a friend of your sister?" He leaned forward, his eyes penetrating, and he seemed more than curious. He was uncommonly interested, there was no doubt about that. I went on, for I had to talk to someone. I was past worrying about what he was getting out of it. "Nat, she's—sinister. Honestly, she is. She is—I cannot describe her. You would have to see her for yourself. She is all tightly folded up inside. Layers of—something—resentment, perhaps, or even

hate. My sister is the sort of person who's easily frightened. Irene would scare the wits out of her. And it just
isn't on that basis she probably isn't a friend. She
thought I was Lee. Now if she had known Lee so very
well, she wouldn't. I mean, not looking square at me,
standing only a few feet away. But that's not all. When
she saw me, or Lee as she thought, she got the most
terrific shock. The sort of shock a person gets when it's
just . . . not . . . possible for the person she sees . . . to be
there. *Impossible*, Nat. It scares me rigid to think . . ." I
could not go on.

"Then don't," he broke in gruffly, and for the first
time there was genuine sympathy in those tawny eyes.
"If you're so close, you would probably know by some sort
of mental telepathy if your sister was dead."

I wanted desperately to believe that, and perhaps it
was true.

"Here, drink this down," he said. It was an order, and
clearly he expected to be obeyed. "Come on, drink the lot.
And mine. Better to be aggressive than in a stew."

I drank the brandy and put the glass down, my throat
burning. "Help! Is that therapeutic?"

"Yes. I think so." He grinned. "Now, tell me exactly
what happened. Exactly."

There was exceptional urgency in his face and voice.
Far more concern than one would feel when setting out
to help a comparative stranger. The brandy was beginning to take effect, but then it had near-virgin ground
on which to work. Some hours had elapsed since Nat
had brought me that coffee, and Spiro's breakfast had
been no more filling than any continental breakfast I
had ever had, as well as slightly less palatable. I was indeed hungry at this point but my fear had obliterated
the signs.

"You went to the boutique, and these two people who
said they were friends of your sister told you she had
gone on a buying trip."

"Yes. And they were lying," I told him. "This chap Kriton Fileas said it was Lee's business. Well, for one thing, Lee hasn't the money to start a boutique."

"She could get a loan."

"I don't think she would do it, Nat. Lee is not that sort of person. She isn't a women's-lib, boss-girl type. She wouldn't take on anything that meant borrowing money. Responsibility isn't her scene."

"Could she not have changed? How long has she been abroad?"

"No," I replied violently. "No. I know her, Nat. And another thing. This Kriton was talking a whole lot of rubbish about Lee being independent and very efficient and she simply is not. I mean, she's neither. She is very artistic and rather lazy . . . He doesn't know very much about her, Nat. I am quite convinced he hasn't really seen much of her at all."

Nat had set the remains of his meal aside. He put a hand in his pocket and produced a packet of cigarettes. "Do you smoke?"

"Not really." Nonetheless, I eyed them hesitantly. "Well, perhaps I will just this once." I really needed it.

He lit our cigarettes. "Where does your sister live? Here, I mean."

"On the premises of the boutique. There were some stairs going up at the back. I imagine her flat is there. She wrote me she has only three rooms. She was going to give me a bed somewhere. I noticed there was a sofa in the boutique. Perhaps I was to sleep on that."

"Did you see her rooms?"

"No, I didn't. There was no way I could. They were so busy trying to get rid of me. And there's another thing. They said Lee had only just gone, but there was very little sign of her. I mean, I simply can't believe she had bought the junk in the boutique. It was not her sort of stuff."

Nat said, "I don't know how you could judge that way.

She would surely supply what the tourists want. A mighty lot of them want junk."

I rubbed my forehead, feeling bewildered. "Maybe you're right. But she would at least have set it all out artistically. There was this patch of wall that had Lee's stamp. Just one bit. She had arranged a really Lee-ish thing with a bit of fishing net and shells and a pretty little kettle." Nat's brows rose quizzically. "Yes, I know it sounds odd, but Lee has a way with things. You have to see it. Well, that's that. But I reckon she has been gone for long enough for all the rest of the stock she kept to have been sold and new stuff put in. It is about ten days since she wrote saying things had gone wrong and she was a bit alarmed."

"You hadn't told me that," said Nat quietly.

"No." I felt the color rise in my cheeks. "We hadn't talked about Lee," I said. I could not very well say, "I did not trust you, before," because it was a fact that I had no reason to trust him now. All I knew, in my help-less and frightened state, was that I needed an ally, and an ally of whom I was not quite certain seemed better than no ally at all.

Perhaps he would talk to me now. "Nat," I began, "will you tell me what you—" Something flickered in those eyes and I knew it was pointless, even before he broke in, to go on. My spirits took a running dive.

"One moment," he said lightly, "we must get back to the subject of food. Anyway, it's now obligatory for you to eat some garlic, otherwise you will have to move to windward." He licked a finger and held it solemnly above his head. "Yes, there's a faint breeze. You'll have to have some garlic. That settles it. Now, if you would like a light dish I can really recommend aubergine Imam Bayeldi. It's all vegetable. Tonight, when it's cooler, I'll see you through a really good meal." He looked up, clapping his hands in the accepted Oriental fashion: "*Garçon, parakalo.*"

I was being put off. I had told him what he wanted to know, he had stored it away for his own use, and now, because he had no intention of helping me, and had never had that intention, he was assuming a social façade and getting ready to play the host. He had changed the subject with a strength of purpose that I could not match. I stared down at the rock floor on which our table stood, feeling emptied of everything, just despairing. An orphan cat came and settled hopefully on thin haunches a yard away. The animal struck a chord of sympathy in me and picking up Nat's fork, I shot a bit of lamb over the side of the table. The cat leaped on the food with the speed of an arrow and disappeared behind the restaurant with the morsel in its mouth.

I looked up into the cautionary eyes of a waiter. He said something in Greek, shaking his head. "Don't feed the cats," I suppose. I did not care. Nat was talking to him in Greek now. "I have ordered for you," he said. "Aubergine Imam Bayeldi. You will like it. You've jumped straight into the national habits, haven't you? Lunching at four."

I did not answer. I was past caring. The waiter went away and we sat in silence. Then suddenly Nat said, "What are you doing about a bed?" and I found myself going on compulsively with the story. What was to be gained by not telling him? I was in a blind alley and there was nothing I could do but talk to Nat. Something might come out of it. Might not some important piece of information he could uncover turn out, incidentally, to be something for me as well? At least he wanted to find my sister.

"When I refused to go back on the steamer," I began, "the Irene woman gave me an address. It turned out to be the last house on the hill, up a very steep climb, on a blind road. With no one there who speaks English."

"Meaning?"

"I wondered if it was deliberate. This did seem like

the next best thing, since they couldn't persuade me to return to Athens. Putting me among people I couldn't communicate with, I mean, and as far as one could get from the boutique. I know it sounds highly dramatic," I added apologetically, "and maybe rather silly, but—well, anyway, I've got a good enough excuse not to stay. There is no water. The woman said it would be turned on tomorrow."

Nat laughed. "Don't believe it. There are parts of Mykonos where the water is always going off. You'd best pick a room where it's always on. I'll take you up to have a look at my place. There may be a vacancy there."

I scarcely saw the waiter bring my plate. Nat and I were staring at each other, a great wall of silence between us. He had not recognized his slip until he saw the bleak look in my eyes. I have said I am a poor drinker. On two brandies I will be bold. I sat up straight, willing him to meet my eyes. He did, but with discomfiture. "You have been here before. You know about the water. You know this island," I said. "You speak the language like a native."

He did not answer, and clearly because, for once, he was at a loss for words. A certain tightness about his mouth told me he was angry with himself, but his eyes continued to smile. I leaned across the table, pressing home my advantage.

"I'll stake my life you've got Greek blood," I said. "And you didn't jump off the *Opollon* because you follow blondes, but because you thought I was Lee." Still he did not reply, but his expressive face told me a thing or two. He had forgiven himself. His poise was coming back. He was about to grasp the initiative again.

CHAPTER 6

With enormous *sangfroid*, he said, "Such humility! And such an imagination! But why should you be so sure something disastrous has happened to your sister? The very fact that the boutique stock is poor is surely indicative that she has gone on a buying trip. As to this theory you have that the Fileas chap owns the boutique, it's possible your sister got herself a license from the Ministry of Commerce in Athens to run it, so it could be said to be hers, even if Fileas is backing her. He might not want you to know that." He had receded from me with jet speed. He might have been a thousand miles away.

"Why?"

"Who knows?" Nat asked carelessly. "He could be on a tax fiddle. It's probably only something like that."

"I told you Lee said she was alarmed."

"What was she alarmed about?"

"I don't know." I told him the story about deciphering the partially obliterated words in Lee's letter.

"I do think you're overplaying it a bit," said Nat soothingly. "After all, your sister did cross the words out. It's natural to turn to one's family when one is a bit upset, but in this case it probably wasn't much and very sensibly, she decided not to bother you. You have had a long and tiring journey, and—"

"Nat!"

He ignored my angry interjection the way a father might ignore a fractious child. The waiter returned and set my meal before me, but I was too upset to look at it. Nat smiled at me.

"I am sorry about yesterday," he said kindly. "About upsetting you. I should not have followed you like that. You're obviously overwrought. Why don't you settle down to enjoy yourself for a day or two? Your sister will probably breeze in tomorrow. She cannot have gone far. It stands to reason she wouldn't go to Athens to buy. She would stock island stuff. She has probably nipped across to Milos or Syros for fine lace or loukoumi."

"Loukoumi?"

"Turkish delight."

"*For a boutique?*"

"Why not? They sell a great mixture in these places. You said yourself—well, never mind. Eat up your lunch and let's enjoy ourselves," Nat said.

I regarded him bleakly across the table. "You do take me for a fool, don't you?"

The bitterness behind my question must have got through to him. He looked thoughtful. I could almost see his mind turning over. Then, a decision, and he leaned toward me. "Yes," he agreed, his voice low, conspiratorial, a little amused as though he were making a joke of it and did not really expect me to take him seriously, "I am half Greek."

"Why were you trying to hide it?"

"I did not want you to think of me as a foreigner," he said smoothly, his eyes on mine. The arch enchanter. "I consider myself to be English. I was born, bred and educated in England. I happen to speak a little Greek because my mother talked Greek to me as a child."

"You have been here before?"

"Yes," he admitted, "I have been here before."

"Then why did you not want me to know?"

He pondered my question, deliberately taking his time, fiddling with a knife and fork. At last he said, "I can answer all your questions, but it's going to spoil things."

"For you or me?"

"For the two of us." His handsome head came forward, set at an angle. He was deliberately wooing me now. "Isn't it rather nice, when one is attracted to a person, to be starting even, so to speak? Seeing a new place from the same angle? Discovering something together?"

I looked into his eyes. If he was trying to get me to trust him, they ought to have been soft and appealing, but they were wary. He was weighing every sentence before he spoke. I did not answer him. He was playing a game, but I could not work it out.

"I thought the Greek might turn you off," he said at last. "That's putting it in plain words."

It was all lies. He could not act at all. "Then why do you speak to waiters in Greek?" I asked bluntly. Did he really think that old line was going to have me blushing and coy?

He grinned disarmingly. "It makes life easier," he replied. "They don't speak English."

And it's not important enough, I thought. *My knowing is not important. It doesn't matter that the waiters know, either. He prefers to pass for an English tourist, but he is too impatient to play the game properly.*

"What about your name?"

"Look here, aren't you going to eat that food?" Nat

asked, honestly concerned, I'll swear. It came over quite differently from the garbage he had been tossing at me in the past few moments. I picked up my fork.

"Yes," I said, "I am going to eat it." I am also going to find out about you, I thought to myself. I already knew he was vulnerable. It was up to me to find the weak spots. I made a stab at the eggplant thing. "What about this name of yours?" I repeated. "Nat Ross. It's a bit English, isn't it?"

He chuckled. A very infectious chuckle indeed. "It's real. Nathaniel Pericles Ross."

I put the fork down with a clatter. My mouth was full and I was determined not to laugh. "You're joking, of course."

"Not at all," he returned, eying me so steadily I felt the color rise in my cheeks as I recognized my *faux pas*. Pericles might be a joke name for an Englishman, but of course it was a Winston or Horatio to a Greek. "It's not too bad a thing to be called after the architect of Greece's golden age," Nat said confidently. "The man who built Athens and gave the Greeks their original concept of liberty."

"Yes—er—yes," I could not make up my mind whether he was putting on an act or not.

"And my great uncle Nathaniel was very rich."

That made me laugh. He said it with such an absurdly straight face. "So he is the cause of you swanning around Greece instead of strap-hanging on the eight-ten?"

Nat said casually, "Not at all. The old boy didn't even come to the christening. It was reported to my parents that he had been heard to say he hadn't come down in the last shower and he thought my father ought to be horse-whipped for loading an innocent child with a name that was such a stumbling block."

Nothing touches this man, I thought nervously. His confidence was secure and unshakable.

"How astute of him." I managed to sound as casual as he.

"Yes, wasn't it?"

"And school? How does one get on at an—er—English school with a name like that?"

He ignored the question. "My father held a theory that a boy who has to overcome a name early in life will acquire a lifelong habit of overcoming obstacles."

"Your father seems to have made his share of human errors," I said lightly, but without taking my eyes from his face. "How do you get on with obstacles?"

"He was thinking in terms of handling people." Our eyes met. "Yes," said Nat, "I handle people quite well."

I have always thought myself to be a person of considerable strength of character. On my home ground I am not easily thrown. But I was not on my home ground, and I had never met anyone quite like this man. I could not have said at any point that he was a threat to me. In fact, there had been many isolated moments, such as when he brought the brandy, that he appeared to be on my side. But the feeling persisted that he wanted something of me, and I had a suspicion that he was going to achieve this end over my dead body, if need be. Handling people! That was what he was good at. Achieving his own ends.

"Ah," said Nat. "You have finished. Now, how about something else? Honey cakes? They are very nice."

"No, thanks, but don't let me stop you having a go at them. I expect you're accustomed to them," I said a little ungraciously. I maintain you have to be a native to enjoy any of the cloyingly sweet Greek desserts.

He called for the bill. I felt him slipping through my fingers and panicked. What was I going to do if he left me? To whom could I turn? I made a last, desperate bid.

"Nat, tell me why you've come to Mykonos. Who are you?"

I timed my question badly, as one always does when panic swoops. By the time the words were out the waiter was at our table adding up figures on his order pad. Nat paid, then rose composedly, pushing his change down into his trousers pocket. "Who am I?" he repeated, looking amused, picking up my shoulder bag and handing it to me. "I am a friend of Greece. Now, let's see if there is a room at my place for you."

I walked beside him in sullen obedience. What else could I do? It would take someone with a name like Nathaniel Pericles to make such a pompous statement. A friend of Greece, indeed!

He led me up some narrow marble stairs between a tiny jeweler's and a shop specializing in crocheted shawls. I knew where we were. About a hundred yards from the Boutique Cleopatra. I had passed these shops when I was searching for Nat. There was a dark-eyed girl on the landing sitting on a hard chair with some lacework in her hands. Nat spoke to her in Greek. She nodded. He opened a door close by. It was the same familiar type of room. A bare floor, a hard bed, a small table. One icon print on the wall. There was a green wooden balcony beyond folding glass doors. Nat opened them and I went out, resting my hands on the railings and looking across a mobilization of squat roofs in an assortment of sizes running down to a pale evening sea and sky.

The man Fileas had said I would find this area claustrophobic! "It's wonderful, isn't it? Is that girl out there in charge?" I nodded toward the open door that led onto the small landing.

"No. She is the landlord's daughter," Nat replied. "She is merely there, I presume, to keep people from coming in off the street. They don't seem to issue keys, and the front door is always open. If you think you would like a room here, I'll go down and ask her father."

"It's very kind of you." I spoke automatically because,

grateful as I was that he had not abandoned me, the unpleasant thought persisted that I was being used.

At the door he hesitated, half turned, seemed about to say something, then stopped. "What is it?" I asked.

"I was wondering—" He broke off. "No, no. It doesn't matter." He left and I went back to the contemplation of this unique view of earthbound roofs assembled in disordered ranks across the town. Here and there the round dome of a chapel stood with its lifted cross. An occasional palm tree reared up in one of the tiny, arid squares fighting off the invasion of white-mortar eaves and decks. And above, a vast pale emptiness of sky. There was a sound behind me. I turned to see Nat enter the room wearing, I thought, an expression of disappointment.

"They're full," he said. He sat on the end of the bed, looking up at me.

Neither of us spoke. I tried to read his expression. I really wanted to know if this setback might be a blow to his plans, but I could not tell. He was rubbing his forehead. The soft brown hair fell forward, masking his downcast eyes. "I say," he said, "I've just thought of something. Why should you waste money on a room when the flat above the Cleopatra is vacant?"

"You mean I might still sleep there?" So I was wrong when I thought he had some reason for bringing me here!

"Why not? It is your sister's boutique."

There was no doubt I could well do with a free room. I had no drachmas to throw around.

"This Fileas chap and the woman—they won't be able to keep you out, since they have said they're not in charge," Nat went on. "And if you want to find out where your sister has gone and why, I can't think of a better base to start from. You'll be able to check and see if her things are there . . ."

That convinced me. My desire to save my few traveler's checks was nothing compared to my vivid preoccupation with Lee's disappearance. I picked up my hold-all from the chest of drawers and spun around toward the door, my mind so taken up with this idea that I forgot Nat had been trying to convince me only an hour ago Lee did not need finding, that my imagination had run riot, and that my sister was on Milos or Syros buying fine lace and Turkish delight.

"Come with me for moral support," I suggested eagerly.

Nat opened the door of the wardrobe and took out a light jacket. "I'll walk down to the corner with you, but then I must be off to see a chap in one of the shops on the quay. I promised to return before five-thirty to decide about a—er a souvenir." He glanced at his watch. "It's nearly that now." He gave me a little push. "Go on. You've already got the light of battle in your eyes. You'll do better to tackle this on your own. I'll pick you up later."

I went out onto the landing. The girl looked up brightly from her crochet work, saying something to Nat in Greek. I had not the slightest idea what it was, but when he replied "*Óchi*," the Greek no, I swung around. Nat gave me a friendly look. I let it pass because my brain was in a turmoil about what I was about to do. I reckoned it would take more than Mr. Kriton Fileas or that strange woman to stop me.

"But I could not possibly give you the key," protested Kriton. "I mean, I haven't got permission to let anyone have it."

The boutique looked very pretty with the lights on, and one could see how glamorous it might appear under Lee's artistic hand. The hideous lamp with its hat-like shade was awful, but the others glowed softly and warmly against the pale walls.

"I am hardly 'anyone,'" I said, digging in my toes.

"Lee intended to put me up."

He lifted that grand, imposing head, speaking rather patronizingly. I sensed something else in his voice—darker and sharper—just under the surface. "So far as I know she was not even expecting you. Frankly, if you weren't so obviously her twin, I would not even be inclined to listen to you. I mean, anyone could walk in and say, 'I am Lee Sandersen's sister.' As a sort of caretaker, I have got some responsibility here."

He had just thrown out something new, but I was not prepared to argue. And I bypassed the fact that Lee was not expecting me since, as he knew very well, my letter had not been delivered. "It's a hypothetical situation we don't need to bother with," I said, giving him as cool a look as I could muster. "This is my sister's home and the truth is, Mr. Fileas, I haven't budgeted to pay for accommodation."

He walked slowly across the room, fingered a green bottle wrapped intricately in silver wire, then turned once more to me. "You have put me in a very awkward position, my dear."

"I am sorry," I said. "But I will take the responsibility."

He took his worry beads from a pocket, frowning at them.

"Well?"

"I had better consult Irene."

My fighting blood rose. "I don't think you need bother. She told me she was not responsible for the boutique. That she had merely opted to open up when she could find the time."

"Oh, I don't think that's so."

"Perhaps you two ought to get together," I said cuttingly. Our eyes met and I saw his harden to a cold ice blue. Whatever friendliness had been there was gone. He was sizing me up, but not as an equal opponent. This man knows how to deal with women, I thought. They're important to him. If he thinks of something fast enough, he will let me stay, but it's going to be on his terms.

I gave him time. My suitcase had been placed in the corner near the door. I crossed to it, stood looking down at it for a moment, then picked it up. Short of admitting that he actually owned the Boutique Cleopatra, Kriton Fileas could really do nothing about stopping me from moving into Lee's quarters. And it was his shop—there was no doubt in my mind about that. I would have given a good deal to know why he would not, or could not, claim it.

"Okay," he said at last. "You stay. But it's on your own head. I accept no responsibility."

"Thank you. May I have the key?"

With a casual flick of one hand he indicated the narrow rise of stairs that went through the ceiling to the floor above. "There is no key."

"You mean Lee has gone away leaving her place unlocked?" I asked in consternation, meaning: *I shall have no key to lock myself in up there?*

"The street door is locked," he returned curtly. "It is enough."

CHAPTER 7

It was a shock to realize I had settled for accommodation to which this man had access, but there was no turning back now. I crossed the floor of the boutique and made my way up the narrow and perilous flight of wooden stairs. Kriton stood with feet apart, hands clasped behind his back, staring out of the door. I guessed this was a symbolic gesture meaning: *Look, no hands,* or, *Carry your bag yourself, damn you.*

When I reached the top, I came upon a narrow landing not more than ten feet long, with three doors opening off it. I tried the one on the right. It led into the ubiquitous Greek bedroom except that here there was a hand-woven bedspread, dark blue and putty-colored to match the floor tiles, and a colorful dyed wool mat upon the floor. There were two tall windows with a shelf above, holding some Greek pottery of the typical functional design. A kylix, the two-handled drinking cup. A water carrier with handles on either side. The standard wine jug and a very pretty midget amphora, the urn the ancient Greeks used for storing supplies. They were all hand-painted and very well made. They bore no relation to the junk in the shop.

Above the small bed hung a terra-cotta mask frozen into a frown. It was a copy of those linen and plaster masks the ancient Greek actors used to portray characters. Puzzled, for Lee had never shown any interest in Greek drama, I carefully took the mask down. A small card, attached by a ribbon, fell out. On it was written: *To Virginia. Happy Birthday. Love from Lee.* I turned the mask over in my hands. King Creon? I felt sure it was. I was deeply touched that she should have chosen my birthday present with such care. But why would she leave it here, not even prepared for the post? Our birthday, Lee's and mine, had been a week ago.

I knew the answer to my question, and I did not like it: my sister had left in a hurry. With apprehension I looked around the room. A cheap wardrobe with oval mirror stood against the inner wall, next to an ugly chest of drawers. I made a beeline for the wardrobe. It could tell me something.

There were not many clothes in it. A couple of pairs of cotton trousers, a shirt, a long checked skirt and one dress of flimsy material with a pattern of white daisies. I did not recognize any of the clothes, but that was to be expected, since I had not seen my sister for more than a year. I took the dress out, examining it closely. A deep scooped neck, small puffed sleeves, a fitted waist. It was the sort of garment either of us might buy. Certainly all the clothes were in our colors, mainly the blues and greens and aquamarines that flatter blonde hair and fair skins. There were no shoes, and neither was there a coat, but a girl living in this climate would keep shoes

down to a minimum, and she would be unlikely to own
more than one coat, which she had no doubt taken with
her.

I pulled the drawers out one by one. Here was a handbag, unfamiliar in itself but of a familiar style. It was
crocheted in a colorful silk mixture with a pretty
wooden clasp and a handle of plaited braid. I opened
it. It was empty. The drawer below gave up some bras
and underpants. One could say they belonged to Lee, or
for that matter to any girl. I pushed the drawers shut,
no more informed than when I had opened them. There
were no cosmetics and, predictably, no brush or comb. I
went down on hands and knees to peer beneath the narrow bed. Ah! There was a large suitcase, and I recognized it as the one Lee had used at home. I pulled it out
and unzipped the lid. There was not much in it. A blunt
pencil and ballpoint pen, a Penguin edition of Homer's
Odyssey, and my own volume of Byron's works with "V.
Sandersen" written on the flyleaf. *My* book. I wondered
why.

I leafed through. There were pages marked that took
me back in time. The lines in *Childe Harold* underlined
with an indignant black pencil after a visit to the Elgin
Marbles in the British Museum:

The last poor plunder from a bleeding land;
Yes, she, whose gen'rous aid her name endears,
Tore down those remnants with a harpy's hand,
Which envious Eld forbore, and tyrants left to stand.

I sat back on my heels feeling, without much reason,
vaguely comforted. Lee had lived here, and when she
left she had intended to return. But something else I
knew that I had not known before. I had thought she
wanted to sever our relationship. Perhaps after all she
had decided to try to share my interest in something
she discovered really was of value, and the young doctor

who loved us both had served merely as an incentive to get off on her own for a while. I felt considerably warmed by the discovery, mere assumption though it was. I picked up the mask again and gazed at it with a lump in my throat. This gift was kindness indeed.

The room next door was a tiny windowless bathroom containing a sit-up bath and toilet jammed side by side. The door opened only halfway because some wooden structure was wedged between it and the wall.

The third door off the landing led into a kitchen. There was a shallow marble sink with one cold tap over it, a pair of gas jets on a metal framework that passed for a stove, some cupboards containing a meager collection of cups, saucers and plates tastefully decorated with classical Greek figures. There was also a teapot, some cheap utensils and, in a corner, a bowl of fruit gone bad that emitted, as I raised it, a turbulent cloud of fruit flies. I looked around for a bin, found one beneath the sink, tipped the fruit in, washed the mold away and put the bowl upside down to drain.

The kitchen and bedroom windows looked out on a small square with a hard dirt foundation. There was a stunted pepper tree in one corner and a row of neglected geraniums in small pots along the base of the opposite wall. A tall wooden gate, the same height as the stone wall, presumably gave access to the lane in which the boutique lay. I decided it had to open from the outside, since there seemed to be no way into the square from either the boutique or the flat. Come to think of it, I said to myself with a pang of alarm, there was no access to the flat at all except through the boutique! If fire broke out, one would be caught here like a rabbit in a trap.

I went back to the bedroom and stood looking at the windows. Yes, it might just be possible for a person of my size to squeeze through one of them. The apertures were narrow, certainly, but they were tall enough. Below, a tiled roof sloped away toward the ground. From the roof one could possibly drop to the square enclosure, though it would be a tricky jump onto the hard-baked earth. Whether one could then climb the tall gate was another matter. *Heavens!* I said to myself, *what chance would a fire have in a Mykonos house with tiled floor and rough-cast mortar walls?* I knew full well that I was considerably less concerned with the thought of fire than with some undefined necessity for escape.

My attention was arrested by voices from below in the boutique. They were speaking in Greek with a touch of alarm and a great deal of urgency. I went quietly out to the tiny landing and caught the words *óchi*, and *né*, *né*, *né*,—the Greek no, and yes, yes, yes. Kriton was giving orders to someone and the visitor was sounding acquiescent. Involuntarily I moved forward. My rope-soled sandals were silent on the stairs but I must have been heard, for the talk broke off. When I had gone down far enough to see, Kriton stood alone in the shop waiting for me, his face expressionless. I stood there foolishly for a moment.

"Well?"

I ignored his implied criticism of my entrance. "What time do you close?" I asked briskly.

"Seven perhaps. Or half past. Or eight. It depends."

"I shall want a key," I told him. "I am going out to eat."

There was a faint but telling reaction in those blue eyes. Oh, but he was a much better actor than Nat! "You have friends here?" He managed to make the question sound casual, though I knew it was not casual at all.

"I have a friend," I said. "He is coming to pick me up shortly." I kept on with the businesslike manner. "Now tell me, how many keys are there? Since there seems to be no way of cutting my rooms off, I must know who has access."

Our eyes met and I was chilled, for his were as hard

as the rocks of Mykonos itself and as cold and sharp as knives. "I've really no idea," he said. "After all, that is your sister's business. If she wants people to keep the boutique going for her, obviously she has to provide keys for them. It's not a very private place. I did warn you you might not like it. I only hope," he added, "I am not going to get into trouble for letting you take over the flat. As I said, if you didn't look so like her . . ."

His eyes suddenly softened and flowed over me. I had the urgent desire to turn and run. "I shall need a key," I said, and waited, my heart hammering.

His eyes changed again. They seemed to be cutting right through mine. "Well now," he said at last, with open malice, "what are we going to do about that?"

"Hadn't you better give me yours?" We stared at each other and I knew without the slightest doubt that Kriton was struggling against a violent desire to tell me to get the hell off his premises. I suppose I was deliberately courting danger, pushing to see how far he was willing to go in his pretense that the boutique belonged to Lee.

"Perhaps you would like to take the place over yourself," he said, and waited sadistically.

"Why not?" I returned, speaking with miraculous calm since I was going up a blind alley and had no idea either where it was going to end or how I would get back. "So long as the prices are all marked it's pretty straightforward, is it not?"

He made no reply. If he was taken aback by my bravado, then I had not the pleasure of seeing it, for that steely look gave nothing away.

"It's not as though we are on a main shopping street," I added, outwardly impassive. Actually, the statement was a very volatile one. Such words could easily push this man to action. "And there isn't even a sign at the corner directing tourists down here. I am sure I would not have found it if I hadn't been looking really hard. I mean, tourists wandering casually up and down would probably miss it, wouldn't they? So you cannot be terribly busy—ever."

I saw by an expression of thinly veiled hate in the Greek's eyes that I had indeed hit a sore spot. He moved closer in that tomcat way he had. His mouth was at once carnal and callous. "You're possibly right," he said. "I haven't been here much before, so I wouldn't know. I have no wish to spend my valuable spare time as a salesman. You're welcome to take the place over altogether."

Under the immense pressure of his threatening sexuality, I felt my nerve going. With iron control I said, "Thank you. Yes, I will. And by the way," I tried to take a step backward and came up against a chair, "what do you do here? Are you in business?"

"I have interests," he replied, "if it is any affair of yours." He looked right down the front of my blouse, and at that moment, Nat walked in.

The two men faced each other, and for one electrifying moment, I thought they knew each other. Then Kriton said, "You wish to look around?"

I began to breathe again. Was he putting on an act for my sake? Was Nat pretending? Were they shocked to see each other? I could have sworn Nat's interest in my story of Irene and Kriton had been genuine.

"Thanks," he replied, apparently casually. "I have come to see Miss Sandersen."

As I introduced them, I watched them both closely. I thought Kriton seemed faintly interested, but Nat's manner was so casual as to be almost discourteous. Turning back to me, he said, "I'll pick you up shortly. No, why don't you go along and meet me at the restaurant? It's a stone's throw from the place where we had lunch. You go back into the town. It's called The Pantheon and there is a big eucalyptus tree outside. You can't miss it."

I had hoped he might stay talking to Kriton while I changed, but I was disappointed, for Nat seemed in a hurry. He shot out the door saying, "See you."

I glanced toward Kriton, but he had turned away. He was lighting another cigarette. Even with his back to me I had an overwhelming sense that he was totally aware of what I was doing. I felt alone with him, not in the casual sense of two people being in an empty shop together, but alone as though in a house, in a quiet street, with the light fading. There was something almost obscenely intimate about being within four walls with this man. I shot up those perilous little stairs like an arrow from Apollo's bow. I should worry about the lack of bathing facilities at Madame Georgidaes! Wild horses would not drag me into this bath with Kriton downstairs and no lock on the door. I would just make a quick pass over my face with a washcloth, put on a bit of lipstick, and I would be out of there in five minutes flat.

CHAPTER 8

Hurrying into the tiny bathroom I pushed the door so wide it bounced back, hitting me on the side of the head with an impact that sent me reeling. I collapsed on the rim of the bath, rocking back and forth with my head in my hands. A lump rose above my right ear with alarming speed. When the pain cleared I saw that the reason for the door's swing was the structure lodged behind it. Obviously, it did not belong here but I could not make out what it was. It looked like some large wooden lid, almost square. It appeared a bit heavy for me to lift. Perhaps Kriton would move it or help me to do so, I thought, as I rushed through my preparations for departure.

I had brought nothing as suitable for dining out as Lee's long checked skirt. Feverishly, I took it down from the wardrobe, held it against a turquoise blouse of my own and decided to team them together. At home Lee and I had always worn each other's clothes. The handbag with the carved wood top was a good match. All too conscious that possession of Kriton's key did not insure that my rooms would be inviolate, I crammed that little bag with all my most precious belongings. Passport, money, insurance certificate.

He was watching as I descended the stairs. He came a step nearer. Clearly, he recognized my sister's clothes and seemed to be searching for some reason as to why I should take them. He came right up to me and looked into my face.

"People will think you are Lee," he said. If ever anyone handed me the opening for a leading question, he had then.

"Does that matter?" It took all my self-control to speak casually.

He watched me, as though trying to make out whether it mattered to me. He was not bothering with the sexy pose now, and without the charm and seductiveness, he was a man even another male might beware of. Evening gloom had crept through the boutique, shadowing some of the decor, masking corners. Only one lamp was lit, and it was small with a dark red shade. The corners of the room had become cavelike. Now I could not see Kriton's eyes, only the powerful profile with its long nose, its jutting jaw. "Who is this man?" he asked. "This man you're having dinner with—Nat Ross?"

"I don't know him very well," I replied truthfully. "We met en route."

"Does he speak Greek?"

"How would I know? Nat Ross is an English name." I cannot imagine why I was protecting Nat. Some sixth sense perhaps?

"What is he doing here?"

"Holidaying, I imagine. What else?"

Kriton did not reply, but he regarded me with the same intentness. I went to the big lamp with the ugly shade Lee would never have bought and would never even have tolerated in any shop she ran. I switched it on. The flood of light brought me some courage. "There is a great wooden thing behind the bathroom door," I said, putting off the important moment of asking for the key. "If it's not there for any particular purpose, do you think I could put it somewhere else? Does the little square next door belong to the boutique? Would it matter if that object went outside?"

This man had the fast reactions of a jungle beast. He was up those stairs almost before I had finished talking. "I'll get it," he said. "Sorry about that. It's not supposed to be there." I heard a window open, heard a scraping noise, and then he came back down the stairs brushing his hands together, looking pleased. "I have tipped it outside," he said.

"What was it?"

"Just a bit of wood." He was wearing the amused look of a man who sees someone making a fool of herself, and suddenly I had the oddest feeling I had asked him to rid me of something I might need. Unhappily, the brandy had long since worn off. I was not as confident as I had been earlier.

"Now about the key," I said, assuming an offhand air that I was very far from feeling. "Don't you think we might close up?"

He glanced at his watch. "Oh, I don't know. Lee usually stays open until eight." I thought he was starting a battle of wits, but I was not sure.

Somebody walked along the street outside, glancing in. His appearance gave me the excuse I needed to act defiant. "There has not been a single customer since I returned," I said briskly. "We might as well close."

Kriton raised his brows. "In fact, there have been half a dozen customers. You wouldn't know, up there with the doors closed." He emphasized the final words of his lie. They pointed up my hidden fear. I was suddenly tempted to have it out with him then and there, and to hell with the consequences: *This boutique is in the wrong place. It's too tucked away. There really is not enough to make a decent living from the cheap stock it carries. The other shops selling junk are spilling over with it. One wave of tourists from a cruise ship washing up that little white lane and the Boutique Cleopatra would be as clean as a tree after a swarm of ravening locusts has passed by.*

He knew I was on the brink of wanting a showdown. He moved so that he stood between me and the door, then waited, and it was the quality of his waiting that silenced me. "The boutique keeps quite busy," he said at last, speaking slowly and deliberately, as though telling me something he wanted me to assimilate and remember. He paused, looking predatory, like a great black mountain eagle.

The memory of Nat's swift departure struck me suddenly as ominous. Perspiration began to stand out on my forehead and trickle down my back. Kriton Fileas was not, I could see clearly now, a man a girl ought to tackle on her own, with one narrow door as escape route and he standing between it and me. But oh, dear God, the key! I was so certain he had no intention of giving it to me, and I could not bring myself to ask for it. I simply could not stay here. I would have to find a room somewhere else after all, and perhaps it was better that way. I had seen all there was to see.

He was waiting for me to speak. *Say something and go. It doesn't matter what.* I said what was in my mind, and the words were brave enough. "Where does Lee keep her boutique stock?"

As though he saw my fear and it convinced him he had done his job well enough, he moved over to the

counter, picked up a packet of cigarettes, offered me one,
then lit one himself. He drew the smoke down very deliberately, coughing a little, playing for time. "She has
stock," he said. "I haven't got access to it, though." He
waited again, almost as though he dared me, maliciously,
to pursue the subject. My nerve gave way. I turned and
made for the door.

"Your key," he said smoothly. I took it from him without a word. "I'll go," he said, "so you can lock up. I
hope you'll be comfortable. If there is anything I can
do . . ."

I found the restaurant where Nat had asked me to
meet him, but I did not find Nat. Inside there were a few
diners. Outside a cluster of sparsely occupied tables were
set out within the shelter of a beautiful eucalyptus tree.
A party of American tourists occupied three of them.
The only other diner out here was a bearded student
deeply immersed in a thick, dog-eared paperback. A
waiter was busily engaged in a debacle with a Greek
family who occupied an inside table with the confident
air of ownership. He saw me and broke away with a
flourish, straightening his white jacket as he came, his
eyes still snapping. I asked him if he spoke English.

"But of course. Yes. Yes." He flashed some gold teeth.
"You would like a table? You will sit here—or here?"
His footwork was splendid.

Diners are always welcome in restaurants, because
they propose to spend money, but in Greece you have a
feeling of being welcome just because you are yourself.
Eat my bread and drink my wine, the Greeks infer, and
yes, pay for it, but first please enjoy it. I smiled at him
for his friendliness. He was just the man I needed. "I am
waiting for someone."

"Yes, of course." He was pleased that I should have a
friend with whom to dine. He pulled out a rush-bottomed

chair for me. "You would like a drink? What can I bring you? Ouzo? Some retsina? Or a local wine? What is it you like?"

"Thank you. It's very kind of you. Not at the moment."

"Your boutique is doing well."

"You have taken me for my twin sister," I said. "I am visiting her." I looked anxiously into his face, waiting. He saw her yesterday? He had not seen her for ages?

"Oh?" The man stood with one hand resting on the back of the chair opposite, surveying me with astonishment. "You are very much alike."

"Yes, we are. Do you know my sister?"

"No," he replied, and my heart sank. "I do not know her." His eyes strayed to Lee's skirt and he said in that disarmingly friendly way in which Greeks make personal remarks, "You wear her skirt. Sometimes she comes here. Not often. But I see her in the street." The gold teeth flashed again and he flicked his fingers as though demonstrating Lee's top-to-toe attraction. "I notice. She is a very pretty girl. Twins, huh?" And then he was off, sliding between the tables in that smooth, efficient, unobtrusive way waiters have, attending to another new arrival with equal interest and courtesy.

Nothing there. I drummed my fingers nervously on the table. The lump on the side of my head began to hurt. I fingered it, wondering about that wooden object Kriton had taken out. Above my head the eucalyptus rustled faintly, its liquid grays and greens sliding and shifting against its reddish trunk. The Americans were growing noisy. One of them had a parcel and they were all exclaiming over the contents. I tried to interest myself in them, but my dark thoughts came swirling back. Might not Kriton be merely a Casanova with a penchant for interfering in women's affairs? No. My brain reacted violently to that. All right then. Don't think about him. There is nothing you can do for the moment. First, talk to Nat, and then if he can't, or won't, help, go and seek aid from the police. If Lee has really been mixed up with that man . . . Stop thinking! What are those Americans fussing about? What have they bought? I craned my neck but only some peaks of tissue paper came into view. One of the women noted my rudeness and smiled good-naturedly. Faintly embarrassed, I glanced away and returned to my own troubled thoughts. One thing was certain, I could not possibly sleep at the boutique tonight. Now that I considered the implications, I was frankly scared. What on earth had made me think of sleeping there in the first place? If a room in Piraeus cost a mere forty drachmas, it might cost even less here, for the season had not yet started. If I were careful, I could make my traveler's checks last. I kept imagining the possibility of some person with a key coming up those stairs in the middle of the night.

What had made me think of going there in the first place? Then, abruptly, with an anesthetizing shock, I remembered it had been Nat's idea, not mine! And he had insured my acquiescence by cutting the ground from under me, telling me his rooming house was full. With a cold feeling in the pit of my stomach, I remembered the girl's query, spoken in Greek, as we crossed the landing. I remembered Nat's swift response, "*Óchi*," the negative, as he hurried me down the stairs. She may have been asking if I wished to take a room. And remembering that he had boasted of his ability to make people do what he wanted, I wondered if he had ever had such an easy victim as I.

I suppose an unwelcome revelation of such immense proportions always comes as a severe blow. When I was calm again I did not want to think. I picked up the menu, but it was in Greek. Numbly I put it down again. Then I heard one of the Americans at the table near me say in a high, astonished voice, "You saw Ghent's yacht? No!"

"I reckon I did," another answered.

"Gee, where was it?"

"The other side of Naxos."

"Who is Ghent?"

"Earl Foster Ghent. Who else?"

"Gee! *Him!*"

A hand stole across my table with a glass of wine and I looked up with a start into the waiter's friendly black eyes. "It is retsina," he said, "for you to try. As you say, on the house."

"How very kind!" I exclaimed warmly. He shrugged, smiling. "You like retsina?"

"I haven't tried it yet. Yes, I am sure I will." Lee had said it was ghastly. Someone had told her the Greeks at one time were considered to be drinking too much wine so the government, in an abortive effort to stop them, had added resin to it.

"Nice?" the waiter asked.

It must be said, to my eternal credit, that even with my mouth filled with something that tasted like a mixture of sewing machine oil and paraffin, I smiled and took another sip. "It's lovely," I lied. Friendship is not so easily won elsewhere. The Greeks are truly named as the most hospitable people in Europe. And sometimes one needs such kindness.

He looked pleased. "The tourists do not always like it," and then he was off at the clap of a hand from a newly arrived group. I returned to my anguished thoughts. I was working myself into a state. Concentrate on these Americans; listen to them, I advised myself desperately. One of them was saying in disbelief, "You never heard of Earl Foster Ghent?"

". . . richer than Croesus."

"He keeps a lot of his collection out of sight in a secret gallery under his . . ."

". . . half of it's talk. Nobody ever sees him—"

"If I had *Fall Tide* . . ."

". . . aping Howard Hughes, I'd say."

"But it's one of the biggest collections in the States."

". . . Mexico . . ."

The waiter was skirting my table and saw the look on my face. Mistaking my despair for repugnance, he asked, "You don't like it?"

"The wine? Oh, yes, thank you. Yes, it's very—unusual."

He gave a shrug of amusement and resignation. "It is an acquired taste."

Some new arrivals stepped between us and I turned to watch the passers-by, blocking my ears to the broken sentences escaping in frustrating fragment from the table next to me. *Why did Nat want me to sleep at the boutique?* A peasant idled, scowling, into view with his head down and his hands deep in his pockets. The black peaked Mykonian cap that he wore looked strangely new with his old and faded trousers and his washed-out shirt. I kept my eyes on him, thinking about his brand-new cap, trying not to think of Nat. All the tourists bought these caps as souvenirs. This man was scarcely a tourist, but he wore his headgear as the visitors wore theirs, with the incongruous neatness of a city gent in a bowler hat. As he passed the restaurant he glanced up idly, still deep in thought, still frowning, until he saw me . . .

His eyes flew wide open. He stared at me mindlessly as though struck by one of those thunderbolts the great god Zeus threw around with such abandon. Memory flooded back across the hours and I thought, amazed: That is how the woman Irene looked at me! As though I, or Lee, and of course he would think it was Lee, should not be here! As though Lee *could not* be here! I struggled to my feet. The man saw me move and took to his heels, darting away into the shadows beyond some steps where he was immediately masked by a shiny-leafed tree in an enormous pot.

"Oh Miss! Miss!" the waiter exclaimed in consternation. In my haste, I had caught my foot in the chair, tipping the wine, splashing it across the table and shattering the glass on the stones. A young waiter came running. "Oh dear!" I exclaimed, "I am most terribly sorry."

"Miss, it is all right. Please do not worry. Please take this seat, this seat over here, and I will have it cleared away." The Americans stopped talking and turned to stare at me. "Please sit down, Miss," the waiter begged me. "There is no need to go. It was an accident, and we do not mind." Effectively, he blocked my departure with his kindness. Anyway, by now I knew I had lost the man. He would disappear in that warren of streets like a rabbit. I sat down, bewildered and upset, while the staff busied themselves clearing away the wet table cloth, brushing up the broken glass. The Americans' chatter started up again. ". . . I tell you he is mad. Mad Midas, they call him."

". . . all sorts of absolutely priceless stuff that no one has seen. Half a dozen Rembrandts above the ground and God knows what below . . ."

An English voice said, "Sorry to keep you waiting," and I looked up into Nat's apologetic eyes.

CHAPTER 9

"Sorry I'm late," he said. "I was drinking ouzo down on the quay and watching the backgammon." He pulled out a chair, glancing casually round at the diners, giving me only half of his attention. "Did you know it's illegal to play backgammon on Mykonos? And yet they all do."

If ever a man lied about where he had been, Nat was lying then. I could see it in the breeziness of his manner, in his unwillingness to meet my accusing look, in the way he had set up a transparent social scene between us that was polite and impersonal. "Now, what are we going to drink? Have you tried the retsina? It's a curious wine," he chatted. "When the Cypriots ran out of oak for barrels they built them of pine. The Greeks got accustomed to the resinated taste the wine acquired, but it's not every foreigner's cup of tea—er—glass of—Do you want to try it?"

I shot him a venomous look. "I have already tried it. I tipped it over and broke the glass. Lee told me the authorities put that foul stuff in it to stop the Greeks drinking so much." I was frightened and, as usual in such situations, I reacted angrily. I was frightened then because Nat, my one possible aid, had proved himself to be a devil.

"Broke the glass? Well now, there was no need to do that," Nat said tolerantly. "Yes, you're right, some people do say . . . Anyway, let's call for something else. Brandy? Gin? Whiskey? What would you like? Although, when in Rome . . . You really ought to try the ouzo now." He gave me a quizzical look, yet managed not to meet my eyes. "Do you always break things when you're displeased?"

I said, "I'll have an ouzo. I quite like it." I added with what social grace I could muster, "I am sorry for having blown up like that. I've had a fright and I was here a long time on my own."

"Sorry. Was I that late?" Nat glanced a bit too noticeably at his watch.

"No. You weren't. I was very early. I had to get out of the boutique. Nat—" But he was not listening. The waiter had returned to the table and was standing with pad and pencil poised. Nat had the menu. I could see his ears were closed to whatever I might say.

"The lady hasn't made her choice yet," Nat said. "Meantime, two ouzos, please, while we study this." The man went away. Nat flicked a corner of the menu with his thumb. "Have you tried moussaka? Everyone likes that. It is mince and eggplant and a whole lot of other nice things."

"Yes, all right." If he had said sawdust, I could not have been less interested.

"And for starters? Do you like squid? It's tough but really very tasty. Or soup? It's not marked here. You can't always get it, but I'll ask if you like. Not that one can always recommend it. It can turn out to be floating boiled potatoes. Well," he grinned, "that is a slight exaggeration. Ah! Here's the ouzo." He gave me a faintly ridiculous social smile. "Squid or—"

I said, "Squid." Anything to damp the phony chatter and get his attention. "Listen, Nat, I don't want to sleep in that flat. Are you sure there isn't a spare room in your place?"

He was scanning the surrounding tables with a genial expression on his face, for all the world as though this was his local pub and he had an eye open for friends. Only half attentive, he nevertheless managed to look surprised. "But you know I asked this afternoon. What's the matter with your sister's flat?"

"I am scared to sleep there."

"Why ever should you be? You've got the key, haven't you?" He picked up the wine list and studied it.

"Yes. But I cannot lock the flat. How do I know who has a key to the boutique?"

"People don't hand out keys to their property indiscriminately," said Nat with common sense.

"I told you, I think it's Kriton's shop."

"Uh-huh." He was running a finger down the wine list. "Demestica! Ah, yes. I can heartily recommend it. Red or white?"

"Nat." Something in my voice must have got through to him for he paused in his concentration and my heart lifted, but before I could speak he had deliberately shut himself off from me again.

"I think you're too easily frightened by half," he said lightly. "Now, you've told me Lee is like that. Are you sure you're talking about the right twin?"

"Nat, let me tell you something." I was desperate. I had to talk to someone, and in my panic-stricken state a man I did not trust seemed better than no one at all.

"Not if it's going to spoil our evening." He gave me his

complete attention for the first time. "Listen, Virginia, I am serious about this. You've got yourself into a stew over something that is probably a figment of your imagination. If you're still worried about your sister in the morning, we'll go into it, but really, I do think you're making one hell of a fuss about nothing. I've met your Kriton chap now, and he looks normal enough for his type of Greek."

"Nat, that is what I am trying to say. I am scared of him."

"I'm sure there's no need to be. Has he made a pass at you?" And without waiting for a reply: "You've got to remember that the Greeks are a naturally sensuous, amorous lot. You've only been in the country a day and you've probably never met a chap like him before. Ride it along, Virginia. Since your sister wasn't expecting you, there is reason why she should not have gone off for a day or two, and there's no reason either why she shouldn't show up tomorrow. I've been thinking about what you said this afternoon. You've done a heck of a lot of jumping to conclusions with regard to the stock of the shop and Lee's choice of friends. Don't you think so?"

I said feverishly, "Nat, a workman went past—past here—and when he saw me he ran as though he'd seen a ghost."

Nat looked incredulous.

"I—spilled the retsina—trying to run after him."

Nat's incredulity changed to blank disbelief and my face flamed. "Here, have a cigarette," he said. "You're distraught."

Without looking at him, I took one. He lit it and I drew some steadying breaths.

Nat said solemnly, "I was beginning to feel a little apprehensive about dining with a girl who breaks glasses if she doesn't like the taste of the wine. Then I am reassured only to be told I am dining with a girl who runs after peasants. What would you have done if you had caught the chap?" He raised one eyebrow, regarding me with mock caution.

"Snob," I said, laughing, and then to my distress two tears rolled down my cheeks.

"That's better." Then he saw the tears, hesitated, and briefly I thought I detected a faint softening about the mouth. He seemed about to say something, then changed his mind. I brushed the tears away.

"I have found a place where we can watch the local folk dancing tonight and join in," Nat said, "if you've an ability to pick up steps fast. How about that? I think the answer is to take you out of yourself, don't you?" With his full attention on me it was like the warmth of a midday sun.

Nat convinced me, albeit only for the duration of time we spent together. We ate such marvelous food: the squid, that octopus-like abomination that I would never have ordered on my own but which tasted of lovely, mysterious sea things; the creamy, spicy, wonderful moussaka; and then the feta cheese, white as Mykonos itself. Perhaps it was the red demestica, more heady than I'd supposed. I ate that meal with appetite and then joined in the lusty village dancing in a quaint taverna somewhere near the sea with the lilting tones of the bouzoukia in my ears. Afterward we walked back to the boutique and listened to a far-off sea cry like a shell echo behind us. Nat convinced me all was well with Lee and the Boutique Cleopatra for the length of time he was with me, but the next morning rude consciousness broke over me again like a wave hurtling upon the shore.

I rose early. The bed had proved hard and comfortless, the two rather worn blankets inadequate. I knew, though, that the bed was only partially to blame for the fact that I lay for five hours half awake and chilly. Kriton had

said I might find the town claustrophobic. This set of
rooms, overlooking the minuscule yard and so shut in,
the yard itself girded on every side by high walls: none of
it made me feel very free. I was fully dressed at seven
o'clock and in a rush to be out of it and warm myself
beneath Mykonos' rising sun.

Last night Nat and I had seen a cruise ship arrive
and anchor offshore. A Chinese lantern of a vessel with
every porthole a golden pool, and a necklace of bright
lights strung out from the tip of the foremast to the
stern.

"If you're serious about opening the boutique," he had
said, "you will have to be pretty quick. Ships often stay
only an hour or so. Long enough for the passengers to
get rid of their spending money. Then they're away
again." To the news that Kriton had offered to hand
the business over to me, he had replied offhandedly,
"Well, why not? It's something to do while you're waiting."

As I came downstairs now, I had the feeling I was in
an alien territory. The boutique was a place of gloom
and shadows. Repressing a desire to look back over my
shoulder, I crossed the tiles swiftly and unlocked the
door. Slipping out into the side street, I locked it again
and ran the short distance to the corner, then turned
right at the main street and hurried toward the waterfront. Here, my footsteps slowed and I breathed an enormous sigh of relief.

The quay was alive with sea scents, sea sounds and
movement. Solid, seagoing caïques lay like brightly
colored toys on an aquamarine sea streaked with the
glassiness of early morning. Two pelicans were happily
involved with the brown, weatherbeaten men of the shore
in their battered black caps and blue dungarees. I stood
there on the quaint white-ringed paving stones, breathing deeply of the fresh, salt morning, glad to be free. Oh,

so glad to be surrounded by people again. Never before had I been conscious of feeling safe like this.

I skirted a mess of dun-colored ropes that smelled of tar and fish and paused to watch a Greek, his shirt puffed out by a breeze, busily painting the interior of a dinghy a bright orange. Someone shouted, and a woman called shrilly from a maroon balcony above some white arches. The lusty, lively Greek day had begun and I was glad to be a part of it. I would not sleep another night in that boutique with its skulking, crawling silence. I would turn over every stone this morning in search of my sister, then if I did not succeed I would go to the police. I began to walk fast, thinking of what it might mean if she could not be found. Then realizing I was going nowhere, I stopped where a ring of black-capped fishermen were noisily involved in argument. The pelicans waddled in and out among them with enormous interest and a certain gawky dignity. One of the men grinned at me and the others stopped to eye me with quickened interest. Their reaction, of course, was to be expected since I was a girl alone in Greece.

Here two men were wrapping up golden nylon nets as carefully as a woman folds a tablecloth. Those nets would not make such a bad bed, I thought, if I had to sleep in the open, although I never really felt it would come to that. The promenade was quiet at the town end, but as I neared the quay, shops burst open one after another as though a score of alarm clocks had gone off. They all displayed that riot of shawls and blouses, hats, and bright wool rugs that had dazzled me as I came ashore yesterday.

Momentarily shelving my problems, I watched fascinated as short, dark men bustled out on the promenade carrying shirts and dresses on hangers strung one above the other on long poles, a cascade of glowing color against the snow-white walls of the waterfront houses.

A far cry this was from the ominous stillness of the Boutique Cleopatra only a few hundred yards away. Outside the tavernas, boys wearing workmen-like aprons rushed chairs and tables from their nocturnal stacks. With flamboyant strokes they dusted those that had stayed out all night. A business-like little man with a huge moustache was noisily directing two boys as they unrolled a huge white canvas awning that would shield his tables from the relentless sun. Everyone seemed in an incredible hurry, and suddenly I realized why.

Half a dozen motorboats had shot out from the quay and were scudding around the breakwater, heading for the big liner that lay at anchor, glittering like an iced cake in the cool white light of early morning.

The motorboats came together at the gangway's foot, and passengers came streaming down. The sight of these approaching tourists brought me back to my own problems. *Well, Virginia*, I said to myself, *are you going to open the boutique? It could prove something, if you feel it needs proving.* Indecisively I began retracing my steps. Early customers were settling at the little tables, and on the promenade waiters were bringing out trays with slabs of bread and thick white cups accompanied by flat packets of powdered milk and Nescafé.

Yes, I decided, I would open the boutique, just to find out if tourists actually came there. And then, following a sudden idea that alarmed me a little, I headed up the curving main street. I decided to pretend that I was a newly arrived tourist, and tried to act like one, glancing interestedly from side to side, noting the chapel, the balconies, the geraniums. I came to the street marked with its unpronounceable Greek name, and ignored it as a foreigner always ignores those indecipherable Greek letters. I stopped, turned slowly round. My eyes were wide open and I was looking, really looking.

Yes, it was disquieteningly true. There was nothing to arrest the stranger! Nothing at all! Now that I was not searching for it, now that I had told myself I did not know it was there, I had not even seen the Boutique Cleopatra sign! Something more than fear tightened the muscles in my shoulders and my back. It could be true, then, that the boutique might be here for some other purpose than to sell souvenirs! Though the narrow lane was still cool, I felt the clamminess of sweat between my shoulder blades and in the palms of my hands.

I had turned into the lane, or thought I had. I stopped dead. Where was I? I looked up and down, bewildered. White walls, white-ringed paving slabs. Had I taken the wrong entrance? I retraced my steps, turned. There was no Boutique Cleopatra sign! And yet, this *was* the lane. Here was the unpronounceable ΘΗΣΕΩΣ. And there the door to my sister's shop! But the shop sign had been taken down!

I stood for a long moment, numb with shock, before my mind began to spin. A tourist ship arrives. All the shops throw wide their doors, bringing out their wares. But the Cleopatra recedes, closes, opts out!

Even for me, now, they were no longer pretending. I don't remember what was in my mind as I began fumbling for my key. Nothing, perhaps, but a spasm of panic because I knew that someone had come here in the early hours to remove the sign while I was asleep. I could swear it had been in place when Nat escorted me from the taverna to this door. So a person unknown had been busy at the boutique as I slept fitfully upstairs! I dug for the key, my nerveless fingers missing it as it slid among my papers in the bottom of the bag. Now, not this afternoon, was the time to go. I would take my things and run to the police before anyone appeared. Before Nat, or Kriton, or that weird Irene came to tell me what they wanted me to do.

I had not yet found my key, but I was hurrying ahead, the bag jolting against one hip. Heavens! But the door was open! There was a lamp glowing in the interior. Oh, but I was going mad! Had Lee come back? Had she really returned? I stopped with one foot on the marble step, my breath caught in my throat, the sudden, soaring, crazy hope in me dropping like a stone with a sick thud that left me rocking.

"Hello, good morning," said Kriton Fileas calmly. "And where have you been?"

CHAPTER 10

You gave me the key. Your key. How did you get in?
The question came raging indignantly up into my throat and locked there, choking me, for Kriton was standing in the middle of the room with the dim light from the lamp playing tricks on his face, making what had seemed yesterday merely a callous mouth look cruel. And somehow, he seemed physically larger to me. Though he was no taller than an average Englishman, this man could appear immense when he had a mind to impress and frighten perhaps.

"The sign is gone," I said stupidly.

"Yes, I took it down." He spoke, too, like a man who does not expect to be challenged. "The stock is rather low," he told me with the confident air of one who makes decisions. "There is a cruise ship in. We could be totally

depleted in five minutes." He fixed me with the coldest
pair of blue eyes I ever saw in my life, and this time the
light was not playing tricks. His look was dangerous.
"It is better this way, to keep up a front. Until Lee returns, I mean. With more stock." The staccato style was
deliberate, part of the new image he wished to present.

I turned nervously toward the narrow stairs, feeling
trapped, not knowing what to do.

"There is something I think I ought to tell you," Kriton said.

I spun around. He had gone over to the counter and
stood with his back to it. He looked very dark this morning. Black brows, thick black hair, long black lashes that
seemed to hold his eyes in shadow. I was suddenly aware
of the difference between a friendly foreigner and an unfriendly one. "Your sister could be in trouble," he said.
"You would be wise not to talk too openly to strangers."

"What do you mean?" My throat was dry, and yet a
great wave of relief surged through me. A girl who is in
trouble is a girl alive.

"She has been, let us say, a little careless." Kriton was
no longer threatening. He came slowly toward me, turning his full attention on me. "Perhaps you do not know
there are rules governing what tourists may take out of
Greece."

"*Out* of Greece?" I queried sharply. "You said Lee was
on a local buying trip. Bringing goods into the island."

He looked amused. "Oh, no. I don't mean she has gone
smuggling. Not that I know of, anyway, although it's not
my business to watch every little English girl who comes
out here looking for sun and adventure."

The calculated insult fired my anger and went a good
distance toward quenching the fear. It is not possible to
be angry and scared stiff at one and the same time.

"Then what did you mean?" I asked coldly. "I wish you
would stop hinting and simply tell me. I would really
like to know."

He offered me a cigarette, then lit one himself. "It's in the guidebooks." He spoke patronizingly. "I am amazed that people like you and your sister don't have all the facts at your fingertips. After all, this is a strange country to you."

I could see now that he enjoyed power for its own sake. He liked to needle me. He liked standing over me, close like this, feeling bigger and stronger. I tried to cast out my awareness of his proximity. "My guidebook says that curios from the Greco-Roman and Byzantine period are a bit tricky. Still, one can check on them," I said.

He sucked at his cigarette, then exhaled the smoke in a narrow, fast stream. "Yes, of course. If one is honest."

"What do you mean? What are you insinuating? That Lee is not honest?"

"There is no use in looking angry like that," Kriton advised me calmly, tossing his match into a large ceramic ashtray on the counter.

Now I was not feeling angry. Antagonistic, certainly, but my fear had returned. Lee could be such a fool. I knew that better than anyone. "If Lee has broken the law it would be in total innocence," I said. "I wish you would tell me the circumstances."

"Of course. But you are a stranger here, and first I have to explain. There were some coins. It is possible to trade in coins, for there are a lot of them that are not very important."

"But?"

"One would have to check them with the authorities, for some are very ancient and very valuable. Not just Greco-Roman or Byzantine. Very ancient indeed. B.C. Hundreds of years B.C."

"And Lee sold some? From this boutique? Without checking them?"

He nodded.

"How did she come by them?"

Kriton's big shoulders rose, then settled regretfully. I

listened, half hypnotized. "Someone sold them to her perhaps. Or perhaps she found them. It is easy enough to go
across to Delos. Forty minutes only in a caïque."

I drew in my breath, almost hissing. "You are saying
my sister actually hired a caïque and went over to Delos
to look for antiquities to sell in this boutique? I don't believe you. Lee is not that sort of person."

"You don't know, nor do I," Kriton said.

But I did know my twin sister was not a thief. She had
as good a social conscience as I, and a foreign country's
antiquities simply would not tempt her. "Who is on
Delos? Does anyone live there?" I asked.

"There are hostels for archeologists. And the coffee
house lets out one or two rooms. There are the guardians
of the sights also. It's really no use protesting," Kriton
went on relentlessly, "because your sister did stay there,
at least for one night that I know of."

"Well, why not? That doesn't make her a thief." My
mind flashed to the contents of my sister's suitcase upstairs: the books concerned with Greece. "She has obviously become interested in the local history," I said, "and
literature, too. Well, it is to be expected, isn't it, for there
cannot be much to do here out of season. But as to saying
she would deliberately look for antiquities and sell them,
that's sheer nonsense."

He looked pained. "Will you listen to me? There is
something I think you ought to know."

"I am listening." I managed to make my voice sound
cold, but my confidence was seeping away.

"Lee recently sold a very valuable Greek coin to a tourist, and it's going to come back."

"Come back? What do you mean by that?"

"I mean the Englishman who bought it is bound to get
it valued when he goes home, and there is going to be
trouble then. It was a fourth century B.C. silver coin with
Apollo's head on it."

I stifled a gasp. "Why didn't you stop her if you know so much about it?"

"I would have done so if I had been here. I heard about it from Irene who was interested from an artist's point of view. She had taken a rubbing from it and we could see the signature: Herakleidias. But by that time the buyer had disappeared."

I passed my tongue over dry lips. I was not going to lay myself open to further insult by asking about that signature. It sounded grand enough. I knew that the Herakleidae were the descendants of Heracles, or Hercules, chosen by Zeus to rule in the Peloponnese—that was legend. A coin was fact, but Greek myths and history tended to merge. The coin could be priceless, anyway.

"Nothing has happened yet," said Kriton, making the word "yet" sound ominous, "but the necklace is another matter."

Apprehension tightened my muscles and set my nerves throbbing. I think he sensed how I felt and was gloating. I did not believe Lee had knowingly done anything wrong, but I could see how such a thing could happen. How could an English girl like her recognize a valuable archeological find? "Tell me about the necklace," I said.

"It was Egyptian," Kriton explained. "The Egyptians had the island for a long period, do you know?"

I knew Delos' history. Everyone had the island at some time. Egyptians, Romans, Phoenicians, pirates, goatherds . . . "What happened to the necklace?"

"Lee sold it to an American. I was in Athens at the time. I knew nothing about it until people around here started to talk."

"What were they saying?"

"The woman who bought it put it on show in a museum in Boston and it was written up in the papers. The Greek authorities are interested now. You know, it is a very serious crime to sell loot."

I felt myself grow hot and cold at once. "But if she did it innocently?"

He shrugged. "After all, Lee might have a—now look, I don't like saying this, but for all the authorities know, or for all I know, your sister might have a source she is milking."

Anger hurled my fear adrift. "You're out of your mind."

He seemed very interested in my reaction. I had an unpleasant sensation of having been tried out and of having shown him what line to take.

"Perhaps she simply made a mistake," he said smoothly. "You must realize it is not so easy for a foreigner to run a shop in a strange country."

I looked him squarely in the eyes. "Then why is she doing it?" I asked with chin high.

"Why does anyone run a shop?" He turned half away, indifferently. "It is a nice thing to do."

The sun had made the lane outside into a cube of solid light glaring whitely toward the sky. There was a whole shipload of tourists in town, perhaps already pouring up the main street not fifty feet away, and I was about to be surrounded by people who spoke my own language. The knowledge filled me with confidence. And I was very angry. Needless to say, I was angry with my sister for getting herself into this idiotic mess. But the real object of my wrath stood before me. "I put it to you," I said, watching that powerful face in profile, "that this is your boutique."

He turned on me with such suddenness that I jumped. "The Cleopatra belongs to your sister," he said. "She can show you papers to prove it."

I was surprised, but wary. I could see that he was telling the truth. "Then where did she get the money?" I demanded. "From you?"

He gave me a deliberate smile. "So far as I know, your sister isn't a whore," he said.

Stunned by his offensive words, I took an automatic
step forward. I think I was actually going to hit him.
Certainly my right hand was raised, for he grasped the
wrist, his fingers closing like a clamp, tightening until
the pain drove my breath from my body. "Don't try that
again," said Kriton softly. "Don't try anything like that
with me."

"My God!" I breathed, supporting my wrist that was
now white with red streaks where his fingers had been,
"and you say you're a friend of Lee's! I just don't believe it. Do you treat her like that?"

"Lee never tried to hit me," Kriton replied and smiled.

I forced myself to be calm. Nothing was to be gained
by losing my temper. "Where is my sister?"

"I told you. She is on a buying trip."

I moved tentatively toward the door. "I am going to the
police," I said. "They might be able to locate her and let
her know I am here."

Not by the faintest movement of a muscle did he show
himself to be disturbed. "I would not do that if I were
you," Kriton advised me calmly. "If they were to talk to
me, I should feel obliged to tell them that what they already suspect is true. The Egyptian necklace came from
the Boutique Cleopatra. Such flouting of the laws carries
a very heavy penalty."

"Why would you tell them?" I asked through tight lips.
"You, who say you are a friend of my sister?"

The answer was too pat. "One must safeguard one's
national heritage."

You, I thought, are not a man to safeguard anything,
except your own pocket and your life. "Are you Greek?"
I asked. He looked so genuinely astonished that I knew
my suspicions to be correct. Kriton Fileas might have
Greek blood, but he was not a pure Greek. My question
had been a shot in the dark. It obviously mattered a great
deal to him, although I had no idea why.

"You're a funny girl," he said. To my surprise, he

spoke quite kindly. I had the oddest feeling that he had made a snap decision and decided to consider the possibility of making a friend of me.

At that moment the postman entered. He was a young man in a neatly tailored summer suit of gunmetal gray. He carried a large bundle of letters in his left hand, and one letter in his right. Clearly, he took me for my sister for he smiled, holding the single envelope out to me. It was addressed to Lee and it bore an American stamp. I went over to the counter and put it down.

"I only say all this to you," said Kriton, following me, "because I think you would be wise not to talk too much to your English friend until you know exactly who he is. This Nat Ross. I would find out if I were you. He may very well be from I.C.O.M."

"What is that?"

"The International Council of Museums in Paris. Or he may be a classical archeologist making inquiries on behalf of some similar body. And that means the police in the end."

As Kriton spoke I was looking down at the letter. He was close behind me, and all at once I had a sensation of imminent danger. I whirled around. His arm came across mine, but I sidestepped and left him standing by the counter, smiling in a pained sort of way.

"You have bad nerves." His voice was silky, and while I was recovering from my foolishness and embarrassment, he produced a nail file from his pocket and slit the envelope.

"Look here, that letter is addressed to my sister. How dare you open it!"

I might have been a fly on his sleeve for all the notice he took of me. "We have an arrangement," he said.

"That you should open Lee's letters?" I cried, outraged. "I don't believe you! I simply don't believe you!"

He shrugged faintly. That slight movement of his shoulders told me plainly that he did not give a tinker's damn whether I believed him or not. He was reading the letter. My anger burst forth in an uncontrollable rush and I reached out to snatch the letter from him. "How dare you!" He grasped my wrist. Heaven knows, I had been warned. That clamp closed upon it again and was getting tighter. I gasped and fell back with a sharp cry of pain. A female American voice drawled from the doorway, "Gee, no, it's not a shop. For a moment I thought it was. Maybe it's a private house or something. Better stick to the main street, girls."

CHAPTER 11

I came across Irene by accident. I had left the boutique in a mindless rush and headed away into that maze of streets that could take me anywhere. She was standing behind an easel in the quarter Nat had told me was termed Little Venice.

Over the tops of a crush of dwellings that were lower than the rest I had caught a glimpse of a windmill sail tip as it disappeared—one flag of triangular white canvas and then another, swinging across the blue background of sky. At that moment I needed some cool air more than I needed anything else. Away from these enclosed streets, sitting on a grassy spot fanned by a mill's giant arms, perhaps the knots in my mind might untangle. I had begun to climb up some steep rock steps bordered by pale violet campanula—myriads of little funnel-shaped flowers rioting from the stem—when out of the corner of my eye I saw an opening leading down to the sea. I hesitated and then turned back. Running down the alleyway, I found myself on a bank above the big square with a chapel and that restaurant where I had noticed the salmon-shaded pelican. Beyond lay the narrow beach.

I recognized Irene from behind by her extraordinary hair. The brilliant sun that might, together with some misapplied bleach, have been the cause of its straw texture, glittered down upon it, exposing its uneven color and the tiredness of the strands. She stood behind an easel set on the stony ground just back from the beach. Unhesitatingly I moved toward her. She did not hear my footsteps. Of course, even to one less absorbed than she was, the babble of the water as it raced around the stones would have drowned any other noise.

Irene was working, very expertly, on a picture of the old ramshackle houses that bordered the aquamarine bay. They thrust their colored balconies out over the water to be sprayed by a high sea. A line of washing hung in the still air, and below, tiny windows peeped out of a basement as though waiting for an afternoon wave to splash up in their eyes.

The picture on the easel was a faithful rendering of the scene except that Irene had slashed a blood-red streak across two of the house façades. Though I know little about painting, the picture struck me as superb, but it also chilled me. Looking at the savage, dramatic beauty of this woman's work, I saw there was evil in her brush tip: a strange, painful sort of evil that was nothing like Kriton's strongarm beastliness. I could imagine Kriton picking up a small animal and dashing it against the rocks. I could imagine Irene caging it and waiting . . . But the one thing I could not imagine in my wildest dreams was that either of them could be a friend of my sister, Lee.

I must have made some abrupt movement because she turned. It was a slow, deliberate act, as though she had no nerves at all. She looked at me, her long, sallow face expressionless. "Good morning," I began, smiling uncertainly, "I—I don't know your name. Miss—"

"Irene Woods."

"I don't want to disturb you, Miss Woods," I said, "but there is something I would like to talk to you about. And by the way, I was admiring your painting. It is beautiful. Do you sell your work here?"

"Sometimes." The pale eyes within their surprising lashes were expressionless.

"I am sure you do very well with them."

She turned away. The polite small talk was evidently not worth her time. I hesitated a little too long, thrown perhaps by her disdain for my friendly words. She picked up a brush from an open box, looked at it intently, then with a little sigh dropped it again. The implication was clear: I was disturbing her concentration.

I said swiftly, "I won't keep you a moment. There is something I would like to ask. It is rather important."

"Yes." She seemed totally uninterested.

"It is about my sister—about Lee. Perhaps you can tell me, since you are a friend of hers, if—well, if you have heard anything about—well—about any sort of trouble?" She did look at me then, but there was no movement of the facial muscles or flicker in those strange eyes. "For selling archeological treasures," I said. "Things she perhaps—ought not to sell."

The woman picked up the brush and rolled it against a worm of cobalt blue. "I really don't want to be involved," she returned indifferently. She frowned at the canvas and made some sweeping strokes, darkening the water against the houses. It seemed almost as if she had forgotten my presence.

A group of tourists from the cruise ship burst noisily

out of the square beyond. "Say, there it is! We found it! Little Venice!"

"Come on, Harry, we got no time. Let's get rid of these dollars."

"An artist, huh!"

"Sh-sh-sh." Their footsteps clattered away on the white-ringed stones and I looked hopelessly at the back of Irene's blonde head. "My sister isn't here," I said, "and now I have heard this story. Couldn't you either confirm or deny it? You do know Lee. If there is any truth in it you must have heard something."

"Who told you?" Irene continued to paint, asking the question casually as though she either did not care about the answer or already knew it.

"Kriton Fileas."

"If Kriton says so, then I expect it's right." She turned a brush in a mess of green, then stabbed it gently at the canvas, darkening a shadow on a balcony. "And if it is so," she added with conscious certainty, though still without looking at me, "there is one person you would do well to keep away from. That man Ross."

So she knew about him! Kriton would have told her. That was interesting.

She daubed and stroked with her brush. She frowned over the canvas. "He thinks you're Lee, doesn't he?" she said softly.

"Thinks I am Lee! No, I am sure he doesn't."

A small black cat with hungry eyes came and rubbed around my ankles.

Irene leaned forward, touching a window delicately with a white glow of oil. "It sounds to me," she said, "as though he is investigating Lee. And so if I were you I would take the afternoon boat back to Piraeus. In fact, I'd get out of the country as fast as I could. It's not like England, you know. Police here are inclined to act first and ask questions afterward. And you're the dead spit of Lee. I wouldn't be at all surprised if she has gone home. If she has any sense at all, she'll be there by now."

Why had I not thought of that when Kriton told me about the necklace and the coin? I stood still, shocked and relieved at the same time until suddenly I was jarred back to the present by a sea bird's strangled cry. "Did she say anything to you about going home?" I asked, my voice rising with this new hopeful thought. "She has left a good many things at the boutique."

"If I were running away from a foreign country," said Irene Woods, her strange eyes watching me, "I would not tell my best friend. Nor would I leave with a pile of luggage."

I knew then that this woman had some practice in running. I felt certain her name had not always been Woods. In that moment of tentative relief my heart softened, and I actually felt a little sympathy for her.

Lee's departure for home was a possibility and my heart was lighter for the thought. I left Irene and swung off back into the town. I would telephone home. No, no, I must not do that. If my sister had not arrived, our mother would be very alarmed. What to do, then? I stopped on the next corner, testing the sensation of relief in me against the prickling of uncertainty that still remained. I stared blankly at a bank of sun-washed brilliance that rose from a stack of white-painted tins and tubs. Roses—pink, golden, apricot—bursting out in a great flood; hydrangeas blue as the sea and sky; geraniums flaming across a sun-hot stone; and right next door, small pots of thorned cactus in soldier-straight rows, and a brown lizard sleeping. A thin stray cat in patchwork fur licked its white paws.

I stared at the scrawny, unwanted cat and a small voice at the back of my mind began to chide me. *You fool, Virginia. Isn't that just what anyone would say to get rid of you? Run away from Nat, who might help find Lee. Run home, where you won't be in our hair.* And when you come to think of it, the last thing your willful twin would do in these circumstances is go home. She would run, certainly, and possibly to a chance acquaintance with a convenient offer of refuge. Had she not run to Kriton Fileas when she was having man trouble in Athens? But not home—to Mother or me. And why not?

Because it was I, the other twin, who had wanted to go to Greece. I who had dreamed for years of Athens, "proud in the girdle of her Seven Hills." The world of classical Greece, the world of Zeus, ruler of Mount Olympus; Apollo, god of the sun; Aphrodite, dispenser of love and beauty; Dionysus, of the vine; and the mighty Poseidon, ruler of the sea and earthquakes, was my world, not Lee's. Many was the quiet evening I had spent alone with Greece's heroes. As a child I could recite the twelve tasks of Heracles. Oedipus, the challenger of the Sphinx, was my hero. And Jason and the Golden Fleece was my favorite children's story that had stood me in good stead on many an evening's baby sitting.

Perhaps Lee, inexplicable though it seemed, was suffering from an overwhelming sense of inferiority or even jealousy. Perhaps she felt she might catch up an easier way than perusing the books I loved. Whatever the reason for her dash to Greece when we decided to split, there was something not quite right about it. Therefore, if things went wrong, the last refuge my sister would seek would be our mother, who had been saddened by her act. I recalled again the words crossed out in Lee's letter which I had so carefully deciphered: *When something goes wrong.* My twin, I was absolutely certain, had the moral fiber to cope alone when hoist with her own petard.

Without making a conscious decision to visit Nat, I found myself at the jewelry shop flanking the staircase which ran up to his room. While I was standing there,

shredding a paper tissue in the pocket of my jeans, trying to make up my mind, a beefy, pleasant-faced Greek
with a huge, drooping moustache waddled into the lane
on his short legs, smiling invitingly. "You will come in?
You are welcome to look. I have much good jewelry.
Brooches. Necklace."

His pressing invitation spurred me into action. I
smiled at him, shook my head and, turning aside, I went
up the two flat marble steps leading from the street to
the stairway of the house above. This morning the Greek
girl was probably busy with her domestic duties for she
was not guarding the landing. I knocked at Nat's door.
Receiving no reply, I tried the knob. The room was empty.

At first I felt only numb surprise, and then my skin
began to prickle as if there were needles down my back.
I had a queer, lost, absolutely hopeless feeling of being
totally alone. A feeling that was so utterly unacceptable
that, in a desperate moment of frustration, I lunged toward the wardrobe and flung the door violently open.

It was a poor piece of furniture, made of thin wood.
My action not only jerked the door wide, it set the wardrobe rocking. A jacket that was hanging inside slid off
the metal hanger and fell on the floor. "Help!" With a
gasp, I steadied the wardrobe on its awkward legs, then
picked up Nat's coat. A thick paper folder, torn at the
edges, slipped out of the inside pocket and fell, spilling
some photos.

I gathered them up and was returning them to the
folder when my gaze was arrested by the topmost picture
of a sun-tanned girl in a brief, sleeveless dress. A girl
with wide-set eyes like mine, a short, straight nose like
mine, a cascade of long blonde hair. A girl, in short, who
could be me and yet was not. I turned the photograph
over. On the back was written: *Lee Sandersen, 5'7", gray
eyes, fair skin. About 118 lbs.*

My fingers tightened on the thin card. Of course I had
known, had always known that he was looking for Lee.

But until this morning I had not known why. Now I felt a cold despair. I put Lee's picture aside and looked at the next one. A muscle twisted like a small, sharp knife in my stomach as my eyes took in the hard calculating eyes, the thick mouth, the rich black hair of Kriton Fileas as he might appear in a passport photo. He seemed somehow devoid of his sexuality, as though he had been scraped clean of it. I stared at the likeness, feeling a swell of apprehension. It was not exactly a passport photo. What was it then? I turned it over: *Kriton Fileas, Age 35. Palestinian-Greek. 177 cms. Approx. 81 kilos. Blue eyes.* I examined the picture again. Then suddenly, in a burst of realization, I saw what the harsh clarity of this likeness meant. The photo had been taken in a cold, unflattering light, and Kriton was wearing an expression one would not normally adopt on being photographed.

Last year I had been asked to call at a police station in order to identify a hit-and-run driver. In the police files there had been pictures of wanted men, and they had all looked like this. Likenesses taken in custody, showing a man's identity rather than his attractiveness.

The third likeness was not a photograph, but a sketch. The subject was a man with the low brow of the Greek peasant, a wide, strong mouth, a battered-looking hawk nose, and rather kindly eyes. The hair was cut short and turning gray. On the back was written: *Identikit of Taki Bajanis. Age 50. No identifying marks known.* It was the face of almost any fisherman along the waterfront; the face of a plain Greek man who has perhaps worked a little too hard, spent a little too much time in the sun. There were laugh lines and worry lines, and through them there was an expression of sadness. It was a very good identikit indeed, drawn by an artist who must surely have seen the face at some time and remembered the look, even if he had had to be reminded of the features.

I slid the pictures together and put them back in the

pocket of Nat's jacket. Then I hung the jacket up again. I went out onto the landing. Closing the door carefully behind me, I descended the stairs. I paused at street level, wondering what to do.

A short, very dark Greek in shirt sleeves came up to me, smiling. "This is my house," he said. "You are looking for a room?"

"I was looking yesterday," I replied, "but you were full up." I spoke automatically, knowing the answer, but somehow wanting to be proved wrong.

The man's brown face creased into a frown. "Oh no! No, we were not full," he protested. "We have only two people staying at this time. There is an Englishman and a German girl. You would like to look at a room?"

"Not just now, but I may move in later if it's still convenient. I was looking for Mr. Ross," I said bleakly. "The Englishman. Do you know where I might find him?"

"I did see him," the man replied, eager to please a potential guest. He extended an arm. "That way, toward the quay. You will find him at the kafenion, I expect. But I will tell him if he comes back that you look for him."

CHAPTER 12

He was there, outside a taverna, where he had been having breakfast. His eyes were half closed against the glare, his long legs thrust full length, his strong, lean body curved between rush seat and upright wooden back. He did not look at all like either a policeman or a classical archeologist. He looked like a tourist with no more cares in the world than the acquisition of a better suntan.

I turned away, sick to the heart. It is a fact that something totally unacceptable can be driven right from the mind by an effort of strong will. There, amid the rank and pungent scents of fish and sea, before my inevitable confrontation with Nat, I turned my attention to tourists chatting gaily at the little tables beneath the giant awnings; then to last night—I searched for anything that would postpone what I had to do.

The Greeks, who saw more than enough of the sun in their working day, sat inside the large kafenion near the quay. As they played cards and tossed dice, a clamor of talk and argument arose. "What do they talk about?" I had asked Nat, after the dinner and dancing when we had walked down here last night. "And where are the women, for heaven's sake?"

"Politics, mostly. It's the national pastime," he had replied, and then, eyes amused: "Women have their place in Greece, but it's not in the kafenion."

"In bed and the kitchen. I know, poor things," I had replied with feeling. "And, Lee says, in the fields, or leading a donkey while their lords and masters ride. Was it not your own namesake, Pericles, who advised women they should aspire to be anonymous?"

"It is a man's country," he had replied, smiling rather wickedly. And then: "The kafenion is where the heart of each man lies."

The thud of a thrown rope echoed dully on the quayside and an argument started up nearby. It roused me out of my fog of apprehension and uncertainty. I turned and walked across the cobblestones, not knowing what I was going to say. I had been angry a while ago. Now I was scared at the prospect of a confrontation. But surely, I thought, trying to convince myself, there is something to be said for knowing where one stands, even if one's patch of ground is totally untenable. I pulled out a chair opposite him and sat down.

Nat blinked, started to his feet, then relaxed. "You are about early."

"This may be early for you, but I have been on the go since seven." Looking at that classical Greek head set on the familiar English shoulders, I thought: how could such a man behave as he has done?

He seemed surprised. "Seven o'clock. Whatever for? I thought you were on holiday."

"As you very well know," I replied, coming right to the

point, "I am looking for my sister. And so are you. Do you, by any chance, still think I am Lee?" Those tawny, golden eyes flickered, narrowed. "You see," I added, deliberately but not without some difficulty, "I have just come from your room. I have seen the pictures in the pocket of your jacket. Why are you carrying photos of Lee and Kriton, Nat?"

His expression hardened. "Do you always go to the rooms of your friends in their absence and search their things?" Nat's voice was calm enough, but there was a sting behind it.

"Not often. And it does seem you're stretching it a bit in calling yourself a friend," I replied. "I could explain, but you wouldn't believe me, so I won't try. It was a fortuitous accident. What do those photos mean? You are looking for Lee and Kriton and somebody else. An older man." To my distress, my voice cracked, and I looked away quickly. "What has Lee got herself involved in?"

He signaled to a waiter. "I don't suppose you have had any breakfast," he said to me, his voice unexpectedly gentle. "There is no toast, but the bread is quite nice and the Nescafé water is warm."

"I don't want anything," I said.

Ignoring my ungracious reply, he said to the hovering waiter, "One English breakfast, please."

"You needn't bother," I told him. "I could not drink anything, and I certainly couldn't eat whatever an English breakfast is."

He reached for a packet of cigarettes that lay on the table between us, took one out, lit it and turned to me with a wry expression. I gave him a sour look. The smoke was going straight up like a gray cord in the still air. A bearded student with AUSTRALIA written in large letters across his T-shirt slid an enormous pack from his shoulders and settled down at the table behind us. He glanced at me with a friendly smile. I turned back to Nat, but at that moment the waiter came, bringing a china jug of water, thick cup and saucer, some chunks of bread, and a small plastic container of honey. Nat asked for an extra pat of butter. How could he be so kind and considerate, I asked myself in despair, and yet so foul? Nat tore the packets open and brewed me a cup of lukewarm coffee. "Greek honey is the best in the world," he said.

I reached for the knife and began to butter the thick slab of bread in the palm of my hand. There were never any bread and butter plates at these tavernas. "Why did you push me into the boutique last night when there was plenty of room at your place?"

"You are looking for your sister," he replied. "It's just common sense to investigate her flat."

"*You* are looking for my sister," I corrected him. He glanced down at the table. I scrubbed my sticky fingers with a paper napkin. "Go on," I said. "I think you owe me an explanation."

He gave a little sigh. Was it regret for having to tell me? Or regret for what he had to tell? I waited apprehensively.

"I am searching for someone," Nat said, "or rather, some people, and I thought you—your sister, I mean— might lead me to them."

"You know I am not Lee, don't you? You're not pandering to me by saying 'your sister'?"

He smiled. I had to admit it was a rather nice smile. "Of course. But I had to be sure. You must understand that. You did behave pretty suspiciously, racing down from the Acropolis and whipping through the flea market, looking behind at every step. I never saw anyone so circumstantially guilty in the whole of my life. If I had been a policeman I'd have arrested you on the spot."

"So you're not?"

"What?"

"A policeman."

"No, of course I'm not."

"And yet you searched Athens until you found me."

Nat chuckled. "You underestimate us both."

"What do you mean?"

"You're tall. In a Greek crowd that yellow hair stands out like a beacon. And I am over six feet. I could see you in front." He grinned. "It was, really, no trouble."

"You mean you followed me all day?" Even forty-eight hours later I felt a little chilled.

"All morning," he replied. "Then when you sat down for lunch I went off and—" he shrugged deprecatingly, "I misjudged the time. I bolted my food, but you were quicker."

"Why didn't you sit down beside me, as you did when you found me in the evening?"

"I told you. I was waiting for you—Lee—to lead me to someone. You might have done it in the afternoon."

"Nat, Lee isn't a thief."

He did not answer. He was watching my face.

Two long warnings from the cruise ship's funnel blasted across the water. There was a cry of anguish from a tourist at a table nearby. "Oh no! And I haven't even been up to the windmills yet!"

"Nat, *Lee is not a thief!* I know about the silver coin and the necklace. Kriton told me. Perhaps—look, I am not saying this because she is my sister. It is a fact that Lee would not steal anything. If she is mixed up in this necklace and coin thing, then she—" I could not produce an explanation. I lifted my shoulders and made an empty gesture with my hands. "—she must have been—I don't know—blackmailed—used . . . She wouldn't even do it under pressure, Nat. She can be a fool sometimes, but she is honest. I swear it."

He had not said a word. He kept on staring at me. I thought he looked a little bewildered, but he was covering up, the way he covered his intentions and his emotions all the time. "What necklace?" he asked quietly when at last my blundering excuses ran out. "What silver coin?"

It took me a moment to get my breath. I could see he was not putting on an act. He really did not know. The waiter came at that moment and asked if I had finished. Absently, Nat answered him in Greek, then we sat in silence until he had gone away. Nat put his elbows on the table and leaned toward me and asked pointedly, "What would Lee not do under pressure, and what about this necklace and coin?"

I was stunned.

With one movement I was out of my chair. My mind was frozen on the thought that Lee was indeed involved in something illegal and I had been tricked into betraying her. Nat grasped my wrist, but it was a very different grip from the one Kriton had employed. Perhaps it was the comparison that stopped me, for I didn't really want to tell him any more at that point. He said, "Don't you think you had better come clean about this?"

I sank into my chair, knowing with a cold despair that I really had nowhere to go. But there was something in Nat's voice, too, a certain sympathy, that was persuasive. "What do you know about Lee?" I asked.

"Nothing, really. You, in fact, served the only purpose I thought she could serve, and that was to bring Kriton into the open. He was holed up until your appearance shocked him out. But I have nothing against your sister, Virginia."

"Then why are you here?" I asked suspiciously. "You followed me in Athens, stayed at the same house to watch me in Piraeus, and stayed as close to me here as possible."

"To find out what Kriton and Irene are up to."

I stared down at the table. Nat's fingers were still on my wrist, but he was not holding it. His touch was warm and, inexplicably, I found it comforting. "Do you want to tell me about this matter?" he asked. "You don't have to, of course." And then: "Oh heck, I am sorry, Virginia. I had no idea your sister was involved."

It was a turning point in our relationship: the moment when I knew he was telling the truth. But I was too distressed to appreciate the fact. "Yes, that's it, isn't it?" I looked at him with unseeing eyes. "She is involved."

"A silver coin? A necklace?"

I sighed, feeling resigned to confiding in him. "First I have some questions," I said. "Why do you pretend not to speak Greek?"

"I want Kriton and Irene to think I am an English tourist."

"They don't," I said. "They think you're from I.C.O.M. Are you?"

"That's to further implicate Lee in your mind, isn't it? If you had turned up with a Martian they would have found a way of saying the same thing." But a sharp intake of breath told me he was startled and annoyed. "This is where it has gone wrong," he admitted a moment later. "Teaming up with you, I mean. The wrong girl. I was to come here and get to know your sister, using her to find out what Kriton and Irene were about. It would have appeared perfectly natural, an Englishman chatting up an English girl. Damn." He looked very impatient. His mind, I could see, had already swung off to investigate new routes.

"So who are you?"

"He's wrong about I.C.O.M., but warm enough," Nat said absently. "I am an archeologist. I am in Greece for a year at my own request." He seemed startled when I asked, "Why?" I think he had all but forgotten me. Courteously, he pulled himself back to our conversation. "Oh, no particular project," he said casually. "I am merely having a look at the alluvial debris that has been working its way to the surface all over the country for hundreds of years. They're making things very pleasant for me because of my uncle."

"Who is your uncle?"

"He is head of an antiquities service."

"A Greek uncle?"

"That's right. My mother's brother. In return, I have offered to come over to Mykonos to help them, unofficially, with a problem." Nat grinned. "I am known to have a nose like a gun dog. I don't want to boast, but I haven't bought a golf ball for years."

"You sniff them out of the rough?"

He saw my relaxation and his question came like an arrow. "Did you see anything odd last night?"

I thought of Kriton opening Lee's letter, of the fact that the boutique was practically out of stock and closed when tourists arrived, and he probably knew the sign was down, anyway. I knew that Kriton could not afford to go back into hiding until I left. That he wanted me, most urgently, to believe Lee owned the boutique. Yes, I had some information. And Nat could see that.

"My priority is my sister," I said. "Yours is a lot of old stones. I'll tell you what I found out when I know some more about you."

"About my mission?" He hid his irritation rather well. "Yes."

"The authorities think Kriton got Lee to open this boutique in her name to give him an untraceable base on the island."

I mulled that over in my mind. If what Nat had said was true, then Kriton's threat to expose Lee for selling the loot did not make sense.

"Do you want to tell me about Lee?" Nat asked.

I turned away from this new, soft, kindly man. "Not particularly."

"I would like to help."

"Would you? I wish I could be sure." And then, remembering the silent shadows and the apprehensions of the night: "Half of you is descended from a people who made one of their greatest sons drink hemlock."

He looked a little shocked, and then, recovering, he laughed. "You've a sharp tongue. But in defense of my mother's people, I'd like to say they have softened considerably since Socrates' day."

"I hope so," I said fervently. "Tell me about Kriton and Irene. What have they done?"

CHAPTER 13

Nat leaned back in his seat in order to survey our neighbors more easily. They were obviously not interested in our conversation, however. On our left a heavy German girl was talking to a young Egyptian in a red fez who was trying, without much success, to convince the girl that he was what she'd come to Greece for. On our right two Greek boys were trying to induce an independent pelican to eat a biscuit. Beside Nat an old man was reading a newspaper, and the table directly behind me was empty.

A passing waiter paused and Nat, without consulting me, ordered two Greek coffees. He left and Nat looked at me gravely. "The authorities are keeping a close eye on an artist called Irene Wurtenstein because she always seems to be in the area, allegedly to do some painting, when a really brilliantly planned theft takes place."

Irene Wurtenstein. Nat had pronounced the name the German way: Ee-raina. I said tautly, "I knew her name could never have been Irene Woods. Is she the brains behind a gang?"

"No one knows," Nat replied. "It's something they have set me to find out."

"What sort of thefts?" I asked.

"Archeological. An illegal excavation in southern Italy last year. Two in Sicily. Some priceless stuff has got away. Nobody knows who is involved. They only know that Irene was living close by, and that she disappeared about the time the thefts occurred."

The cruise ship's siren suddenly rent the air with what sounded like a final blast, and a spattering of anxiety ran through the groups of Americans along the quay. Around us, they began calling for waiters, paying bills and gathering up their plastic bags. Our man arrived with the two tiny cups and put them down on the table. We sat in silence. The young Egyptian blundered to a stop in his negotiations with the German girl and went off in search of easier game with a cigarette hanging from his lower lip.

I began to think again about Lee and about the possibility of her getting mixed up with Kriton and Irene without knowing what she was doing. But why would they threaten to report her to the authorities? It did not make sense. If they were up to some monkey business of their own and, as Nat had suggested, were using the boutique as a front, they would want to stay as far away from the police as possible.

"I begin to think Kriton was bluffing," I muttered.

"About what?"

"About Lee. I said I was going to the police, and that is when he came out with the—" I stopped. For all Nat's apparent candor, I had to remember he had trailed me all one day. And he had put me up to sleeping in that boutique last night.

I said, "Before we talk about Lee, I would like you to tell me all you know about these two, Kriton and Irene."

He did not like me laying down the rules. I saw that in the flash of those unusual and highly intelligent eyes, in the faint but perceptible hardening of his mouth. He had no idea how much his expressive face gave away. What it was saying now was that he did not easily tolerate a woman holding the reins. An Englishman he might well be by birth and education, but the Greek blood in Nat was pretty potent all the same. And Greeks are fighters. They have a heritage of battle, and, with their backs to the wall, will get what they want the best way they know. Putting a woman to work for them could be as natural as putting a beast to work in the field.

> *Therefore, I hold to the law,*
> *And will never betray it—least of all for a woman.*
> *Better be beaten, if need be, by a man,*
> *Than let a woman get the better of us.*

I shivered, but at the same time I lifted my head high and gave Nat a straight look. He said the Greeks had changed since Socrates' day. At least I was holding my own for the moment. I crossed my fingers superstitiously and repeated in a voice that was braver than I felt, "I want to know more about those two."

"Irene has a grudge against society," Nat said. "These are the facts I have been given: The family were displaced persons. They escaped the Nazi atrocities after seeing the grandparents shot. They arrived in Palestine penniless and starving. Her father was apparently a brilliantly clever artist, but he never had a chance—his health was broken. They lived in transient camps all the time. Then the parents died. More recently, Irene was a member of an anarchist group. But she cut away from that. It's thought she may prefer to be on the dishing-out rather than the receiving end when it comes to orders."

"I can imagine," I said thoughtfully. "Yes, I can imagine all that. It's in her face—the resentment, the suffering, the hate." I suddenly felt cold. "She doesn't care about people," I said.

"Maybe. She has contacts, I am told, but she doesn't seem to have friends."

"And what can she be up to on Mykonos?"

"That is the mystery. There is nothing here."

I was thinking of Kriton's saying Lee might have a source she was milking on that neighboring island. "Is there anything still to be found on Delos?" I asked carefully. Delos, the Sacred Isle. "You do know all about it, don't you? We have finished with all that stuff about guidebooks?"

"Sorry," said Nat. He touched my hand in that gentle way which, juxtaposed with his toughness, baffled me. "It was better that you should think of me as a tourist. I didn't know what sort of actress you were and it was important that Kriton and Irene should not notice me. Of course they're suspicious now, but if everything had gone according to plan . . . Anyway, to go back to Delos. In antiquity it was a very prosperous cosmopolitan city. You know, I dare say, that it had the nearest safe harbor to the Ionian coast of Asia. When the Romans made it a free harbor, that is, released it from all customs dues, it became the center of commerce between East and West. Archeologists have unearthed the remains of some grand houses with wonderful mosaics. But as to actually digging up a treasure trove, it's a long shot. Of course a lot has been found in the past and removed. That is why the rules are so stringent now. You're not allowed to pick up a pebble."

"Couldn't they be plotting to steal something from the museum there?"

"Museums are closely guarded."

"Well, yes, I dare say. Anyway, assuming they did get off with some old bit of mosaic, or whatever is offering, who would buy it? Surely only other museums would be interested, and they would ask questions, wouldn't they?"

"That is part of the puzzle," Nat returned. "None of the stuff Irene is suspected of getting off with has ever been found. Thanks to liberal Swiss laws there is a free market in Switzerland, but none of her loot has turned up there. It's as if it had been removed from the face of the earth. It's frightful, really, for some quite fantastic stuff has disappeared."

"Could she be a procuress for individual buyers?"

"Maybe. Or maybe she is shoving it in a dusty attic for the future. Or maybe, and this is almost worse from an archeologist's point of view," said Nat with feeling, "she is just shoving it in a dusty attic, and that's the end of it, taking her revenge against humanity. That's the sort of thing that really gets my blood up. It's so wasteful and pointless. A marvelous urn bearing Euphronius' signature disappeared from Rome last year after Irene had spent three months painting there."

"Pardon my ignorance," I said, relaxing.

He smiled. "Of course. Why should you know! Euphronius was the Michelangelo of sixth century Greek pottery."

We seemed to be talking above our differences. The gap between us was closing unobtrusively, and my hackles had certainly flattened. I liked the way Nat showed genuine indignation over the loss of things that were not his. Nevertheless, I was still smarting over the way he had used me last night, and was on the alert for tricks. I decided to take a risk. "Do you know about a silver coin with a head of Apollo on it?"

Nat smiled wryly. "Which one?"

"Oh, I see. They're two a penny are they? Well, what would you say about one signed Herakleidias?"

"Ah, now that is a very different matter. There is one in the British Museum—410 B.C., I think."

I blinked. "I say, you do know your stuff, don't you?" He replied modestly, "I worked there for a while. What about this coin?"

"Well," I began carefully, "let's put it this way. Would one be likely to find this coin's twin on Delos now?"

Nat was looking hard at me. I could see his mind was churning with this new lead. He did not bother to answer. He was working it out. I did not want him jumping to conclusions, so I asked him swiftly, "Is Kriton the sort of chap who would know of the existence of this coin in the British Museum?"

"Kriton has been around," Nat replied. "He may well have some superficial archeological information. Anyway, he can get this sort of thing from Irene. She's obviously no slouch in the field. I take it this coin is the one you spoke of earlier?"

"Wait a minute," I said. "We will go on to that. First tell me about Kriton. Who is he?"

Nat ran a fingertip thoughtfully around the rim of his empty coffee cup. "The authorities wondered why he should set up an English girl called Lee Sandersen in a boutique on this island and then disappear."

"Disappear?" I repeated in astonishment. "He is very much here."

"Yes, isn't he, now! But the fact remains that he had not been seen here until you turned up and brought him out of his hole."

"I see. He became quite violent and insulting when I suggested he had put up the money for the boutique."

Nat nodded. "You are the only person who could say Lee was not in a position to finance the thing."

"Nat, Kriton has a record. That is a police picture you're carrying." The anger I felt at having been pushed into sleeping at the boutique gave my voice an accusative quality. The man at the next table heard me and looked over his newspaper. We sat in silence for a moment, toying with our spoons, until the man lost interest. Then I said, "Look, hadn't we better go for a walk?"

Nat called for the bill. I rose and went to stand at the edge of the promenade looking at the fishing boats. Along the quay two caïques were filling up with tourists for the daily visit to Delos. Nat came to join me. "What did he do?" I asked. "What was Kriton's crime?"

I thought Nat looked uncomfortable. "Come on," I said. "And don't try to smooth it over. In my present state of edginess—after last night, I mean—I could see through a haystack at half a mile." And I could still feel the soreness where Kriton's fingers had gripped my wrist.

"Kriton has been in a little trouble," Nat admitted. Turning aside he examined the beached caïques with interest. "Only over a girl, though."

"Be careful," I warned him sharply, "your Greek half is showing. I reckon girls to be important."

He chuckled. "I didn't mean it like that."

"I hope you didn't." He could be terribly nice, and that was the trap for me. He took my arm and steered me around a tight-knit group of chattering tourists. "Who was the girl, and what happened to her?"

Nat was silent. We walked a few paces. I looked up at him, ready to ask the question again, and he said uncomfortably, "I don't know if you are aware of the fact that in Greece virginity is an absolute requisite for a bride. A brother, father or fiancé can get away with mur—I mean, quite a lot, if a girl is, well, deflowered."

CHAPTER 14

My blood ran cold, but I managed to say in a fairly impassive way, "This girl was Kriton's sister?"

"No, fiancée. Daughter of a skilled marble cutter from a village near Amaroussi, not far from Athens. A chap who works on the restoration of the Acropolis. Taki Bajanis."

"The identikit man from your little album?"

"That's right."

"Hence," I suggested, catching up fast, "your following me—the Lee me—to the Acropolis yesterday? You thought I might be contacting him? He has disappeared, too?"

Nat nodded.

"Why should she contact him if, as you say, she is not involved?" I asked suspiciously.

"We don't know how she is being used, do we? I was covering all points."

He was being reasonable. I had to accept his explanation.

"Tell me about the girl." Nat seemed disinclined. He turned his attention to a small brown caïque that was coming in with three weatherbeaten men aboard and a box of gleaming fish lying open amidships. The tables along the promenade emptied as tourists flocked to view its beaching. "Go on," I urged him. "I have to know."

"The girl was either very unfortunate or very foolish," Nat said, trying to sound casual. "The story goes that Kriton caught her under a hedge with a chap called Georgi Latsis. She swore it was rape. Anyway, Kriton did a spell in jail." Nat glanced over toward the lively crowd. "Do you want to go and look at the fish?"

"No," I replied firmly. "I want to know what Kriton did to this Georgi man, or the girl, or both."

"There was a fight. Anyway, it's all over now," said Nat lightly. "Kriton is currently making a fuss of a little tart called Zoe Markopoulou who lives in Athens and who, I understand, is just his cup of tea." Nat turned to me and smiled endearingly. "Or glass of ouzo, since the chances are neither of them takes tea."

The blazing Hellenic morning sun touched me like ice. I said, my voice thin and not very steady, "I want to know what Kriton did to the girl."

"Does it matter?" Nat asked. "For heaven's sake, it's over." He added implausibly, "He has had his punishment. You can't nail a man's past up for continuous viewing." He pulled a packet of cigarettes out of his pocket and became preoccupied with lighting one. We had come to the end of the promenade. He swung slowly around and started back again. I could see he was not going to tell me.

I decided to attack from a different angle. "Kriton

didn't marry the Bajanis girl," I said. "Is she dead or—"

"No, no, no. She is all right," said Nat swiftly, but too lightly, I thought.

"Then, was she not pretty enough to marry by the time Kriton had finished with her?"

His cigarette seemed to have gone out. He examined it thoughtfully, then delved into his pocket for the matches. I could see I was backing a loser. "What about the lover, then? Did he marry her? *Noblesse oblige* and all that."

Nat glanced aside. A pelican was having a last-minute photograph taken by a tourist. "No," he said. "The girl is still single. She is not—er—the kind they would marry off easily."

"In other words," I said baldly, "he bashed her face to a pulp. I don't see Kriton ever contemplating marriage with a plain girl, and so I'll stake my life she was a beauty when he wanted her." I was in a cold sweat regarding the fact that Nat found it easier to answer the question about the girl than the one about her lover. I had to ask, but my voice shook. "Is Georgi Latsis dead?"

Astonishment flashed over Nat's face. "You morbid girl! How would I know if he is dead or alive?"

"I think you do know." But he was not going to be drawn. "Kriton killed him, didn't he?" I asked. "Kriton Fileas is a murderer, isn't he, Nat?"

Nat did not answer. I looked up at him and he looked back at me, his eyes wintry and despairing. As though I had ruined everything by finding out. I hated him at that moment for using me so callously. "*Crime passionnel* is not murder," Nat said, "If you're thinking about last night, consider it unemotionally, Virginia. Whatever Kriton is up to, he isn't going to let you in, then knife you in the night. What could he gain by that? It was very important that you should get into your sister's flat. From your angle as well as from mine. Why don't we get to the basics? By moving into the Cleopatra you had to find out something." He had stopped. He took my arm and turned me around to face him. I could see he was annoyed at having to tell me about Kriton.

"Yes," I retorted bleakly. "I found out a few facts, but in view of what I have just learned they don't add up to anything. I learned the hard way that my sister's employer is a brute and got my wrist crushed. And now I have discovered he is a murderer into the bargain. *Crime passionnel* indeed!" I repeated tartly. "There is no such thing in English law, and my sister and I are English." I waited for him to inquire about the crushed wrist. It had not passed him by. There was something in his face, but he had himself well in hand controlling the concern, or was it merely curiosity? After all, I said to myself a little sourly, a man of the caliber of the warrior-statesman Pericles would never arrive at the top if he let a mere female stand in his way. I did not want to believe that Nat thought a woman's place was leading the donkey while her man rode, but some of his sophistry were highly suspect. "I am going to the police," I said.

"What police?"

The tone of Nat's question threw me.

"They are down there opposite the quay," I said.

There was something about his silence. I eyed him uncertainly. "There is a building marked Tourist Police."

"Don't imagine that the police, and it's not the local tourist police I am talking about, but the ones back in Athens behind the desks, don't know everything there is to know so far," he said. "They even know your sister is missing because I have telephoned them, and they're concerned about it. I tried to keep the facts away from you because we reckoned you would be more useful to us if you believed Kriton's story and behaved naturally, but it hasn't worked."

"In other words, you took me for a dumb blonde?"

"Let's say I hoped you would be a little dumber than

you turned out to be. Perhaps this isn't the most tactful thing to say at the moment, but it is an explanation: I was told your sister might be—er—easily handled. My back was to the wall last night when I was pulling that 'Eat, drink and be merry, life-is-sweet-on-the-island-of-Mykonos' stuff."

"The proper end to that quotation is 'for tomorrow we die,'" I said, openly hostile. "I thought yesterday that Kriton Fileas was a potential killer if ever I saw one. But he has more than lived up to that potential, hasn't he? And I'll not easily forgive you for putting me in his hands, whatever you may say about the safety of the operation."

Nat said, "I hope you're going to cooperate."

"Cooperate?" I repeated bitterly. "I want to find my sister. What choice have I?"

"It involves staying on at the boutique."

"No," I told him violently. "No, I will not sleep there again." We had reached the end of the waterfront. Olympic Airways and the post office were on our right. A sudden panic gripped me, and I moved involuntarily a few paces toward the post office doorway. Then I stopped dead, remembering one did not telephone from there in Greece, but from the OTE which lay on a rise at the other end of the quay.

I don't know what Nat thought I was doing. Perhaps he guessed, but he made no comment. "Let's get down to brass tacks," he said. "Kriton's willingness to come out of hiding and stay out, plus his closing the boutique this morning, can only mean that they are about to move. Thefts of the kind Irene goes in for need precision planning and timing. Once the starting pistol has gone off, there is likely to be no turning back because too many people are involved. A well-planned crime, and a feature of Irene's operations is that they have been very well planned indeed, has to have a tight schedule. There is transport, for example. Say they have a contact in Cus-

toms. The right person has to be on duty at the prearranged time. That sort of thing. Do you understand?"

I swallowed.

"We are hoping the wheels are so far set in motion
that your presence cannot stop them. All you have to do
is hang around and look innocent. Pretend not to see
anything."

I felt physically sick at the thought of exposing myself to whatever Kriton had in mind for me. "Perhaps
Lee was hanging around looking innocent," I said bitterly. "Riddle for today: what is worse than one missing
twin? Answer: two."

"Virginia," said Nat quietly.

I said angrily, "My sister has disappeared and the
police in Athens are sitting behind their comfortable
desks feeling concerned about it. But they're twice as
concerned, aren't they, about their old stones?" In the
present context, the antiquities of a foreign country
seemed very unimportant.

"I need a hat," I said, having to get away. "I saw one
in a little shop farther back. I must go and buy it."

"I'll buy it for you," Nat offered gallantly. "I seem to
remember promising you one. How very remiss of me."

"A bribe?" I asked unkindly. My voice was shaking,
but if he noticed he made no comment. We had begun retracing our footsteps.

"Why not? You never get anything for nothing."

It was the sort of moment when we should both have
laughed. I suppose it was a measure of the situation
that we did not. We walked back past the little square,
past the tavernas with their tables set up in the shade,
past the shop announcing grandly: *Gold Store.*

"A girl with sunstroke is no use to anyone," said Nat.
"Look! Here's a jaunty little number." He slid an arm
through mine and quickening his footsteps, hurried me
over to a little shop displaying a riot of hand-woven

mats, gay peasant blouses and a shelf of little windmills whose pristine-white cotton sails lay still in the torpid air. Against the wall, topping a spike which held a string of sandals, was one individualistic straw hat. To my consternation I found my eyes were damp. I was truly shaken by this curious man—his thoughtfulness is selecting just the right hat for me; his diabolical use of me.

"Just you," averred Nat, taking it down and putting it on the back of my head.

I looked up at him, swallowed and said quietly, "It's like the one the donkeys wear, without the flowers."

Our eyes held in a queer sort of silence. Then the shop owner came fussing out, both hands spread and shoulders hunched in an ecstasy of admiration. "It looks beautiful on the lady. You will buy it for her, of course."

"Of course," agreed Nat. His mouth was a little tight and the lightheartedness had gone from his manner. He took the hat off my head, turned it up at the back and down at the front, knocked a man's dent in the top, gave it a pinch here and a jerk there, then put it back on my head again. "That's more you," he said briskly. "A smart hat for a smart girl." He took a little roll of drachmas out of his pocket and handed them to the man. "Don't think I don't appreciate your sparkling wit, Virginia," he said as we turned away.

We walked a few yards in silence. "That was very kind of you," I managed at last.

"It's nothing."

And that was right, too. Payment for services about to be rendered. There must be a streak of masochism in me, I thought. "If spending another night in that beastly place was going to produce my sister," I said, "I would be prepared to go through anything. But frankly, whether Greece's antiquities are under a rock here, or whether they're in Boston . . ." I broke off, remembering Lee's potential involvement.

"Boston?" repeated Nat shrewdly.

I looked up at him with despair. What was the point of fighting? Where was I going if I did not go with him?

"Come and sit down," he said, tucking an arm through mine and leading me purposefully to the nearest group of tables. "I'll buy you an ouzo, and you can tell me everything."

CHAPTER 15

"That," said Nat unequivocally, "is sheer tommy rot. If there was a splash in Boston about an Egyptian necklace from here, we would know. And as to the coin, it sounds mighty like a useful working fact handed out by Irene. It's too much of a coincidence that Lee should dig up a coin that is a replica of one kept in the British Museum."

"Nat! You're sure?"

"Of course I am sure. I've been briefed with all the facts, and those are not among them. I wouldn't be at all surprised if this was the trick they played to get rid of your sister." He rested his elbows on the table and leaned toward me. "It's not too difficult to see through this one, Virginia. They could arrange for Lee to buy the stuff. It would be no trouble to put it in her way—they could use

one of the gang to offer it to her. Another member of the
gang could buy it. Then, after it had been sold a reasonable length of time, they would tell her the story they
told you about the police making inquiries. If she had in
fact served her purpose here, and they wanted to send her
packing without pausing to shut the shop and without ill
feeling, it's not a bad way of getting rid of her."

My head was spinning with excitement. The waiter
came and I gave him an idiotic grin. He smiled as he
put down the ouzos, the inevitable glasses of water that
accompany them, and two tiny plates on each of which
lay one potato chip, one olive, a piece of sausage and a
tomato slice.

"Oh Nat, do you think this is a real possibility? That
Lee has gone off to some other island or over to Athens?"

Nat smiled. "Why not? When you think about it, if Lee
knew nothing of antiquities, it would be easy enough to
fool her with coins. And any necklace. I don't see that it
matters whether it was loot or just some old junk. Is
your sister easily thrown?"

I was suddenly so excited I almost knocked over my
ouzo glass. "Easily thrown? If Irene told her what she
told me, that police here are inclined to act first and
ask questions afterward, I would certainly think she
would run. And that would be a very sensible thing for
her to do. I am sure our Foreign Office officials have
enough to do without pulling English girls out of Greek
jails. Is it true?"

"That they act first? I should think Irene's views are
highly colored by what happened to her parents at the
hands of the Nazis," Nat replied, not without sympathy.
"Tell me a bit about your sister. How did she get involved
with Kriton in the first place?"

"You see, she had this *au pair* job. She seemed well
settled, but her employer made a pass at her and she took
fright and fled. If Lee was scared and had nowhere to

run to, she would be a sitting duck for whoever came along and showed her a way out."

"Okay. Let's say Kriton offered her a refuge on Mykonos and she settled down quite happily, stocking the boutique with his funds and running it alone. All went well until Irene and Kriton moved over here and they pulled the fast one about the necklace and coin. That's when Lee got scared and wrote to you."

"I told you," I said, "that Kriton doesn't seem to know her. He obviously hasn't spent any time with her."

"Yes, that adds up. As I said before, Kriton was in hiding until you turned up and shocked him out of his hole. So far as the police knew, he had simply disappeared. The only clues were that he was short of money, and that he had been in touch with Irene. The authorities are keeping a close eye on Irene. They know who visits her."

"And how do they know Kriton was short of money?"

"He seems to have got some mysterious remission of his sentence. He has always been involved in a small way with politics. He may have been able to supply some useful information. Anyway, let's say he is free so long as he keeps his nose clean. He doesn't know it, but he is being watched pretty closely. It is known he was trying to raise money around Athens, apparently without success."

"What for? What does he want money for?"

"We're not sure. But the police have worked out a possible reason. It is known an offer has been made for Katerini Bajanis' hand, providing the dowry is big enough."

"That girl! Is Kriton really going to find the dowry as a penance? You're joking!"

"I should think," replied Nat, "if things run true to national form, Kriton would be more concerned with the possibility that one day Bajanis might want revenge. So if Kriton is involved with Irene in a plot where the mar-

ble cutter might possibly come in handy, he is bright
enough to see a way of giving Katerini's father a dowry-
sized pay-off. Anyway, that is all part of the theory the
police hold. You see, Kriton visited Irene and suddenly
he had the cash to set up an English girl in a boutique
on this island. He didn't stay here. He continued to be
seen at the usual places, but the significant fact was that
he stopped trying to raise money. Irene was here, painting. Lee ran the boutique alone. Then Bajanis disappeared, and several weeks later Kriton went. That's all
we know."

"And the police reckon Irene is paying Kriton and
Bajanis to organize an archeological theft, using the
boutique as headquarters?"

"Could be."

"Nat," I said urgently, remembering Kriton's brutality
toward me, "I am worried about Lee. What if she got
in their way? I tried to stop him opening a letter addressed to her this morning. I thought he was going to
break my arm. It's all very well for you to say that she
went off voluntarily to hide, and according to your rea-
soning, that makes sense. However, it doesn't cover the
fact that Irene looked at me as though I had—Oh God,
it's still with me and I cannot get rid of it—" I pressed
a hand to my eyes, "as though I had returned from the
grave."

"You said she is easily frightened. Gullible and easily
frightened was the way you described her," Nat said
comfortingly. "Why should she be in danger if she did
not get in their way?"

I sipped the heady ouzo, hoping it might steady me,
but I could not block out that expression of utter disbelief
in Irene's eyes when she first came face to face with me.

"What excuse did Kriton offer for opening the letter?"
Nat asked.

"He said he had 'an arrangement' with Lee concerning
mail."

"You must realize," said Nat thoughtfully, "a man in hiding doesn't have mail sent. He could have been getting his letters addressed to Lee."

Along the quay an engine fired and one of the Delos caïques, loaded to the gunwales with tourists, headed out to sea.

"Hey!" I exclaimed, "I've just remembered something rather odd." I swung around, digging in my hold-all that was slung across the back of my chair. I pulled out my own letter, remembering that I had noticed it looked un-opened. I turned it over, examining the edges carefully. It seemed to be intact. "This is my letter that Lee never received."

"It could have been steamed open," suggested Nat, reaching for it, frowning at it, "then glued down again."

"There is absolutely no sign at all. Anyway, the one that came this morning," I told him, "didn't get that sort of delicate treatment. Kriton slit it open in front of me. Why should he treat this one differently?"

"Could be this morning's letter was marked," suggested Nat.

"But he didn't even glance at it. The mark would have to be very obvious indeed.

"Where was it from? Did you notice?"

"Yes, I did. America."

"Does Lee have friends there?"

"Who knows? She has probably met all sorts of people during the past year."

A waiter approached us and Nat shook his head. I glanced along the promenade. A pair of tiny donkeys led by a young woman in a black blouse and spotted head scarf were ambling toward the quay. They stopped by the fishing boats and the woman began unloading pale courgettes, taking them from the pannier baskets and filling up large green plastic bags. A short, heavily built Greek walked past, looking at them with interest. His back was turned to me, but there was something very familiar about his cap. I waited, suddenly alert, and he turned slightly in our direction. Heavy features. A low brow.

"At the risk of seeing you go off into peals of hearty laughter," I said carefully, "I think I see that workman. You know, the one who ran like a startled rabbit when he saw me last night? Over there near the beach. About ten yards to your left."

Nat did not scoff this time. He did not have anything to gain now by denying that Bajanis' presence might be important. His back straightened and his eyes took on a very sharp expression. "Is he looking this way?"

"No. I think he is going to the Delos boat—caïque, I mean. He's heading for the quay now. Yes, so he is. But he isn't going to make it. Look, they've cast off. They're on their way." The solid, seaworthy craft with its happy passengers was well clear of the quay, and Bajanis, if indeed it was he, turned back. He hurried along to the beach, and jumping down onto the sand, spoke rapidly to one of the fishermen. With the irritated gesture of one unaccustomed to wearing headgear, he took his new cap from his head. He had thick hair flecked with gray that grew close around his face, rising from a widow's peak. A peasant's face it was, with a lumpy, hawk nose and a solid jaw. That was the face, I was absolutely certain, of the indentikit man.

"It is him, isn't it? Bajanis."

But Nat was not sure.

"The new hat," I said. "That's the real clue." None of the locals wore new caps, and none of them wore their caps at the angle he wore his. The two men appeared to be bargaining. Now, a matter had been settled, and some money changed hands. They walked off across the beach together, stepped up onto the promenade and began striding briskly in the direction of the yacht basin.

"Okay," said Nat. "Let's investigate." He motioned to the waiter and paid the bill.

"That was the last boat to Delos for today," I said. "I looked at the sign. There are only two, and the other one has already gone."

"Then the chances are he is hiring a caïque. Let's follow and make sure. I'll go first," said Nat. "You keep me in view. But stop well behind. Just in case he recognizes you, he must not see us together. And if he looks around, get out of sight if you can." Nat strode away.

The two Greeks were keeping up a good pace. They had turned and were going along the little strip of paving just short of the yacht basin. Nat with his long strides was already well out in front of me. I quickened my steps. A moment later the men had jumped down on to a sandy beach beyond the last row of buildings. They disappeared behind a corner of wall. Nat was level with the post office. I saw him turn aside and enter the door. I paused outside a chemist's shop, pretending interest in the window, but with one eye on Nat's doorway. When I looked across the beach again I was just in time to see the two Greeks jump aboard a small caïque that was tied up by the breakwater.

Nat came out of his doorway like a torpedo. "Come on," he said. "We've got to follow him."

CHAPTER 16

This new side of Nat was short on manners, but exhilarated by his dynamism and excited by the fact that something was happening that might lead me to Lee, I did not care. "Wait outside that shop," he said brusquely and I did so, fingering some shining tiles painted with wildflowers, pretending not to be watching him as he strode off toward the quay. He returned accompanied by a young Greek with a lively face and boot-black eyes. "I have explained to him that we've missed the boat for Delos."

"I speak English," said the young man, addressing me with pride and the studied concentration of one whose vocabulary is both small and rusty. "You, Americans?"

"That's right." Nat spoke offhandedly, at the same time darting a warning look at me. And then, in a lighthearted aside: "I make it a rule to take camouflage when it's offered."

I said nervously, "It's cloak and dagger stuff, isn't it?"

"I hope not. Right-o. Jump."

We went over the low wall onto the beach. The Greek pushed a dinghy into the water, then pulled it back to the water's edge so that Nat and I could step in. He rowed us out into the center of the bay and we climbed aboard a nut-brown caïque. The inside planks were painted crimson and the wheelhouse green. Nat spoke to our boatman in Greek. "I've told him we're in a hurry."

And, of course, we were. Although the signs were that our quarry had gone to Delos, we could not be certain. Besides, Delos covered more than a square mile—maybe two—and if the man we were following milled around with the tourists from the excursion caïques it might be difficult to find him again.

Out here, beyond the breakwater, there was a warm, buffeting wind that hurled the white-topped wavelets up against our prow. We could see Bajanis' caïque ahead of us now, forging its way swiftly across the roughened sea. Nat and I settled amidships, our arms stretched along the gunwale, our faces to the sun, listening to the shush-shush of the waves against the sides of the caïque. Small, gray islands rose all around us out of the brilliant sea.

"That's Reneia," Nat said, pointing to a stony hump crouching mouse-like on our starboard side, "Where women went from Delos to give birth to their children and where the sick and old were sent to die. It's full of the bones of the ancients."

I knew Apollo's birth had given Delos this sanctity. No one could be born there again. Or die. "My guidebook says—" Nat looked down at me and laughed. His reaction was not derisive, but I felt the warm color rise in my face. "It's all very well for you. Everybody can't be a learned archeologist," I said defensively.

"Sorry. What does this splendid guidebook say?"

"That Athenians actually carried out several purifications of the island. They removed all human remains already buried there."

Nat grinned. "In 427 B.C. they went further than that. They deported all living Delians to Asia Minor. Look at our man! He *is* making for Delos. That's Delos, now, in front."

Nat stood up, then went to the bow. From here Delos was just another gray island. Could my sister be there? All at once my heart began to beat a little faster. Might not this man we were pursuing, having taken me for my sister last night, be on his way to warn her to stay away from Mykonos? And yet, could she remain incognito in the one tiny hotel that Delos boasted? We weren't exactly nondescript, Lee and me. My mind swung back to the night before when I had been waiting for Nat in the restaurant and first the waiter had recognized me, and then the peasant. The restaurant! The Americans! What about that conversation I had overheard?

A man called . . . Ghent? An American who was a collector, and who was mad . . . I leaped out of my seat, stumbled on the uneven surface of the boards and scrambled forward. The caïque was jumping on the lively water. Nat turned. His face and hair were wet from the spray that misted up over the bow. "Watch it," he said, warning me. "It's a bit damp here."

"Listen, Nat. I've just remembered something. Bajanis could be going out to a yacht. Last night when I was waiting for you at the restaurant, I overheard some Americans talking about a collector called Ghent. Have you heard of him?"

Nat's eyes sharpened but he shook his head. "Go on."

"His yacht is here. One of them said it was behind Naxos. Isn't Naxos over there, where we're going?"

Nat nodded.

"Well, they did mention its name, but I forget. I wasn't really listening, and the waiter kept coming along and chatting. Then I saw this Greek, Bajanis, and ran, and forgot all about it. It must be quite a splendid yacht anyway, for it to be so obvious to tourists."

"So?"

"Well, the point is, they were talking about Ghent being mad and rich, and having, I think they said, one of the biggest collections in the States."

"Collections of what?"

"I don't know. But when you think of it, if he is mad and rich, and has stuff hidden underground—"

"Underground?" asked Nat sharply. "You didn't say that."

I rubbed a hand across my forehead. "Look, I find it awfully difficult to remember, because I wasn't really listening. But I am sure that is what one of them said. Half the stuff is underground. Isn't he, I mean, his yacht, the sort of thing you ought to be investigating? You were talking about Customs and transport and a free market in Switzerland, but wouldn't a private yacht be a whole lot simpler? There must be a lot of unguarded shore in America for night landings. And if he sailed in close here, late at night—" I broke off on a gasp of astonishment. While I was talking, a pretty caïque with a scarlet life belt hung on its white wheelhouse had been approaching fast from the opposite direction, and as it came abreast of us, to my utter disbelief, I saw two cows and several goats standing patiently amidships. I laughed aloud.

Nat said dryly, "How else? There are no bridges, and the islands provide grazing."

"It's all so marvelous," I said in a rush. "Or could be, if Lee was here and we had never heard of those beastly people. I hadn't dreamed the Aegean was like this. Not really as magnificent, I mean."

I don't think he was listening, for as soon as I finished he said, "Let's go back to this American. What did you say his name was?"

"Ghent. They called him Mad Midas. Bajanis could be making for the yacht now."

"He tried to catch the Delos caïque," Nat reminded me.

"Perhaps he is being picked up from Delos. Perhaps the people from the yacht don't want to be seen on Mykonos."

Nat looked at me curiously. "What makes you think he is going to the yacht?"

I said unhappily, "I am not really thinking about your antiquities. You know that. I am thinking about Lee."

"That's understandable," said Nat, looking faintly irritated.

"So Bajanis thought he saw Lee last night. So . . ." Even when one is as worried as I was, the desire not to look ridiculous dies hard. "Lee might be on the yacht," I said defiantly, and then in order to avoid his eyes, I put my hand over the side, sliding it through the bright, clear wash.

Nat did not laugh. After a moment or two he said, "Look, a dolphin! Two of them!" On our port side, dark, glittering bodies rose in a scimitar curve and dived again. But Nat was not looking at the dolphins. He was frowning, and his eyes were on the distance. He is taking me seriously, I said to myself, half elated, half sick with apprehension, for what might be the penalty for sending this man on a wild-goose chase? I turned my attention to the view. Delos was coming closer. *The desolated lands* of Byron. *The ravaged isle.* I watched its approach with a kind of hunger, and after a while actually forgot the trauma of the moment in sheer ecstasy. I leaned over the bow and a mischievous wave leaped up, splashing me in the face.

. . . there, there the waves arise,
Not to be lulled by tyrant victories.

Indeed! I thought, as I blinked the salt out of my eyes.

Delos had never recovered from its tyrants' victories. Its good days, long before the coming of Christianity, had never returned. Who knew, though, what treasures still lay beneath that rocky surface, left over from the time when the island, inhabited by merchant princes, had been the center of trade between East and West—a thriving city of rich homes and architectural glories.

"Good God!" Nat broke in with a loud exclamation. "He isn't going to land *there?*"

I came back to the present with a jerk and turned my eyes sharply to the caïque we were pursuing. It had rounded a rocky point and was now heading in to the shore. "Why not?" I asked.

He said, looking puzzled, "It's the ancient harbor. A stony beach. There's no pier. How extremely odd!"

I pulled out my sunglasses. The fine spray swept up over the bow, clouding them, and I took them off again. The caïque had turned in toward a shallow sickle bay.

"We can't go in there," muttered Nat. "He will see us. And yet, if we go right around the point to the harbor proper, we're going to lose him." He threw out his hands in an angry gesture and exclaimed, "What the devil are we going to do?"

"Go to the point beyond the bay," I advised him promptly, "then turn back. And look around now. There are lots of caïques to take Bajanis' attention." It was true. We had been so intent on the approaching Delos and the caïque in front that we had not noticed there were more than a dozen fishing boats, lying serenely still between the crouching islands. Another of those low, wide vessels, full of goats and one resigned-looking black and white cow, came put-putting by. A small yacht and two hurrying caïques very like ours were closing in, perhaps from Tinos, the big island we could see hazily through waves of heat in the center distance. It was as though a shroud of thin sky had been drawn down across it to the water's edge.

"There is no reason why he should notice us specifically," I said. "We can cut the motor and lie around for a while. If he looks up, he will think we're fishing. Then, when he has gone ashore, we can follow him."

It happened just like that. Before we reached the rocky promontory we saw the other caïque had grounded on the beach. Two men leaped out. Nat put his head in the wheelhouse to instruct out boatman and the next moment we were swinging around in a wide circle. Before we regained a straight course, our man had crossed the beach and disappeared among some stunted trees behind.

"That's a puzzle," said Nat, rejoining me in the bow, frowning deeply. "He didn't mind being seen by the boatman and tourists in the excursion caïque he was trying to catch earlier, so he isn't hiding."

"What is in the bay that might interest him?"

"Nothing, really. Market gardens and a whole lot of wild stuff. But there is a track into the ruins and the Sacred Lake. He could easily walk across to the harbor if, as you suggest, he wants to transfer to another boat without being noticed. And when you come to think of it, he could hardly lift something from here in broad daylight with two caïque loads of tourists looking on. Of course, he might be coming to have a look, and using the tourists as cover. The guardians of the sites would naturally be curious if a lone Greek turned up and started examining some particular object with undue interest."

"Do you mean there is no potential booty on this track?"

"Oh no. There is potential booty everywhere. Just through those trees you see at the back of the beach, there is the start of an old avenue, and there are mosaics in some excavations there, but hell, you can't steal mosaics!"

"Why not? Couldn't a craftsman like Bajanis lift a mosaic floor?"

Nat turned to me, his eyes dark and intent behind their thick, dark lashes. But he was not intent on my face. He had that withdrawn look of a man whose mind has moved several steps ahead. At last he said with assurance, "Every museum in the world would recognize a Delian mosaic floor."

"You did say Irene might be stowing her stuff away in an attic."

"That's horribly true."

We were coming in to land. Nat said, "I'll tell our chap to drop us and go around to the quay to wait." He moved off amidships. The engine cut and the caïque drifted in across the clear, deep water to nuzzle gently into the big, smooth stones that fringed the Sacred Bay.

CHAPTER 17

The other caïque lay not more than ten yards distant. Its owner looked at us without interest. He was already half asleep in the sun. Nat and I scrambled ashore and wobbled across the stones to a sandy track on the other side.

Here there were wild figs, giant bamboo, tall dry grasses and some scrubby undergrowth. There were also a lot of flies that gathered irritatingly around our heads. A green lizard appeared near our feet and sped away in crazy zig-zags. We walked a short distance and there were the market gardens Nat had mentioned. Potatoes in flower; lush blue-green onion tops drooping over the gray, sandy soil. Here, where the stone walling began, the path rose steeply.

"This is the start of the excavations," Nat said. Gay scarlet poppies nodded to us from mounds of dry soil on the walls, and at our feet, nudging the path, was a pumpkin vine. Nat stamped a big golden thistle aside with his foot and I went past. On our left now, within a tall gray wall, there was an open doorway. "Look casual," said Nat in a whisper. "You never know. This is a sanctuary with an excavated mosaic floor."

We went into a biggish room. The floor was gray-white and surrounded by a square of magnificent columns all broken off several feet from the base. It was the first time I had ever seen an excavated room and I gasped, not at its present beauty, but at the sublime magnificence it conjured up. The grandeur that had been.

"Mithridates and his army did that in 88 B.C.," said Nat dryly. "He made quite a job of Delos. Those stumps of columns are made of the finest Parian marble."

I was too moved to answer him. I was here, at last, in such a place as had inspired Byron to write:

> *There is a temple in ruin stands,*
> *Fashion'd by long-forgotten hands . . .*
> *Out upon Time! who for ever will leave*
> *But enough of the past for the future to grieve . . .*
> *Remnants of things that have pass'd away,*
> *Fragments of stone rear'd by creatures of clay!*

"No time for dreaming," said Nat brusquely, but he smiled and I felt he may have understood.

He crossed the room by a little stone path that ran outside of the mosaic. He looked around another doorway into a room beyond. "There is no one here," he said. "Let's move on. This lane leads to the lake and the Sacred Way."

We went out beyond the excavations and onto a wide area of flat, dry ground where more poppies grew and brown lizards scurried across our path. Huge snails—brown and cream whorls—clung to the fine, tough stems of sea lavender, and more snails clung, less precariously, to stones. In front of us and to the left was the low wall of flat rock that surrounded the Sacred Lake.

I stopped and clasped my hands in ecstasy. "Oh Nat! The palm tree! Is that it?" It stood alone among the wild grasses and stunted bushes that filled the dry lake, its huge fronds moving elegantly in a faint breeze.

"That's it," replied Nat lightly. "The repro job."

I laughed. "In another twenty years or so it will be an antique and perhaps you will treat it with respect," I said. I supposed the late nineteenth century seemed pretty recent to an archeologist who spent most of his thinking time concerned with affairs of the era before the birth of Christ. Nat was striding ahead up the path.

"How long has the lake been dry?" I asked as I hurried after him, scuffling my feet unavoidably in the dust and stones.

Preoccupied with his thoughts, Nat did not answer immediately. A moment later he said, "Sorry. Since 1926. Its feeding stream, that came down from Mount Cynthos —that's Cynthos, that hill behind—ran dry. The soil from the diggings has gone in there since, of course." He was frowning as he stared at the hill ahead, his eyes roving over the gray excavations that ran up to a rocky summit. Ahead of us, the path split. One branch led left around the Sacred Lake and the other to the right.

"No one is going to pinch the Sacred Lake," said Nat facetiously, "so . . . let's put our minds to . . ." Eyes squinting against the glare, he looked over to our right where there was a great mass of walls—gray, white, cinnamon, black, all colors converging to a muted mixture broken by horizontal black shadows where they met. "Now, that is the Sacred Way to Apollo's Temple." A trail of tourists was progressing slowly through.

"There is a headless statue over there, but I can't imagine anyone going after that," Nat said. "Not Irene, anyway, if one can judge by her past form. She set a pretty high standard with her other loot." My eyes followed his. I could not see a headless statue, but the lovely columns of a chalk-white temple loomed against the sky. I wanted to ask what it was, but hesitated to disturb Nat's train of thought. "If they're thinking about statues . . ." he muttered, then paused again, deep in contemplation.

"Would it be necessary to bring a marble worker here to dislodge a statue?" I asked. "Wouldn't they simply lift it off the ground?"

"Who knows? If they were taking something really big, I should think the advice of an expert wouldn't go amiss." We stepped aside to allow a party of French visitors to pass. They were taking their time. One of them carried a guidebook and was reading directions out loud. Nat was chafing at the delay.

"What about the lions?" I asked.

"Come off it." Then, looking down at my face: "Sorry. I didn't mean to be uncivil. You haven't seen them but they're huge, and out in the open. They're very, very obvious. If one of them disappeared, the hue and cry would be on before it was down from its plinth. The thieves would never get away." Our path was unobstructed now. I moved forward but Nat arrested me with a touch on my arm. "I am going to leave you here. I think perhaps I might take up that lead of yours and nip down to the harbor to see if you're right and Bajanis is picking up another caïque. If he isn't, then I'll go on to the excavations on Cynthos. I'll see you back at the harbor." He pointed across the arid land beyond the Sacred Lake. "There is the Sacred Way straight over there. You go and have a look at those lions," he said kindly. "They're well worth seeing. Seventh century A.D. Naxian work."

"You're giving me something pretty to keep me occupied?" He looked surprised at my angry reaction to his suggestion. A girl can have enough of being used, and of being shoved aside in this patronizing fashion, especially when there is an exciting job in the offing.

He contemplated me thoughtfully for a moment, looking annoyed, but I could not tell whether he was annoyed with himself or me or circumstances. It seemed momentarily as though he had something to say, but he only told me, "Get your hair under that hat. It's the Sandersen sisters' trade-mark."

"That is why you bought it for me, isn't it?" Earlier, I had seen the hat as a bribe. Perhaps it had been, but it was camouflage, too. He thought of everything. I removed the hat and, holding the brim between my teeth, pulled my hair back from my face with both hands, twisted it into a coil and, pressing it down on top of my head, set the hat on top.

"Suits you," remarked Nat cryptically.

"Is that a compliment?"

His face softened, then he grinned. "We English have a saying: Don't gild the lily."

Heavens! Don't think you understand this man, Virginia. "There is nothing very English about you," I retorted, and without waiting for his protest, added, "I'll go and look at the lions. And then I'll find the hotel or coffee house or whatever, and ask them if Lee has stayed there."

He switched to business fast. "*Unless* you see Bajanis. If you do see him, and I am not there, follow him. If he goes back to the caïque, trail him."

"Trail him to sea?" My throat was suddenly dry. Another time, I might think twice before complaining of being treated as just a pretty face.

"Find out where he is going," Nat said. "See if he makes for that yacht you're talking about, and if he does, meet me back at the quay. But if by any chance he goes to Mykonos, follow him right to his destination. Find out where he lives. He may be hiding your sister on Mykonos. Remember that." The carrot was thrust right down in front of the donkey's nose again.

I asked in a voice I thought sounded reasonably steady, "And how will you return if I take the caïque?"

"I'll do the same as you will do if I spot him and take the caïque. Return with the tourists at midday. Right! I'm off!"

I came up to the flat ground that formed the Sacred Way and there they were. Proud, angry, sleek as greyhounds, they crouched on their rocky plinths side by side, glittering white marble thoroughbreds with the scarlet poppies blowing in the grass behind. I caught my breath in awe.

"Say," said a friendly American voice, "would you care to take a photograph of my wife and me standing by that lion? I hate to bother you, but we'd like a picture of the two of us together here. The camera's quite straightforward."

I came back down to earth. "Certainly." One for the family album. They thanked me and went on their way. There were half a dozen groups of tourists within fifty yards, looking in their guidebooks, taking photographs, staring. I walked among them, gazing at the lions or what remained of them. They were magnificent. The famous one, the one pictured on the front of my guidebook, was at the far end of the line. He was elegant, fierce, almost perfect. I walked toward him.

It was then I saw the Greek. His head was bare, his new headgear in one hand. His mahogany-brown face was raised in the full light of the sun and I could see the battered hawk nose, the wide mouth drawn back and tightly closed. He seemed rapt in bleak concentration as he stared at the lion on the end of the row. Instinctively I moved out of sight, edging swiftly behind a plinth, using a lion's rump as a shield. I was in a perfect position to watch his movements because, though there should have been two beasts between the Greek and me, only the hindlegs of one were left, and the other had been removed from the marble slab. The Greek was walking around the lion at the end, examining it from all angles. Once he reached up to touch the exposed rib cage. Then he walked slowly around it again, and this time he was examining its feet. As I watched him, he took something out of his pocket. A notebook? Standing with his back partially to me, he appeared to be writing something down.

I bent my head to peer beneath the belly of the grand beast who sheltered me. Passing tourists stared at me and I straightened, embarrassed, wishing I had a camera or at least a guidebook to give me an air of normality. A man came up to me and asked me if I would mind stepping aside as he wanted a picture of my lion. I apologized and moved away. There was another party coming along. Walking out onto the track, I wandered down it with what I hoped might appear to be an absentminded air. I had studied a map of this area and I remembered that the Italian Agora, the old market place, lay opposite Bajanis and a little farther on. I could reasonably hover there for some time, looking interested.

The Greek stayed all of half an hour with that lion, walking around it, leaning against a wall, examining it from every angle. One of the guardians of the site began to look at me curiously, although he did not seem to notice Bajanis. Eventually he came over to me and asked with a friendly smile, "You are archeologist?"

"No," I replied. "I am having a rest." I sat down on a jutting end of excavated wall. "It is very hot."

The man nodded. "Always hot now."

It was at that moment Bajanis decided to go. He pocketed his notebook, swung round, and with long strides and head down, went back up the Sacred Way. I said a hurried good-bye to the guardian and stepped out after him. He left the Way by the path along which Nat and I had come from the beach. I went to stand on higher ground where I would be able to watch him if he made for the caïque. There were some partial excavations here full of big golden thistles and cow parsley, and a blue-veined iris. There were some sections of Doric columns on the ground, and here was the headless statue Nat had mentioned. I edged closer to the statue, trying not to take my eyes from Bajanis in case he should suddenly leave the track and change direction. But he did not. He passed the fork where the other path led around the lake and made straight for the excavations where we had seen the mosaics. I had to stay then, to see whether or not he emerged from the ragged trees behind the beach. Waiting, I looked around and saw with alarm that I was standing too close to a sinister-looking square hole about the size of an average room. It was half filled with black water that was partially obscured by some bright green weed. There were pale cyclamens growing in the crevasses on the stony sides. I backed to the safety of a large marble segment and sat down. A moment later Bajanis appeared and strode toward his caïque.

I looked at my watch. It was eleven-thirty. Three-quarters of an hour had elapsed since Nat left. He would have had time to walk to the harbor, establish that Bajanis was not there and get well up the sides of Mount Cynthos. Not knowing my way, and with all these tourists milling round, it would be useless to look for him now. I hurried back down the Sacred Way, past the excavation which Nat had said was a sanctuary to Leto but which there was no time to look at now, past the temples to Apollo. As I was leaving the area, I turned just once more to see those archaic lions, glittering now against the sapphire sky. There was a hungry elation about that last long look; to stand one moment on a pinnacle and then be ordered down brings on a fire within oneself and is a demand on life. I will be back, I promised myself. I could not know the horror that awaited me when I would return.

The caïque was tied up at the jetty alongside the ex-

cursion craft, and Nat was nowhere to be seen. Our boatman helped me aboard and we cast off. I had asked him
to ferry me back to Mykonos as quickly as possible but I
was not certain he understood. I was not certain either
that Bajanis was going to head for home. If he was making for Ghent's yacht, he would meet us on the point. I
would have to deal with that exigency when, or if, it
came. But if he was going to Mykonos he had a good
five or ten minutes' start and we would have to round the
point before we even made the bay from which he was
setting out. I had little hope of catching up with him. I
sat down in the bow and watched distortions of white
and gray stones in the startlingly clear water as we
pulled away. I couldn't help thinking with frustration
that Nat was on a wild-goose chase; that Lee, because of
the very nature of this tourist-ridden island, could not be
here; that if Bajanis was heading for Mykonos, he was
going to get away and we would be back where we had
started.

And then we rounded the point and unbelievably, just
pulling out from the beach, was Bajanis' caïque. Perhaps they had had trouble starting the engine, for I saw
the Greek emerging from the wheelhouse. If he was
returning, we were actually going to race him in! I moved
to the stern so that I could see better. The little vessel
came out in a straight line and I held my breath a moment before it swung around into our wake. My breath let
out in a great sigh of relief.

Almost subconsciously, I think I had been bringing
myself to a decision. To give Nat his due, I felt he was
concerned, as were the police in Athens, about my sister's
disappearance, but this morning's observations had convinced me that he was only worried about her in relation
to Irene's plans to steal antiquities. In my fears for Lee's
safety, I was growing more and more certain that I was
on my own. Well, here was my opportunity.

I will follow Bajanis, I said to myself, *and if he does*

not lead me to Lee, then I will tackle him. I stood there in the stern with the sea breezes tugging and jerking at the hat that Nat had given me, furtively watching Bajanis' caïque following behind. "Family first," I muttered to myself defiantly, "and to hell with Greece's heritage!"

CHAPTER 18

Back on Mykonos I waited in the middle of the prome-nade with my hat well down on my face, merging with the tourists who drifted up and down the waterfront. Bajanis' caïque had come in. I could see him approach-ing, walking quickly along the beach. He came straight for the square and crossed it, then turned up one of the narrow lanes that led into the town. I sped past the little shops and stopped abruptly on the corner, my heart beat-ing rapidly. There were always people in these streets, so in order to keep him in view I would have to stay close. If I did not, he had only to make a quick move into any one of the dozens of doorways or alleys and he would be lost.

Bajanis forged straight on with head down and arms

swinging. Keeping my hat well down over my eyes, I
trailed him as closely as I dared. Luckily there were
plenty of tourists in the street so I was comparatively well
shielded. We came to an open patch of ground with big
eucalyptus trees, and on the left a building that could only
be a school. Bajanis turned up a steep stony street with
houses on one side. Here an arid patch where pale-yellow
poppies, their petals tissue-thin, bloomed among the dry
grass. I paused, for there were no tourists here to hide
me. A fat woman in a green dress and red hat, on a
cluttered blue balcony, looked up curiously from washing her child's hair. I smiled at her uncertainly and
she smiled back. Here Bajanis turned right into a bare
street, then turned left again, and I dashed ahead to the
corner. The three windmills I had seen so often on posters
were close by on a low hill above a bay, their sails still.
I came breathlessly to the next corner. Bajanis was
going up a wider street, still at a hurried pace, then as
quick as a blink he disappeared into a white house. There
was a Greek sign over the gray door, and outside a jumble of wooden boxes and crates, cupboards, ladders and
one or two chairs. I stood in the street waiting to see if
the chase had really ended here, so precipitously and so
mundanely, at what must be a box factory, or if Bajanis
was merely making a business or social call. I decided to
give him ten minutes and had half turned away when, out
of the corner of my eye, I saw him emerge as suddenly
as he had entered.

The street was empty except for the two of us. I moved
toward an acacia tree and stood a moment fingering the
delicate, drooping leaves, trying to look engrossed and at
the same time keep sight of him. But Bajanis did not
once turn around. He was striding up the street toward
the outskirts of the town and the hills. There were no
more corners. The road was wide and flat. How could I
possibly keep out of sight? A toothless crone in a black

skirt, hunched over crochet work on her marble step, looked up at me curiously, and realizing I was probably behaving very suspiciously indeed, I began to walk after Bajanis.

He came to a crossroads and paused. There was a little group of people standing there. A sign out in front said: *Platiyalos Beach.* A bus was grinding up the hill on the roundabout route that led from the town. Bajanis seemed to be of half a mind to catch it, and suddenly I was in a cold sweat, wondering what to do. I could see at a glance that the bus was laden with passengers. Tourists were packed like sardines all along the center and jammed on the steps by the doors. If I let him go, certainly I would not find him again, but if I should climb aboard, then I would be pressed right up against him and that could put a stop to my tracking him to his destination.

The bus ground noisily to a halt, the driver sounding his klaxon horn. The doors opened and young people who were jammed against each other on the steps protested, half laughing, half indignant:

"There is no room!"

"Tell him to shut the doors or I'll fall out."

More laughter, a harsh order from the driver, a protest from the passengers, a moment of deadlock, and then, with another crazy shriek from the horn, the bus lumbered clumsily on its way.

Half a dozen young people standing at the stop settled down resignedly on a retaining wall to await the next bus, but several others set out to walk. Bajanis had already started, striding through the clouds of dust that swirled and puffed in the bus's wake. Three young people, two girls and a boy, heaved their rucksacks into their backs and set off after him. I moved in behind. If Bajanis turned now, the presence of four of us straggling along should look natural enough.

The steep, narrow road was thickly edged with small, square, flat-roofed, houses painted white, many of which had strange dovecotes, decorated with spike-like projections on their roofs. I was gaining on Bajanis for his pace had slowed. I leaned against a stone wall for a moment to allow him to get ahead.

The town looked strange from here, almost like a neat dumping ground for white marble blocks. Away to the left on a rise stood more of those storybook windmills with thatched roof and sail tips showing. The Greek was now about a hundred and fifty yards ahead. I began to walk again. Here and there a building with a dome-shaped roof and raised cross appeared by the side of the road. *Every family seems to have a chapel of its own*, Lee had written when she first arrived here, *and sometimes, through intermarriage, or maybe if they are well off, they have two or three or even four.*

Here was one of them, right against the road. Bajanis was slowing down again, as were the three people in front. The sun was grueling. I took the opportunity for a look at a chapel. Crossing a strip of grass between the little building and the road, I went up to its green door. Three padlocks lay side by side along a chain. Such distrust! We were told the Greeks were honest! Or were the padlocks for us?

I darted a quick look toward my quarry, not far enough yet in front, then went around the side of the building. There were yellow poppies in the grass, and green shutters firmly closed against the one small window. I returned to the road. Bajanis now had about a hundred yards' start. A taxi passed me in a little swirl of dust. Holding my breath I closed my eyes. Bajanis and the three people ahead of me went around a corner and I set out again. There were fields here, already brown from the sun, and a farmhouse standing back from the road with hen coops, tethered goats, a black-clad woman toiling in her yard which was rimmed with thistles. A mule eyed me indifferently from a stone-walled field, a bunch of weeds and dry grass sticking out from either side of his jaws as though he had taken the food absentmindedly and forgotten to eat it. We came upon market gardens next, spilling over with tomatoes, maize and onions, and opposite, a mysterious building lined with battlements embedded in a threatening nest of yellow flowering cactus, more efficient, I thought, than that triple-padlocked door. Another taxi swung around the corner, its horn blaring, and the driver waved. Surprised and oddly warmed by this show of friendship in what had become to me such a lonely island, I waved back.

We must have been walking for about twenty minutes when suddenly a bus came sweeping around the corner and pulled up just ahead of me. The three young people turned, ran toward it and climbed aboard, but Bajanis kept walking. I waited by the side of the road until the bus went on its way. Bajanis rounded another corner and I started out again. I had no shelter now, but, I thought, I am in Fate's hands. If he looks, he looks.

He did not turn. We passed two donkeys standing together in another field, half asleep in the sun. One of them moved lethargically and I saw his front hooves were tied together. A lone sheep, dusty as the land, stood with her two lambs in the shade of a stone wall. Beside them, a little clump of poppies, blood red in the drying grass.

It was now very hot indeed, but as we came to what must be the summit, and the sea on the opposite side of the island came into view, we walked into a welcome breeze. There were sandy beaches and rocks at the end of this road, Lee had said, and some restaurants that served seafood. The houses thinned out now. An occasional chapel, surprisingly enough, lay among the stony mounds and hills quite far back from the road.

We came upon a tiny farmhouse, its railless verandah a clutter of painted cans full of flowering pinks. A carpet of whitewash spilled down the outside steps and across the yard. Another taxi sped by, its horn blaring, and a golden feathered hen, disturbed by the noise, fled squawking across the yard with a clutch of fluffy chickens in dismayed pursuit.

At that moment Bajanis did look behind and I froze. I don't know why, for surely I had been expecting it, and did I not half wish to speak to him? For a split second he seemed to be looking right at me, and then a taxi came screeching around a sharp corner behind him, kicking up a cloud of dust. When the dust cleared and I could see again, Bajanis was climbing over a gate into a field where there were grape vines growing higgledy-piggledy, a fig tree with tiny fruits already formed, poppies red as a flag, cow parsley taller than my shoulders and a grand dandelion three feet high.

The field sloped up toward a mound. On top of it, all alone and half hidden behind a sheltering outcrop of rock, lay one of those little pale-blue chapels with a crimson dome roof. Over the hill there could only be more hills, or fields sloping toward the southern end of the island and the sea. I walked on as far as the gate and paused, half hidden by the stone wall and a wild rose, considerably taller than myself, that stood by the wood-slat gate. Filling time, I picked one of the brilliant vermilion blooms and sniffed it. It smelled faintly of musk. Bajanis was going through another gate at the opposite end of the small field. A taxi raced up behind me, honked an impatient horn and sped on, leaving me enveloped in yet another choking cloud of dust. Bajanis had climbed over a second stone wall and was ascending the steep slope below the chapel. Without a backward glance he went right up to the door, opened it and went in.

So! This was the end of the line. And what a peculiar end it was! I stood there with my arms resting on the top of the gate, baffled. What on earth could Bajanis be doing in a chapel? When I had decided to beard him in his den I hardly thought that den would be so isolated. The building was two fields' distant from the road. I

looked behind me. The road was empty. After being be-
leaguered by buses, taxis and tourists for the past half
hour, I was suddenly, frighteningly on my own. Should
Bajanis turn violent, no one would ever know. On the
other hand, if I were to give up the chase it would take
an hour to return to Mykonos, find Nat and bring him
here. Meantime Bajanis might disappear.

I took a deep breath, and with my heart hammering
mercilessly, I heaved myself over the gate. At least the
windows were not facing this way, and all the chapels I
had seen so far were either barred or shuttered so that he
was unlikely to see my approach. The going here was
rough, the soil hard-baked, the thistles cruel. Two goats
tethered to a bush eyed me with interest and some flies
hovered round my face, refusing to leave when I brushed
at them with my hands.

And then I saw that there was a grassy track running
from the gate around the inside of the stone wall. I made
my way across. Here golden daisies formed a miniature
forest reaching to my knees, but some of them had apparently been flattened by a vehicle passing over them as
they grew. The buds were mutilated so that they had
never flowered. The wheel marks led me to the other
gate over which Bajanis had climbed.

The chapel stood above me on the hill. I climbed over,
skirted the boulders and came out on the track that led
to the door. I paused, looking at a side window. Yes, it
was barred, but unshuttered. I advanced toward it, then
hesitated. With Bajanis inside, I could scarcely look
through the window, but what about the keyhole? Treading carefully on the dirt track, I made my cautious way
up to the front door. There was a heavy knob and here,
a keyhole. I bent down, putting my eye to it. Nothing but
darkness. Either the key was in the door, or else the hole
had been blocked up. Covered over with a curtain perhaps?

I went back to the corner and stood looking along the opposite side. This window, too, was barred. I returned to the door and tried the handle. It was locked. Then, I thought faintly, I heard a sound. Clip. And then another. Clip. I looked behind me. There was no one in sight. Perhaps the noise came from an insect tucked away in the olive tree close by? I knocked, but my knuckles made little impact, for the wood was very thick. I thumped with my fist, then picked up a piece of stone and rattled it against the door, raising a small racket. Bajanis was in there. He had to answer.

But he did not. I waited a moment, then went around to one of the windows. I peered in, seeing nothing. Perhaps my eyes were full of sun. I put my face as close as the bars would allow. The recessed glass showed the walls to be a good ten inches thick and I could see my reflection in the glass. One of the bars was broken. I gave it an impatient shove and looked again, my face a little closer now, but could see nothing except my own reflection. A trick of the light, I thought, and went round to the other side. The bars were rusted badly and in the process of being eaten away, with the shutters firmly held against the wall as though they had not been used in a long time. My reflection came back at me again.

Puzzled, I stood back a pace and looked up at the sun. It was almost directly overhead and was not casting much of a shadow. I should be able to see. Unless someone had drawn a curtain. I went back to the door and beat on it with angry fists. Now that I had made my presence known, I might as well go all out for the information I wanted. There was no reply. The chapel was still as a morgue.

I turned away feeling frustrated, and now that I had achieved nothing, I also felt guilty and not a little upset. Here, where the olive tree stood, poppies bled above the sun-bleached grass. The land sloped away to a little bay tightly enclosed between two ridges oddly free of stones. I stood beneath the silver branches of the olive tree listening, but those curious sounds did not come again. I looked out to sea and, perhaps a mile from the shore, one sleek yacht with a tall brown mast and magnificent lines lay steady, its sails furled. There were no caïques over here, no fishermen. A breeze had begun to feather the water.

I looked at my watch. It was nearly half past one. Nat would be waiting for me at the waterfront. I turned back toward the sea and found myself looking closely at the yacht. It was a beauty. The plaything of a Greek ship-owning millionaire? Or—and now I caught my breath—did it belong to Mad Midas, who had all those treasures hidden underground? I stared at it. Naxos, the man had said, and there was Naxos now, in the background. It might indeed be the yacht of which those Americans had spoken. Why was it not coming in closer?

Irene and her accomplices were about to move, Nat had said. To steal that Naxian marble lion from Delos and transport it to a yacht? It was surely possible to do almost anything if one had the money, the time, some ardent collaborators and a bit of luck. But why would Bajanis, whose marble-cutting skill they might need in order to safely remove the lion from its plinth, be skulking in this tiny chapel? Did it have an underground passage leading from it? And if so, to where? There was nothing of any significance in the area. In the distance were several tiny innocent-looking houses, another chapel or two. I walked around the side, scanning the fields. A cow with sharp horns stared at me. A sheep bleated and her lamb came running. There was no other sign of life.

Nothing made sense. I cast a lingering, angry, puzzled look back at the door and then went off down the hill to the road. Let him see me now, if he wished. I would tell Nat that Bajanis was holed up here, and he could tell his policemen, or archeologists, or whoever cared. I did not care. By the time I got back to the town, unless I could catch a bus, the siesta would be in full swing, but come five o'clock I intended to be on the steps of the OTE, ready to telephone London.

I was past caring whether our mother would be alarmed or not. I had to share my own alarm with someone to whom Lee's safety was a number-one priority. I had to have help and the right kind of advice, or I felt I would go out of my mind. That banging on the door had been a stupid act. I had alerted Bajanis, and to what avail?

And then, with stunning shock, an idea hit me. Could Lee be held prisoner in the chapel? I went back, picked up a big stone and banged like a madman on the door. There was no answering sound. The chapel was still as the grave. I went off down the hill feeling shaken indeed.

CHAPTER 19

The Delos tourists had long since scattered, the caïques gone to anchor. I walked along the waterfront searching the tables, but Nat was not there. Neither was he in his room, and he had left no message. I went back to the promenade and pulling out a chair at one of the little tables, I settled down nervously, and unhappily, to wait.

There was little activity on the shore. The steamer from Piraeus was on the horizon and a queue of luggage lay beside the quay. A score or so of holiday-makers were scattered among the open-air tavernas, idling over coffees and drinks. Two Greeks were untangling a net. A girl in checked jeans was perched on a bollard reading a paperback.

Nat did not come. I waited for an hour beneath the awning, drinking a Greek coffee I did not want, shrugging off the men who tried to pick me up. When the strain became too much, I rose and walked the length of the quay and back, only to settle at another table and order yet another coffee only to begin again the annoying task of avoiding men's advances.

Had Nat found something on Delos? And then, having missed the excursion caïques, could he find any alternative transport for his return? There had been talk of archeologists on the island, and if they were there now, surely they would need a ferry boat. But were they there now? Should I take another caïque and return to the island to look for him? Somehow it seemed ridiculous to think in terms of Nat needing help from a woman—a mere woman.

Suddenly I saw a familiar figure walking down toward the beach. Kriton, wearing a blue-and-white striped shirt and jeans, jumped down onto the sand and began untying a dinghy. As I watched, he pushed it into the water and jumped aboard. I got up from my chair and walked over to the low wall that ran from the beach along to the quay. Kriton seemed to be making for a sturdy, russet-colored caïque that was tied to a blue buoy some distance out. Shielding my eyes with one hand from the sun, I tried to read the name on the bow. It was short and might, I guessed, be *Ajax* but I was not sure. He climbed aboard, untied the caïque and tied the dinghy to the buoy. I sat down on the wall to wait. No one else appeared, and a few moments later the caïque began to move out to sea. At the end of the breakwater it turned in as though it was heading around toward the opposite side of the island. I went along to the quay and watched it until it disappeared behind the point.

After a while I went back to Nat's room. The young girl was settled on her hard chair on the landing with her crochet work in her hands. I gave her a sick sort of smile as I opened Nat's door and she eyed me suspiciously, then followed me in, making agitated signs to tell me he was not there. I took a pencil and notebook from my bag, wrote:

Waiting on the waterfront. V., tore the page out and, making apologetic signs to the girl, put it on the bed.

I returned to the waterfront and walked the length of the promenade and back. The Piraeus steamer lay at anchor and the caïques were dashing back and forth bringing the passengers ashore. The black-clad widows who let rooms were gossiping together. As each little ferry arrived and discharged its passengers, they broke off their chatter to make forays into the crowd, looking among the new arrivals for potential paying guests. On the other side of the quay the queue of departing passengers had grown. I eyed it uncertainly. What could I do in Athens that I could not do here? I looked at my watch. It was nearly four o'clock. What on earth could have happened to Nat?

Restlessly, I returned to the boutique. It was closed. I unlocked the door and pushed it back on its hinges. Illogically, for Kriton or Irene could close it if they appeared, I then felt better about going upstairs. Would I pack my bag swiftly and catch the steamer? There was an air letter on the counter addressed to Lee. I looked around guiltily, then pushed it into my bag.

The bedroom was as I had left it. My bag beckoned me invitingly. It would be so easy to go. Hesitating, still uncertain what to do, I went to the kitchen for a glass of water. Turning the tap on, I glanced casually down into the yard, and then, sharply alert, I looked again. Surely that wooden box had not been there before? It was standing against the near wall, partially concealed by an overhanging sloping roof that jutted out below my window. I put the glass down and hoisted myself up on the sink. Balancing precariously, I leaned sideways out the narrow window.

It was a big box about eight feet long and six feet deep, perhaps three feet wide. I blinked, shook my head, then blinked again. No, my imagination was not going berserk. That box would hold one of the marble lions from Delos. And had I not seen Bajanis pay a visit to a box-making establishment this morning? So why had he gone to Delos? To take a final look, in daylight, at a job that had to be tackled at night, without lights?

I unwedged myself from the window and went back to the bedroom, feeling disturbed. There were some things that scarcely made sense. Bajanis' movements had not been totally those of a man who plans to remove a statue from its plinth. He had spent a considerable amount of time viewing the lion from all angles. He had reached up to touch its ribs. Could it be that he, as a patriotic Greek, was doing something very much against his will? Was this morning's visit a last act of homage? Of penitence?

No, I decided conclusively. I would not return to Athens. Back to the waterfront and make another all-out effort to find Nat. I slung my bag over my shoulder and started down the stairs. I have said they were precarious and that there was no rail. I was treading carefully, looking at my feet as I descended, so I did not see Kriton standing in the middle of the room. He spoke and I jumped nearly out of my skin.

"You are going to meet Lee?"

My fright gave way to a burst of giddy excitement. "Lee! What do you mean?"

"Both of the steamers are in. The *Opollon* and the *Oïa*. I thought you would be down on the quay waiting."

My heart sank. I managed to say steadily, "I have no reason to assume Lee is back. But I am going down to meet the boats all the same."

"Were you having a siesta?" Kriton was looking at me as a cat looks at a mouse, challenging me to produce an answer that he could catch me up on. He must have known I had not been here when the box was delivered, because he could have suspected that I might be spying for Nat and would have checked the flat. But perhaps he had been out in his boat when the box came. He had discarded the striped seaman's jumper and now he wore a blue shirt open down the front and tied in a knot at the waist. Around his neck he wore a leather thong strung with those strange evil eyes and it ended at rib height with a small tassel.

"A siesta! You should know English tourists don't waste time that way." I gave him what I hoped would look like a friendly smile. "I came in only a moment ago."

He seemed relieved. "What are you doing this evening?"

"Having dinner with my friend."

"Oh, I am sorry. I nearly forgot to tell you. Your friend has gone to Athens."

"Nat?"

"Yes. He dropped in, carrying his bag."

My first reaction was one of disbelief. "Nat! Gone to Athens! You're joking!"

"He seemed in a hurry," said Kriton. "Rushing to catch a plane, I suppose."

"And he didn't leave a note for me?" My voice was a giveaway, high and unsteady.

"As I said, he was in a hurry." Kriton glanced away, the insolent lids drooping, almost as though he did not wish to witness my embarrassment at being ditched. My fingers tightened in the palms of my hands as I fought down the growing hysteria of shock and despair. Why should Nat disappear like that without letting me know? Yet, would Kriton say he had gone if there was a chance of Nat walking in here at any moment? Kriton raised his great head. There was a glint of amusement in the black eyes. I could see he was conscious of his power by the way he held those overdeveloped shoulders. He flaunted his sexuality, lifting one slim hip, lowering the other. "Perhaps you would like to have dinner with me?" Sensuous lips parting over white teeth. The eyes watchful.

My mind began spinning around. Was Nat marooned

on Delos? And did Kriton somehow know? Was Nat even in danger? Incredibly, as those thoughts rushed through my mind, I believe my eyes remained steadily on Kriton's face. Then, equally incredibly, I heard myself saying quite calmly, "Do you mind if I let you know later? After all, as you said, my sister might arrive."

Kriton had his back to the doorway so I saw the girl before he did. She was a small, pert creature with long hair back-combed on top of her head. She had brown limpid eyes heavily lashed and weighted with mascara and was wearing an embroidered blouse and a very short black skirt belted in tightly at the waist and flaring out at her rounded hips. Kriton must have realized my eyes were looking past him for he swung around, but only halfway, so that I saw the expression of incredulity that crossed his face.

"Zoe!" he exclaimed. It evidently took every ounce of self-discipline he possessed to restrain himself at this but I could see that he considered greeting her arrival a disaster. Angry lines formed swiftly between his brows and down from his heavy mouth. I could see it in the gleam of sweat on his low forehead, his quick, shallow breathing. "This is a surprise."

With her eyes on Kriton's face, Zoe could see she was not welcome. She came hesitantly down the steps and put a small suitcase on the floor. "I came," she said, in heavily accented English, "as you say, for a surprise." Her voice sounded uncertain and nervous.

"You should have let me know," said Kriton, chastising her with a velvet tongue, his anger hidden behind the iron-hard chin, within the hands that locked and unlocked at his sides. "Since you knew I was here, you could have sent a letter or a telegram."

She had a soft mouth. I saw it tighten. I saw the hurt and disappointment in her eyes. Perhaps it was not so much disappointment, as a confirmation of something she had not wanted to believe. In my situation, anything that got in Kriton's way had to be an asset for me. I found my emotions ranged between pity and relief.

Kriton said, "Let me introduce you two. Virginia Sandersen. Zoe Markopoulou."

Kriton is currently making a fuss over a little tart called Zoe Markopoulou, Nat had said. Well, he was in no mind to make a fuss over her now.

"Do you work in the boutique?" Zoe asked, looking at me directly, as though she were giving Kriton time to take that unwelcoming expression from his face.

"My sister does," I said, "but I am staying here. Are you looking for a bed? You may sleep on this couch if you like. I am sure my sister would not mind."

I suppose ideas for self-preservation come to us in various ways. Nat had disappeared. I was on my own and I turned to this poor, unwelcome waif. Maybe she could be an ally. There was a naked silence in the room. I had that weird sensation of split seconds stretching out like thin rubber bands. I became intensely aware of the gloom and went to the big, awful lamp, groping blindly as I kept my eyes on Kriton's face. Perhaps my fumbling fingers caused some damage for there was a small pop! and the bulb burned out. I went to the smaller lights, feeling a terrible need to get them lit as quickly as possible. The little red lamps sat in their own pools of light. The center of the room and the corners stayed shadowed.

Kriton's black eyes were slitted, but he managed to say lightly, "I'll have two girls to take to dinner, then. But we'll easily find Zoe a bed. She doesn't have to sleep on that hard thing."

I went to the couch and sat down. I needed to sit, anyway. "It is very soft," I said. "Very comfortable. And I would like Zoe to sleep here. I did not much enjoy being on my own last night." I addressed the Greek girl directly, trying to sound merely hospitable when there was real entreaty behind my words. "You will, won't you?"

Zoe looked at Kriton—a purely instinctive glance to gauge his reaction. He did not so much as flick an eyelid, nor did he speak, but his stillness was a symptom of something else. Something too evil to come out and face the light of day. Then, breaking the deafening silence between the three of us, Zoe's small voice said, "Thank you. Yes, I will stay."

I think I knew, at that moment, she was making the biggest mistake of her life. I think I knew by the way Kriton's face slowly relaxed, the way his foot came forward deliberately. I think I knew then, that for the rest of my life I was going to be troubled by Zoe Markopoulou.

Somewhere a bell sounded, reminding me to look at my watch. The OTE would be open again, and I could telephone home. "I won't hold you to your offer," I said to Kriton. I was not looking at Zoe, but I had an impression of her rising a little on her ridiculously high platform-soled shoes. I knew she was suspicious of Kriton and me. I had to put that right, and fast. I said, "In case you are under a misapprehension about me, I only met Mr. Fileas yesterday." I thought she registered relief.

"Where are you going?" Kriton asked, looking annoyed.

"To meet my sister, if she is there. It was your suggestion." I turned to Zoe. "Do put your bag upstairs." I started for the door, then paused. Kriton was blocking Zoe's way, although he did it gently.

"I will find you a room," he said. "A friend of mine has a house where you will be very comfortable." He looked across at me. With one foot in the doorway, I paused. "I'll get Irene," he said.

I came back, trying to look casual, and not succeeding. My desire to talk alone to Zoe must have been written in large letters all over my face. The Greek girl sat down disconsolately on the couch.

"I won't be long," said Kriton. He did not even seem interested in the fact that I had changed my mind. Going to get Irene seemed to absorb his entire consciousness. In some way it was extraordinarily important.

I went over to the counter and stood facing Zoe with my elbows resting on it.

"I suppose it's just as well," she commented as Kriton went out the door. Her heavy accent was surprising considering her excellent command of English. "I am not mad about sleeping here. It's eerie, isn't it?" She looked at me forlornly, then said, "Who are you?"

"Virginia Sandersen."

"Yes, I know that," she retorted pettishly. "I mean, in the setup. Kriton is up to something, isn't he?"

"I don't know," I replied. "And I don't know what you mean by a 'setup.' I came here to visit my sister and found her gone. I am waiting for her to return. Kriton is supposed to be looking after the boutique for her."

Zoe's eyes roved around the room. "For a man who is looking after someone else's shop, he seems very much at home," she said bluntly. I was about to agree with her when she fired her next question. "What is your sister to Kriton?"

"Absolutely nothing," I replied, hoping desperately that such total confidence was not misplaced.

"And you?"

"I told you why I am here. I met Kriton for the first time yesterday. You must believe me."

She picked at the goatskin cover on the couch.

"Why have you come?" I asked.

She said diffidently, "I don't know whether you have noticed anything about me."

I had not, but in the face of such a loaded remark, I realized that in this era of flat-bosomed, flat-hipped girls, Zoe was perhaps a trifle overripe. I said, "You're not pregnant, are you?"

"Kriton doesn't know," she said, "but I think it's time he did."

Yes, perhaps it was. I eyed her with a good deal more sympathy than I had felt before.

"I heard a rumor he was getting out of the country," she said.

"Who told you that?"

She watched me for a long moment before she answered. She was summing me up, I thought. Those overpainted eyes weren't exactly suspicious, but they were certainly watchful. Zoe Markopoulou might be a little tart, as Nat had said, but she was sharp about people. Basically underprivileged, I thought. She may have learned the hard way never to take people at face value or even at their word. At last she said, "I wasn't exactly told it. I went to his village. To the Bajanis house. He was going to marry the girl, you see. Katerini."

"When was this?" I asked sharply. "When did you visit the Bajanis house?"

"Yesterday."

"And you saw Bajanis? Katerini's father?"

"No. They wouldn't let me in. They don't let anyone in now. People think they're going mad," said Zoe, looking up at me with a heavy frown. "It's all to do with some accident the girl had. The doors and windows of the house are always shut. Only the old woman goes to the market, and she doesn't talk to anyone. They say in the village that the man doesn't go to work either. He doesn't even appear. Madame Bajanis sent me away, but Katerini must have seen me from a window because she ran after me. She is very ugly," said Zoe with stunning innocence. "Her face is all twisted. But she's kind. She said Kriton had come over here to Mykonos with her father, and I should hurry if I want to catch him."

"I thought you said her father was holed up in the house," I said, frantically sorting out her confusing story.

"That is what the villagers think. But Katerini says he is over here."

"What did she mean by 'catching him'?"

"He is leaving."

"Is he? I didn't know." Zoe made no effort to reply and by way of encouragement I remarked kindly, "You speak very good English."

"My mother lives with an Englishman. I don't want to live with anyone. I want to get married. That is why I came after Kriton. If he is leaving the country, I want to go with him."

We stared grimly at each other, both in our separate ways needing help. I was thinking of the lion-sized box, and Nat's departure and the possibility that Lee was somewhere near. There was no point in worrying my mother with a useless telephone call. There was something to be done here, if I could only find out where to start.

"Did Katerini tell you what her father was doing?" I asked.

"Working," she replied. "It's strange, isn't it, to let people think he is hiding in the house, when he isn't there at all?"

CHAPTER 20

"Yes," said Zoe, "I know Mykonos well. I used to have relations living here. My uncle died and the rest of the family went to Tinos. That's a bigger island over there." She waved one hand vaguely at the side wall.

"Then perhaps you can tell me about the chapels," I said.

"What about the chapels?"

"What they mean. Why there are so many. Did your family have one?"

Zoe was relaxed on the goatskin, her legs drawn up under her, her back against the wall. "Of course. They're just private places of worship."

"They seem to be firmly locked." Trying to appear casual, I picked up a keyring and tossed it from one hand to the other. "Are visitors ever shown inside?"

"I dare say anyone would let you in," Zoe replied straightforwardly. "The islanders are friendly to tourists. I can show you ours tomorrow, but it is quite a long way out of town. We would have to take a bus. If you're interested, I will get the key from Kriton."

I moved away from the counter and picked up a leather-thong belt, fingering it so that I might avoid Zoe's eyes. "Why does Kriton have the key?"

"He said he was going to marry me." She added, a little defensively, "It is usual enough for a fiancé to be shown family property. He asked to see it and I gave him the key then. I never thought to ask for it back."

"What is there? I mean, is it as it appears, one room with—er—nothing underground?"

I caught her look of astonishment and rushed into an impromptu explanation: "I mean, in England some of the old churches have secret passages and secret rooms where the clergy hid in troubled times."

"Oh, nothing like that. It's just an ordinary little chapel. And not very old. We don't hide things there," she added severely. "There is only an icon or two and some holy pictures."

Kriton's large figure appeared in the doorway, blocking the brilliant light from outside, suddenly throwing the entire boutique into shadow. A pair of black eyes glittered, and that sinuous body swayed in on light, animal feet. He crossed to the counter. Zoe looked up at him, her eyes liquid, large. She had a curved shell of an underlip and she pressed it with small, neat teeth. Suddenly she looked guilty, frightened and a little desperate. Without taking her eyes from Kriton's face, she swung her legs to the floor. Perhaps accidentally, she flicked the short skirt a little higher on her overdeveloped thighs. "Virginia wants to see our chapel. I said I would show it to her tomorrow. You have the key."

Those black eyes narrowed and I shrank instinctively. "Tomorrow?" he echoed lightly. "Sure. I'll take you there myself." He pulled something from his pocket and tossed it down on the counter. "There's the key." He was looking directly at the girl now, speaking with an odd sort of weighty, even ironic deliberation. As though he were having a little joke at Zoe's expense. Last night when I had asked him to remove that board thing from behind the bathroom door, he had reacted the same way, as though I had invited him to take some advantage over me.

There was a faint footfall in the street outside. Nervously I swung around toward the door. "Ah! Irene!" Kriton said and stepped forward lightly to meet her, clapping his hands, smiling, surprised. Too surprised perhaps. "I was looking for you. Could you put up a friend of mine?"

Irene's eyes had gone straight to Zoe. She knew the Greek girl was there, all right. Kriton went through the motions of introducing them.

"Pleased to meet you," said Zoe, that open expression drawing in with dismay as she met Irene's unfriendly flat stare. She added swiftly, looking to me for help, "Virginia says I can sleep here, and I would rather like to, thank you all the same." Eerie the Boutique Cleopatra might be, but only half as eerie as Irene. She certainly did not seem detached this evening. Her eyes had that burning look I had seen in them the first time she met me.

"It isn't really convenient," Irene said.

"Then that settles it!" I exclaimed heartily. I did not at all mind the idea of sleeping in the flat with this girl downstairs. Especially now that she seemed to be looking on me as an ally. Illogically, I was also drawing confidence from the fact that we had Katerini on our side. It occurred to me that I might even confide in Zoe. That we might take that key later and investigate the chapel together. Last night there had been a moon which was full enough, I thought, to show us the way. I had seen an ironmonger's shop in the street Bajanis had taken this morning. I might be able to buy a flashlight there.

I turned toward Kriton, realizing he was watching me. His shirt open almost to the waist exposed a mat of black hairs in a sensuous curve. He was fiddling with that leather necklace and the evil eyes shone in the lamplight as they swung back and forth. I was reminded that even this chauvinistic half Greek was probably riddled with superstition. Something is up, I said to myself with conviction. What god had sent Zoe here in my hour of need?

"Right," said Kriton, totally in command. "Let's all go and have a drink."

My first reaction was to excuse myself but then I realized Kriton would not leave me alone here in daylight with the box. Besides, if we were to investigate the Markopoulou chapel together, I needed to work up my new relationship with Zoe. We went to a small bar in a side street with tiny lanterns hanging from a huge beam in the white-washed ceiling and Kriton ordered ouzos. One drink lifted Zoe's spirits. Those big brown eyes glowed with a brazen beauty, and the soft mouth pouted and drooped. On the second drink she loosened the neck of her peasant blouse. With the sinuousness of a young cat, she leaned up against Kriton, brushing her well-developed bosom on his bare arm, teasing him with her nearness.

He caught Irene's watchful, cold eye and gave Zoe a little push, but Zoe threw Irene a defiant look and came saucily back again, soft, perfumed, exposed. At any other time I would have found such play amusing. Now I could only think that Zoe was not going to be much use to me tonight if matters went along these lines.

Kriton said suddenly, "Who wants suckling pig?"

The very thought of food set me aching with hunger for I had eaten nothing since breakfast, but I had to get away from them to check Nat's room and buy the flashlight.

I slipped down from my bar stool. "Thank you for the

drink. Now you must excuse me. I have one or two things to do." I stopped dead as Kriton's fingers closed on my wrist.

"What do you have to do?"

"Let me go!" I was angry, but my voice sounded sharp with alarm. The barman had gone to serve customers who were seated by the door and there was no one to overhear.

Zoe giggled. "He gives man-sized bruises." She added something in Greek that was evidently meant to be provocative, for Kriton made that unpleasant cabalistic sign with his free hand, the five fingers pointing downward. Zoe pouted, slapped his face lightly and got a blow in the ribs that set her reeling on the stool. Irene caught her and said to Kriton in a frozen voice, "Stop it, you."

I was suddenly frightened. I said with icy politeness, "Let my wrist go, or I will start yelling for the tourist police."

He did, reluctantly, then held out a packet of cigarettes. "I didn't mean any harm."

Zoe seemed to have recovered, though she held one arm folded across her ribs. "Englishmen are soft," she said contemptuously. "She doesn't understand."

I said, "You're dead right." Then, speaking pointedly to Zoe, I asked, "What time will you be at the boutique?"

She fluttered those heavily weighted eyelashes: "What time will we be there, Kriton?"

I was keenly conscious of Irene's silence. She had laid her thin arms on the bar, but she was not relaxed. A cigarette hung from her lower lip and her dry, pale hair had fallen forward a little. She, too, seemed to be waiting for Kriton's reply. Testing his attitude to Zoe, I thought. Or her power over him.

Kriton's eyes flicked toward the doorway. The early Aegean night had fallen. He smiled, and I knew suddenly that he was letting me go because the yard, with its suspicious box, would be in darkness. "Don't worry," he said, deliberately spiking my confidence and at the same time giving nothing away. "I have a key."

I guess it was just not my night. Nat's room was empty and when I went to buy a flashlight the shop was shut. I found a restaurant tucked away in a back street where Kriton and Irene would not find me. I had given up all hope of cooperation from Zoe tonight.

The letter addressed to Lee that I had picked up earlier in the boutique rustled against my fingers as I pulled my wallet out to pay. For the first time I noticed it bore an American stamp!

I ripped the letter open. There was no return address. The date was May 9th. That was ten days ago. The letter must have been held up in the mails. *Dear Lee*, it ran, *F.T. will be waiting off S.E. point of Naxos. My experts tell me that weight in water is negligible and you should manage very well with Ajax. Good luck. G.*

Was Lee involved? Or were they really, as Nat suggested, using her name as cover? *F.T.?* I racked my brains, trying to remember the name of the yacht those Americans had mentioned in the restaurant last night. And then it came to me: *Fall Tide.* Had I not seen a luxury yacht off the coast of Naxos today? And the signature, *G.* Mad Midas, whose name was Earl Foster *Ghent.* I folded the letter up tightly and pushed it into my wallet.

What was I going to do now? I could, of course, go to the tourist police and ask for a bed, but somehow that seemed like walking out. Especially when one considered that Nat might not have gone to Athens. I closed my mind to such speculation and to my fears. With a heavy heart, I went back to the boutique to wait for heaven alone knew what.

It seemed only common sense to stay in my shirt and jeans. I kicked off my sandals and lay on the bed. Beyond the window, I could see stars. The moon was high, an imperfect, depressed circle. There might be enough light for Zoe and me to investigate the chapel, in the ever-decreasing likelihood that we should need it. The warmth of the room, the meal, the exceptional strain of the day and my near-sleepless night had begun to take their toll. I must have dozed off for all at once I sat up with a start, not knowing why. I swung my feet to the floor, then felt my way across the room. The hall was pitch dark. And then I heard muffled voices rising from below. I went like a stealthy cat toward the stairs. The voices were directly below me now, still muffled.

Suddenly I realized my foot was sliding across something warmer than tiles, and less smooth. Wood? But the landing was fully tiled! It took me several moments to understand I had no access to the stairwell. That while I slept, someone had blocked it in. The image of Kriton's face flashed across my terrified mind. Kriton being kind and obliging that one time. Kriton rushing upstairs to remove the cumbersome piece of wood from behind the bathroom door. The key that Lee must have used to shut herself in! A trap door to block the stairs and insure her privacy! But Kriton had fixed it in from below, and now I was a prisoner!

Real terror leaves no room for asking questions. I remembered those narrow windows opening onto the yard. They were just wide enough for me to slide through. With thudding heart, I felt my way toward the kitchen door that was beyond the stairwell. I pushed the door open. Pale moonlight lit the kitchen faintly, and yes, with relief I saw that the window was open a fraction, just as I had left it. At least I was not a prisoner. They did not want me disturbing them in the boutique. That was reasonable, assuming Kriton was spending the night on the goatskin couch with Zoe. But those were not the dulcet tones of lovers that came up, muted, from below. I was hearing two people involved in argument.

I went back to the trap door, and going down on my

knees, I put my ear to the crack. It sounded like Zoe's voice, but she was speaking in Greek. Kriton answered, also in Greek, his words calm and cool. Then Zoe's voice rose in a threat or accusation. Still Kriton remained calm. Too calm for one who hit out so easily.

I went back to the kitchen and stood for a moment eying the window. It was unpleasant being locked in, but if I was to leave now, where would I go? In the moonlight glancing in from the window, I looked at my wrist watch. It was half past one. Zoe's voice, raised to a shriek, split through the floor. The chilling thought occurred to me that Kriton did not particularly mind if I overheard, so long as I could not interfere. The memory of what had happened to Katerini Bajanis shot through my mind, and I knew I had to go to Zoe's aid. But not from here. Kicking and banging on the trap door would avail me nothing. If I climbed out the window, I could unlock the door and, keeping to the safety of the lane, yell until someone came. I went back for the key, grabbed my sandals, opened the window as wide as it would go, climbed up on the sink and eased myself through, pushing my bare feet out on the gently sloping tiled roof directly below. But I had forgotten about the box. There it was, in the yard, directly below me now, and half hidden by the overhang. If I slid down this roof, I would land on the box with an almighty crash.

I bent forward awkwardly to see if there was any possibility of my dropping over the side where this half roof ended. And then I saw that curious little square of glass, peephole-sized, that I had noticed the first time I entered the boutique. I lay down on my front on the tiles, gripping the window sill with my left hand for safety. Slowly and very carefully, for if I made a false move now I would go hurtling down onto the box, I wriggled forward across the sloping roof until my head and shoulders were over the edge. From here, I could just see through that tiny peephole window.

Kriton and Zoe were standing in the middle of the room. I saw Kriton in profile, those big shoulders squared, the head lifted. At least he was not, for the moment, knocking her about. Zoe had been crying. The light from the glow of a single lamp showed her face weirdly white, and her eyes looked shrunken. She was talking angrily again, using her hands, sometimes threateningly, sometimes with supplication. Kriton said something and she jerked her head up, her face suddenly contorted with fury. She shouted and the next moment he slapped her across the face and sent her reeling.

I must have reacted physically for I felt myself slipping sideways and forward, hideously close to the roof edge. With my right hand I pushed myself back, gripping the window sill once more. Then I had to work my way carefully across the tiles again before I was able to lower my head safely down to the peephole. I saw then that Irene was in the room. Zoe's head, astonishingly enough, was on Kriton's shoulder and he had his arms around her. I only remembered afterward that he held her awkwardly with one arm around her waist and the other behind her neck.

I edged carefully back, my mission rendered pointless by Irene's arrival. If I put a chair over the trap door, no one could remove it without disturbing me. Not that I was likely to get any sleep tonight. I squeezed through the window and slid down across the sink to the floor. I don't know what made me turn to pull the window closed. As I was doing so, I saw the wooden gate in the outside wall that led to the lane open slowly across the yard.

I drew back behind the kitchen curtain in fear. Had Kriton seen my face at the glass and come to cut me off? But no. Two burly men, light-complexioned with closely cropped fair hair, lumbered in.

I could see them quite clearly in the moonlight. The blank expressions in their pugilistic faces. Just as I knew bit players in a gangster film looked. They were each holding an end of rope. They pushed the gate wide open, then pulled a small trolley through. Drawing it up to the wall below my window, they swung it around to face the gateway. They each took an end of the empty wooden box, lifted it effortlessly onto the trolley and went out into the lane, closing the gate after them.

I crossed the kitchen in one stride, then pulled up sharply in the pitch darkness of the hall. Muffled sounds were filtering through the cracks in the trap door. I was feeling my way along the wall above it when I distinctly heard Irene speaking in English. I dropped to a crouching position over the crack, laying my ear against it.

". . . don't know. How could I possibly know?" That was Kriton, angry and at the same time defensive.

"Somebody told her." Irene's voice was accusing.

"It doesn't matter now. Hell—what harm?"

"If your family or Bajanis have been talking . . ."

"My family don't talk," said Kriton aggressively. "And it doesn't matter about Bajanis. What are you worrying about?"

Irene said something I did not catch and Kriton replied, "It was bad luck. Katerini did it . . . spite."

There was a moment's silence and then Kriton said with what might have been an exasperated sigh, "She's not getting her dowry, is she?"

They must have moved then, for their voices came muffled, indecipherable, until Kriton raised his, saying with aggressive defiance, "Okay. It was your idea, but I've done it. There's nothing more to say. They're waiting."

I drew myself carefully to my feet. The box must be going down to the bay. I felt my way along the hall to my bedroom and slid my shoulder bag with my passport and money under the mattress. If I was going to be creeping silently through the night, I did not want to be carrying anything.

I returned to the kitchen, made certain the yard was

clear, then climbed out the window and slid down the
tiled roof, hurtling six or seven feet into the yard, falling
forward painfully on my knees. I rose shakily and looked
up at the peephole in the wall above me. It was higher
than eye level. Before going into the lane I decided I
ought to check to see who was in the boutique. I glanced
around for something to stand on.

There was a large flower pot in the far corner. I
carried it over and turned it upside down, then balanced
myself precariously on it. Stretching up to the edge of
the little window, I looked in. The light was still on, but
the boutique appeared to be empty. My view was re-
stricted, so I cautiously put my face close to the glass.
By peering sideways, I could just see a corner of the
goatskin. Zoe lay on it, and it looked as if she were
asleep, or maybe she was crying. The street door was
closed.

I was drawing away when it opened. Kriton and Irene
returned. They faced each other, and I could see them
clearly for they were in the middle of the room. Irene
was giving authoritative orders in an autocratic manner.
Kriton went toward Zoe, and Irene, for one heart-stop-
ping moment, seemed to look straight at me.

I slipped down from the flower pot and crouched
against the wall. All around me the night was eerily
silent. I waited, my heart beating a furious tattoo. But
surely she would never see me against a darkened window! I would know soon enough if I had been seen, for I
was trapped here like a rabbit in a snare. Nothing happened, and after a few moments I climbed warily onto
the flower pot once more. The lights had been put out,
and Irene's thin back was silhouetted in the open door
against the white wall of the lane. She pulled the
boutique door shut behind her.

CHAPTER 21

The muted rattle of the trolley's wheels was not coming from the direction of the harbor. With some difficulty, I had climbed over the gate and slid down into the narrow lane close by the door of the boutique. I made my way cautiously forward to the corner and peeped around. But for the whitewashed shop fronts, the street would have been very dark. I could just make out the little cortège perhaps fifty yards away, against the white walls.

I moved into the street, following the sound of the trolley at a safe distance, and nearly jumped out of my skin when something soft rubbed up against my legs. One of those hungry cats! It slipped away in the darkness. The trolley was well ahead now. The rubber soles of my sandals were blessedly silent on the stones. The little procession went the full length of the silent shopping street, emerging in that square where the big eucalyptus trees grew. The building I had taken to be a school must be close by. Here it was very dark, for foliage hid the moon. I drew back against the trunk of a small tree. Now that the sound of the wheels had stopped, the silence was overwhelming. Another cat came out and rubbed itself around my ankles, purring loudly. I edged back a little. A man could lie in wait here, unseen in the darkness. If only that cat would go away. And then I heard two voices, unmistakably American. They were terrifyingly close. I edged further away from the doubtful camouflage of the shadowy tree, but then I had to stop for fear of showing myself against a white wall. My foot touched a picket fence, and I smelled the sickly sweetness of honeysuckle in a front garden. Stop here, I told myself. With the dark vine behind and the tree in front, I might be reasonably safe.

I heard an interchange of voices. The sound of wood knocking lightly against metal, a heavy scraping sound, the rattle of a chain. My eyes were growing accustomed to the darkness. I could just make out the shape of some object beneath the trees. A truck? It could be one of those little vehicles that I had seen scurrying to the waterfront carrying luggage from the hotels. A truck of that type might be just big enough to carry the box. As though to confirm my conjecture, a door banged and an engine started. There was a scuffle of footsteps, a protest, another door banging. My mind shot ahead, remembering that farther up this hill lay the crossroads where the bus had stopped this morning to pick up passengers. One route led directly across the island, the other to a beach on this side beyond the Xenia Hotel. The truck would have to go down the left-hand side of this square and back toward the waterfront to get onto the bus route. But if I could find my way, I could take a short cut between the houses. If I were to run now, I might be able to make

the bus stop by the time the truck arrived. Hiding behind a stone wall, at least I could establish the direction
the vehicle was to take.

The truck had begun to move, but the driver had not
switched the lights on. I went across the right-hand
corner of the square, my feet silent in the dust, and
ducked behind a building on a street corner. It was
lighter here away from the trees. I was on one of those
tiny paths that ran uphill, not, I thought, one I had seen
before, but I was fairly certain it was pointing in the
right direction. I began to run silently in my soft shoes.
If the truck took its time proceeding as it had begun,
without lights, I just might make the corner first.

I do not know what went wrong. My sense of direction
has never been good, and there is no doubt Mykonos is a
very confusing place in the daytime, not to mention the
middle of the night. I turned this way and that in the
freakish darkness that paled against the white walls and
that lunged at me menacingly from trees and overhanging
balconies. I could not find the road that went up over the
hill, or the more exposed one that ran down into the bay.
I thrashed around in street after street, some dark and
narrow, some wide with that pale moon shining kindly
down upon them. Eventually running uphill in a desperate
effort to get clear of buildings, panting and despairing, I
came upon the windmills that stood sentinel on the rise
near the Xenia Hotel. So! Finally I knew where I was,
but the truck must by now be well on its way.

I turned left, ran like a fiend, and there was the silent
crossroads. Perhaps if I had reached this spot in time,
I might have gone back, considering my job well done. I
certainly had some facts for Nat, should he return.
Bajanis was interested in one of the marble lions. Kriton
had taken a caïque out to sea, possibly around to the
other side of the island. A lion-sized box had been sup-
plied, and Americans were involved. Adequate information
indeed, except that by tomorrow morning, if all went well

for them, the lion would be gone. And if my sister was involved, she might be gone as well.

Besides, I liked that lion. It had stood for twelve centuries on its rock plinth guarding the Sacred Way and no one had any right to take it down. Crazy thoughts for an English girl to conjure up on a dark hillside in a country not her own. Of course, I later realized that there was another, rather mundane, reason mixed up with my newly acquired altruism. I wanted to please Nat. All evening I had been trying to tell myself he had forgotten about me in the pursuit of his own affairs, but my heart was not listening. His certainty that Bajanis would not be interested in the lions had endowed him with a new sort of vulnerability in my mind.

In any case, where was I going at this hour of the night? It is one thing to slide down a roof and drop to the ground. It is quite another to get back up again. And what use was this key in the pocket of my jeans if the trap door was still in place? I thought it unlikely that I should be able to take its weight from a precarious footing on the narrow stairs below.

Besides, Zoe was asleep . . . I did not want to think about that.

I struck out up the narrow road that led to Platiyalos Beach and was rewarded by the scent of stale exhaust fumes hanging in the still air between the close-set stone walls and white shuttered houses. Above, the Milky Way was thickly powdered with stars, and the moon gave enough light for me to see.

I must have been following the deserted road for ten minutes when I heard a sound like the sputtering of an engine coming from the distance. I clambered swiftly over a stone wall, scratching my knees in my fevered haste. A thistle pierced the skin on the back of my hand. Some tiny animal, disturbed by my arrival, scudded away. The noise of the approaching vehicle grew louder, and when it came abreast of me I pulled myself cautiously to my feet and peeped over. It was the sort of truck I had remembered in the square and the driver was a small woman in a head scarf. Irene? She was alone, and the truck was empty.

I climbed back into the dust-shrouded road. There was no doubt at all in my mind that the men and the box had gone aboard Kriton's caïque, and were therefore lost to me. But the night was warm, and I had no wish to return to the boutique. I kept walking.

The scent of the wild rose drew me to the gate that opened on the field below the Markopoulou chapel. And it was open! I did not want to go, but I had to. After all, I could not see the chapel, and so no one could see me. Steadying the chain with one hand and lifting the gate slightly, I went through cautiously, leaving it as I had found it, a little ajar. Keeping to the path that ran round the inside of the wall, I crossed the field. The next gate, too, was unlocked. I examined it scrupulously and moved it so that it was just wide enough to slide myself through. Carefully I allowed it to slide back again. I could see the chapel now, looming above me against a starry sky. Moving like a cat burglar, terrified of dislodging a giveaway stone, I skirted the boulders and moved toward the track.

"It's all okay." The voice came suddenly from close by and I jumped involuntarily. I sank to the ground beside a scrubby bush, huddling with my feet beneath me and thistle jabbing my back, agonizing over the fact that I had left the boulders behind, that might serve as a cover and I dared not return.

And then I heard another voice and knew it was Kriton's: "One moment. I must lock it." He came over the bank not far above my head and moved toward the chapel.

An American voice said, "Okay. Can I have a smoke?" Kriton said sharply, "No."

Feet crunched on the stony path unbearably close. There was a split second of terror when I thought I must have been seen, then there was the rattle of a padlock and chain. The thistle dug into my back like a knife. I moved, just a bare fraction, but I must have dislodged a piece of rock for there was a fall of stones and earth. In the silence it seemed to assume the proportions of an avalanche. My legs, bent double and supporting my weight, wobbled badly so that I was forced to put a hand out for balance. I dislodged another little stone that rattled slowly, and then tumbled with a penetrating clunk! clunk! clunk! down the slope below me. My stomach turned over sickeningly, and I closed my eyes waiting for discovery.

Kriton's hoarse demand, "Who's there?" seemed to come from just a yard away. I crouched, as still as death, and then like a gift from the Greek gods some small animal, perhaps a rabbit, leaped away from its lair close at hand and sped across the track. Kriton grunted, and his footsteps crunched once more in the stones and dirt as he walked away. I opened my eyes in a prayer and saw him silhouetted for a moment against the sky as he rounded the corner of the chapel and disappeared. The sweat of terror was running down my face.

Silence, then the rattle of thin metal that sounded like harness. A Greek voice, sullen, thick, said, "You and me hold these."

A mumble of voices, then: "Take it easy. It's gonna be steep in parts. You gotta hold firm at the back, and don't forget." The rattle of metal came again and then more voices, fading into the distance.

Very cautiously I stretched my stiff and painful legs out on the ground before me, then rose, an inch at a time, staying within the shadow of the bush and keeping my eyes fixed on the skyline close above my head. The voices stopped. In the distance I could hear the faint rattle of wheels. I looked around warily. The bush under which I had sheltered cast as heavy a shadow as the boulders by the track, but outside of it, unfortunately, the night seemed shades lighter than when I had left the town. Not daring to stand upright, I crawled on hands and knees across the track and up the bank until I could just see over the hill. The little procession was moving slowly down the grassy slope that ran to the sea. In the moonlight the forms were easily discernible. The box lay once again on the trolley, but now it was being drawn by a pair of mules. Two big men, no doubt the fair-haired ones I had seen come into the yard, walked in front with the animals, and Kriton walked behind by the side of a short, solid-looking man who might have been a Greek. They slid over a mound and disappeared from sight. I stood there looking after them, my shoulders slumped in despair. What could I do to stop a mad American millionaire from taking what he wanted in a foreign country? What could I do to stop a brutal Greek with a criminal record from helping him? Precisely nothing. I cast a puzzled glance at the chapel, then turned and began to make my way back to the road.

What was I going to do now? I did not fancy walking the streets for the rest of the night, and yet, could I return to the boutique? I thought of Zoe and my mind veered away again. If, as I assumed, these men had run an empty box down that hill to a waiting caïque—the one Kriton had taken out earlier—they were probably taking it to Delos to collect the lion. Katerini had warned Zoe that Kriton was leaving the country. Surely, then, the time to leave was tonight, either with the lion or, having deposited the lion at a prearranged site, with his reward as he skulked off in another direction. Either way, it seemed unlikely that he would return to the Cleopatra.

But what of the trap door? If Lee had used it to lock herself in, then it must not be too difficult a job to remove it from below and set it in from above. With that door fixed down and the windows onto the yard closed, Kriton would not be able to get in, if by any chance he should return. But why would he? Well, if he wanted to kill me, he would have done it before going off with the box. What was the point of killing me now? *Face facts, Virginia. You're fooling yourself.* Yes, I was pretending to a courage I did not possess. What I had to do, what I wanted to do, though my whole being shrank from the thought, was go back and find out if Zoe was still there. I turned my reluctant feet in the direction of the boutique.

The key clicked in the Boutique Cleopatra's door. I pushed it very gently, and waited on the lower step, blinking to accustom myself to the darkness. One of those little red lamps, I recalled, lay in an alcove near me on the right. I moved toward it and bumped up against a chair. "Zoe?" The room was silent as the grave. My flesh began to creep. "Zoe!" I said, and then sharply, with uncertainty, "Zoe!" I felt a pricking on my neck as though the small hairs were standing on end. I felt blindly along the wall. My fingers were damp and sticky on the cool plaster. Then my feet scuffed up against something soft, and I stifled a scream. A small object flew in a metallic clatter across the floor. I felt my way frantically down the wall, measuring distance from the golden fishing net to the crude display of leather necklaces. The lamp! I pressed the switch.

I think I knew already that Zoe was not there. I think I had known even when I spoke her name out loud. The place was without breath or scent. The goatskin rug lay askew. And then I saw that the soft object I had kicked was Zoe's shoulder bag; the metal was a silver and black lipstick. It lay against the counter, the cap off beside a chair leg. And there, behind the counter, leaning up against the wall, was the trap door. Without moving more than my eyes, I could see a pair of thick metal staples like slots in the ceiling on either side of the stairwell, big enough to support the bar that was attached to the back of the trap door.

I did not go up to the flat. If my life had depended

on it, I could not have climbed those stairs. With nerveless fingers I turned the lamp out and left the boutique
exactly as it was, with the bag and the lipstick on the
floor. Outside was fresh air and a semblance of freedom.
The sky was growing lighter with the approach of dawn.
I went down the street that led to the waterfront. There
was no one on the promenade. A forest of chair legs rose
above the cafe tables. The awnings had been rolled back.
The breeze had dropped and the caïques in the bay lay
still. I walked to the end of the promenade and stood
beside the quay. Mykonos was asleep. A mess of red
fishing net lay spread out by a flight of steps with some
rolls neatly stacked behind. The Egyptian I had seen
talking to the German girl lay curled up, still wearing his
fez, with his head on a roll of net and his pack beside
him. I may have been deluding myself, but in my hour of
fear he looked gentle and innocent as he snored softly in
the gray light.

I lay down near him, as close as I dared, and after a
while I closed my eyes.

CHAPTER 22

I wakened slowly to sea sounds which merged with my dreams: I was sitting beside Lee on the goatskin couch and Kriton was in the doorway paring his nails with an enormous knife. Lee was saying something about the chapel, but her words were jumbled and I could not hear them. Then a sea gull screamed close by the door and Kriton jumped . . . An unfamiliar, accented voice said, "You sleep long."

My eyes flew open. The Egyptian was kneeling beside me, and slowly I took in his scarlet fez, long beige face and strong pointed teeth within his smile. I sat up with a jerk, the events of the night jumbling through my mind, entangling themselves with my wretched dream. The sun was bearing down on the stone steps and on the cobblestones. I blinked hard and rubbed my eyes. The water, twenty yards away, was flat and still.

A Greek woman in black with black head scarf was coming down some steps. She looked curiously at me before she adopted the far-be-it-from-me-to-criticize-but-if-you-were-my-daughter expression. Two fishermen idled in from the opposite direction, and then a tall man rushed by with a slim girl in shorts, carrying a picnic basket between them.

"We are rather in the middle of things," I gasped, jumping to my feet, smoothing my trouser legs down with the palms of my hands.

The Egyptian said solicitously, "You were comfortable?" He had begun to wriggle himself into a nest in the loose netting.

"Yes," I replied nervously, trying to laugh about it. "Yes, well, obviously." I looked at my watch. Nearly nine o'clock!

"You will have breakfast with me?" the man asked.

"Oh—er—" I began, growing flustered. Sure, we had been bedmates of a sort, but . . . "Er—look, it was kind of you not to wake me. I am sorry, but I have to make a telephone call, and then—er—then I must go and meet someone."

His shoulders slumped. "You have friends?" He seemed surprised, wondering no doubt why they were not lying all over the fishing nets with me.

"Yes," I told him swiftly. "A man friend." My eyes swiveled in embarrassment from his. I looked around for my shoulder bag and remembered, with electrifying shock, that I had left it under the mattress in the flat above the boutique. I had no money, no passport, no comb.

But Kriton would not be at the boutique. He and his helpers would have done their job and left. The place must be empty—except for Zoe's bag. I did not like the idea of seeing it again but it would not attack me. I had better return and pack my case, then leave it at the office of the tourist police. Afterward I would spend the day here, waiting for Nat, and if he did not arrive I would catch the afternoon steamer for Piraeus and go to the British Embassy in Athens with my story.

The Egyptian was still squatting on the net at my feet, looking despondently up into my face. "I am friend," he said.

I gave him a hasty, panic-stricken smile. "It was awfully kind of you not to waken me. Now if you'll excuse me."

He jumped up like an agile monkey and laid a brown, sinewy hand on my arm. "I am student. Cairo University."

"Oh yes." I began to laugh. He smiled uncertainly, then taking my laughter for approval attached himself to my side. *Hermes! Guardian of wayfarers!* I suppose even a god cannot be all things to all people at all times. Hermes, I had to bear in mind, was also protector of thieves and mischief-makers. Well, I thought tolerantly, as the Egyptian padded along next to me, this Greek god may have had his work cut out protecting Kriton and the gang last night.

In the middle of the promenade I paused to look for Kriton's brown caïque. The bay was full of craft but the one he had taken out was still missing.

"You like boats?" my companion asked. "We hire a caïque?"

"Thanks very much. But no."

I did not shake the Egyptian off until I reached the end of the promenade and turned up the narrow lane. "I am meeting my friend here," I announced firmly.

"You come back to me?"

"No. I am sorry. Good-bye."

He hurled what might have been an Egyptian expletive after me, but when I looked back nervously from the next corner he was not there. I went up the little lane marked ΘΗΣΕΩΣ and there, unbelievably enough, was the boutique door, wide open.

I stood numbly on the cobblestones, untidy in my crushed clothes with my uncombed hair. Who could conceivably be in the boutique now? Should I simply go back to the promenade and wait for the afternoon steamer? No, I could not, for without passport and money a foreigner is hamstrung.

I took a long breath and walked firmly, but with heart hammering, to the door. In the dusky, lamp-lit interior, Kriton looked up from a chair set between the ugly lamp and the counter. He was reading a newspaper. "Ah!" he exclaimed by way of greeting. "The early-morning walker. You are—what do you call it?—consistent, aren't you? I thought you might still be in bed."

"I am going on the steamer this afternoon." The statement was not premeditated, and I could not have said why I uttered it. I felt as if I was in limbo, waiting for something to happen and feeling, queerly, that it *would* happen, quite beyond my control. If Kriton had removed the lion, then returned here for the sake of appearance, and Nat was right in saying the loss would be seen immediately, then the police hunt had already started.

"Okay." Kriton returned to contemplation of his paper, but I was aware that he was still concentrating on me.

Uncertain even now that I was going to risk entering the cul-de-sac upstairs, I crossed the tiled floor. Out of the corner of my eye I saw the trap door had gone from behind the counter. "Do you want me to take your bag down to the quay?" Kriton asked, relaxing his studied interest in his paper.

"No thanks," I returned in a ridiculous, overbright voice. "It's not heavy. I'll come back later to pack and carry it down myself. I am going over to Platiyalos

Beach to have a swim. There is a friend outside. I must rush or he will be in to see what I am doing."

Kriton's paper seemed to absorb him totally so he did not see the guilty color in my face as I composed my self-protective lie. I had come to the foot of the stairs and had to go up now. And I did, moving slowly, looking back and watching him all the way. If he knew, he made no sign.

I crossed the tiny landing on flying feet, ran into the bedroom and pulled my shoulder bag out from beneath the mattress. I checked it swiftly for passport and wallet, then picked up my brush and put my hair to rights. I went to the bathroom but left the door standing wide, for modesty was out of the question at this moment. I was straining to listen for soft footsteps on the stairs. I splashed my face and swiftly cleaned my teeth, then with another hasty glance at the silent stairway I returned to the bedroom, grabbed a geranium-colored blouse and fresh pair of jeans, slipped out of the clothes I was wearing and dropped them on the bed.

I eyed my suitcase, pushed half under the bed. No, I could not stay to pack. Not with Kriton below. The afternoon would have to take care of itself. I made for the stairs, then remembering my excuse for coming, shot back for a bikini and towel.

Kriton did not appear to care any more about my leaving than he had about my coming. He had finished with his paper and was calmly smoking a cigarette. Yet there was a watchfulness about him that one felt rather than saw. I had a strange sensation that I was important to Kriton. At the door I turned. My heart began to hammer mercilessly, but my voice sounded calm. "What happened to Zoe?" I asked.

"Irene gave her a bed." His own voice was cool, ordinary.

"She was going to show me the family chapel."

"Was she? Oh yes, I remember."

I went out into the lane with a sensation of reprieve. How could I find out if there had been a theft on Delos in the night? I could not unless some tourists were talking about it and I should accidentally overhear.

I was coming out onto the waterfront when I saw Nat. He was stepping from a taxi in the square with a suitcase in his hand. He paid the driver, then set out purposefully in my direction, not yet seeing me, his broad forehead creased in a worried frown. The jutting cheekbones made his face look thin, and he wore a distressed air.

"Nat!" I cried.

His head came up, those unusual eyes alight, the thick lashes flying wide. "Ginny!" He had never called me that, nor had he ever looked really pleased to see me before. "Ginny! Thank goodness! What a bit of luck! I didn't know where to start looking for you. Where are you going? Swimming?" He put his bag down and clutched my arms above the elbow.

I said a little shakily, "I've spent most of the past twenty-four hours looking for you."

His face darkened. "Sorry. I rushed into the boutique, oh, about half past five or six last night. I damn near missed the plane doing it. But only Kriton was there, and I certainly didn't want to tell him I was going to Athens. I didn't dare leave a note for you."

"He knew. He saw your bag. But—it seemed too convenient—for him, I mean, so I didn't believe him. Heavens," I exclaimed excitedly, "but I was worried! I did not know what to think. Why did you go? So suddenly, like that?"

He tucked an arm through mine and turned me around. "Come with me while I deliver this bag to my room and I'll tell you as we go."

Nat had missed the tourist caïques on Delos. "I wanted to talk to people at the hotel and some of the guardians of the sites. It took quite a while. Someone told me there would be a caïque coming in the afternoon to bring guardians over here, so I decided to settle for that, but it was later than I expected. I had arranged to telephone Athens at five and I had to rush straight to the OTE. My uncle said something had come up and they wanted me to catch the evening plane without fail. There's only one at this time of year. So I picked up my bag and made a run for it. I practically grabbed its tail as it took off," Nat said.

I laughed delightedly. "Well, what has happened? Has a lion gone?"

He looked at me, blinking, half smiling as though ready to laugh when I finished telling my joke.

"Would you have been told if one of the lions disappeared in the night?"

"It's an odd sort of question. But yes, I suppose I would." Still that funny little smile, polite, uncertain. It was almost as though it were on the tip of his tongue to protest there were more serious issues at stake.

I said, "You weren't told? I mean, no one, for absolutely certain, has taken a seventh century Naxian marble lion from Delos in the night?"

We stared at each other, then Nat's lips began to twitch. I turned away to hide the color flaming in my cheeks.

CHAPTER 23

I was sitting on the end of Nat's bed and he leaned against the little balcony rail with the roofs and the blazing sky behind him.

"So Zoe did dash over! We guessed she might. She came to Madame Bajanis with a hard-luck story."

"It's hard luck all right," I said. "She's pregnant . . ." My eyes filled with tears. "She *was* pregnant." I suppose I know now what people mean when they say one should not bottle things up. Better to face them. Bring them out into the open. I took this thing about Zoe out into the open and it shattered me. "I think she is dead." The tears started running down my face.

Nat came in from the verandah. He stood looking at me. I could not see his face for the tears. He put a hand on my shoulder, then slid it under my hair. "Hell, Ginny, what happened last night?"

"Tell me your lot first." I needed to take myself in hand.

"But you said Zoe is dead."

My throat was blocked up. "Please, Nat. Please, tell me where you've been and I—I'll—" I pulled a handkerchief out of my bag and blew my nose. "It's been one hell of a night and I'm all in pieces."

He patted my shoulder, looking grave. "Yes, all right. I had told the police about Bajanis seeing you outside the restaurant, and—"

My distress went in a flash of anger. "Why did you laugh at me, then?"

"Forgive me, Ginny. We wanted to keep you out of it as far as possible."

"Out!" I repeated bitterly, "I'm only alive by some whim of Kriton's. Or maybe they thought two dead blondes might be one too many so they would leave me alone while I was not making any false steps. Or maybe they're timing my demise for their moment of departure."

Nat cut off my angry recriminations. "Your sister isn't dead."

"*What!*" I leaped to my feet.

"I'll qualify that. At least we think she is all right. The police are investigating this morning and I am to ring them later. It's thought she may be in Madame Bajanis' safekeeping."

"Madame Bajanis!" My eyes flew wide.

Nat smiled. "Yes, it is a very real possibility. It would account for Bajanis' shock on seeing you. Kriton's and Irene's shock, as well, if they thought Lee was safely tucked away with the family. Her return here could only mean Katerini or her mother had spilled the beans. It makes sense, if you think about it. From Lee's point of view, she is hiding from her own mistakes—selling the necklace and coin—and the Bajanis are doing her a good turn. But if Bajanis has told his wife and daughter what he is up to, and Katerini decides to confide in Lee—or Lee squeezes it out of her . . ."

"I want to believe your little story," I said gravely. "It's kind, anyway."

"There is *someone* at the Bajanis house," Nat went on insistently. "It is shut tight as a drum."

"Yes, Zoe said that."

"The villagers know about Zoe," Nat added. "Now we don't know if Katerini confided in Lee. It's immaterial, but it seems she had put two and two together and realized that if Kriton was going to skip the country, he was not going to bother to leave her dowry behind, so she ran after Zoe and told her. The dowry, as we"—I noted that, with kindness, he included me in his intelligent conjecturing—"surmised, is what Bajanis is on Mykonos for. To earn the hefty sum of twenty thousand drachmas. That is not far off three hundred pounds."

I had got my poise back sufficiently to whistle. "Isn't that a pretty big dowry for a peasant girl?"

Nat's face darkened. "As you suggested when we discussed this subject before, Katerini isn't very attractive these days. The price of a husband for her is sky-high."

"And it's a highly priced job! Therefore, perhaps, risky."

"Twenty thousand drachmas," repeated Nat, looking hard at me but perhaps not seeing me. "Yes. a risky job and, I would think, one requiring skill. What is this about Zoe, then? You said she is dead."

I stood up. "I think it is better that I take you there. To a chapel on a hill. I have walked twice already, so may we please have a taxi?"

"Of course."

I picked up my bikini and towel. "How about bringing your trunks? I presume you have them. I've a feeling our track is going to lead to the sea."

"By the way," said Nat, "the police think something is going to happen tonight."

"It has happened," I said flatly.

Nat's eyes pierced straight into mine. "Come again."

"It happened," I repeated. "Last night. I am not worried any more about your old stones. That part is over. It's Zoe I am worried about. I tried to tell you. They took a lion from Delos. One of those Naxian seventh century marble lions. In fact, the one from the end of the row."

"Virginia!" Nat shook his head.

I swung my bag over my shoulder. "Come on. You will be a captive audience in the taxi. I will tell you all about it."

Nat was laughing as he pulled his swimming trunks out of his case. "Okay. Over to you."

"And come to think of it, I have missed my breakfast again. May we pause at a taverna as we go?"

The chapel looked so quiet and innocent with the bright sunlight beaming on its lovely crimson roof. The chain was back on the gate. Nat and I climbed over. I continued my story as we crossed the field. "You see the tire marks? The truck would have come in here, right up to the chapel, I expect. Then the mules took over."

Nat had commented only briefly, but I could detect his dismay in the pressed line of his mouth, the genuine distress in his voice. "Hell, Ginny, I am sorry," he said once.

"It's no use blaming yourself," I replied cheerfully. Now that I had unburdened myself my spirits were rising. "It is what the insurance companies call an act of God. And anyway, I didn't come to any harm."

I had pushed my fears for Zoe to the back of my mind and Nat seemed to understand that, for he did not ask questions about her.

The padlocks were on the door. "When Zoe talked

about showing me the chapel, Kriton produced one key," I said, "but see, there are two padlocks. Anyway, the key was not there when I returned to the boutique. He did not mean me to see inside."

Nat examined the padlocks carefully. "We've no hope of breaking them. Besides, the door is locked as well. See! The knob turns loosely. What about the windows?"

"The bars are pretty rusted," I told him. "Come and have a look." He went around to the side. "If we do decide to break in, I think we might bash these two in with a big stone, then break the glass. The window is just big enough for me to crawl through."

Nat reached through the bars and pushed at the window with his fingers. It gave a little. "We might even get it open without resorting to breaking the glass. Anyway, let's see if we can find the track before we start damaging private property. It might not be necessary."

I hesitated.

"What do you want to do? Look in now?"

It was a fact that I did not want to look at all, but was this not what I had come for? To find out what had happened to Zoe? I started for the track, then hesitated again.

"Well?" said Nat, looking at me curiously.

I shivered. The shiver had nothing to do with the weather for the sun was beating down mercilessly. My hat had slid back on my head and my face felt dry with heat. I turned away, trying to will the moment away from me, because now that it was here I did not want to face up to it.

It was easy enough to see which way the men had gone. The ground was too dry for footprints, but the wheels had left faint tracks in the grass, and farther on there were mule droppings. We went over a small hump, and then the ridge proper began to form. There was now no possibility of the trolley deviating for if it took any other route down the slope it would certainly have overturned. The ridge went more or less straight for a half mile. At the start there were gates in the stone walls and then, as we came closer to the shore, there were no walls at all. The coastline was rocky here, the sea penetrating deeply within folds in the hills.

"If Kriton brought his caïque over, he wouldn't have much difficulty tucking it out of sight," I said. "But they would have the devil's own job rolling that trolley anywhere but directly down to the water." Nat muttered in agreement. Out at sea two yachts were scudding along and three more were heading in the general direction of the town on Mykonos. "That fancy job has gone," I said. "The one I reckoned could be Ghent's yacht."

"I dare say. It would hardly hang around in one spot."

We came to a dip. Directly in front of us the ground rose again, forming a jutting point over the water. From either side the terrain fell away into twin bays. We paused, examining the ground for wheel marks. The ground was very dry here, and again stony, the grass tufted, hard. There were a few stunted bushes and some yellow poppies. The trolley could have gone either way without leaving marks. A few sheeps' droppings lay around, but there were no sheep.

"There is one crushed poppy," said Nat.

I laughed. "How very perceptive of you. Let's take this route then."

We turned down toward the water, and there, tucked between the rocks in a narrow inlet, was the sturdy russet-colored caïque. With *Ajax* written on the bow.

Nat asked, "Kriton's?" and I nodded. Hands on hips, he stood looking around the knoll on which we stood. "I suppose four stalwart men could run a trolley across here without mishap, if they were lucky, but I don't see a box such as you describe. And there is nowhere to hide it on that little ship."

"They have taken it to Delos," I told him patiently. "We're on a wild-goose chase."

"In that event, why not return the caïque to the harbor?" We stood there contemplating the caïque, the symbol of a dead end. Then Nat said, "There is obviously no one here."

"Why do you suppose they left it unattended?" I asked.

"Because it's safer that way. Anyone might approach a lone man on a caïque for a chat, but no Greek would go aboard someone else's boat."

"Well, I am not a Greek," I said. "Let's swim out and have a look around."

And that was how we came across the box. Perhaps those Greek gods have a soft spot for a modest girl, for I saw it when I went behind a boulder to change into my bikini. It was not a box any more, it's true. The new, clean wood lay in a neat stack, and it had been pushed as far as it would go beneath the boulder, then covered with rocks and stones. I gave a yelp of delight. "Nat!"

He came running. "That's the sort of wood the box was made of. It has served its purpose so they dismantled it. Look! We had the situation turned around. The box carried something *from* the yard to the boutique *to* here, and then it was not needed anymore. Whatever it held must have gone aboard the caïque and been taken somewhere else. To the big yacht perhaps?" That did not make much sense of my theory about the lion. Nat and I looked at each other. "They took something from Mykonos," I said humbly. "Sorry, Nat. Sorry about my lion story. No wonder you laughed." I grasped his hand and squeezed it. "I'll never make a detective." I turned my back and made my way carefully over the rocks to stand on a projection that lay just beneath the water. I raised my arms to dive. The sea was very clear and ten or twelve feet deep. There were sea urchins and polished white stones on the seabed.

I hit the water and felt the sharp cold numbing me. It took a while before the stunning realization hit me that we were *not* on a wild-goose chase.

A sudden gust of wind had come, as it comes so unexpectedly and often so forcefully in the Aegean after midday. The water in the bay was suddenly ruffled, pitching over my feet and gurgling among the boulders. It obscured my view of the sea floor. I looked across to the caïque, waiting for it to go into the sort of dance one would expect from a small boat in such turbulent waters.

But the caïque lay still. As still as though it were anchored to the sea floor.

"What is the matter?" Nat asked sharply.

"Look!" I exclaimed. "Look! There is a great, thick rope—two of them, going under the caïque. There must be something tied below—something very heavy—" I did not finish. I took a header, and Nat dashed after me.

CHAPTER 24

Even underwater, strung up in an undignified fashion, the lion looked beautiful. One rope was twisted around its front legs, the other around its rump. Its back lay close against the keel with the hindquarters high. The stretched front legs hung down straight, so that it had the appearance of diving head-first into the bottom of the sea. Nat had followed me in and we surfaced together, gasping for air and excited. Together we struck out fast for the rocks and clambered ashore. "Well!" I exclaimed as we pulled ourselves out of the water. "Well!"

If I had expected Nat to look abashed I would have been disappointed. He took my hands and with magnificent *sangfroid* kissed me on either cheek. "Good girl," he said. "Very good girl indeed."

I was nearly beside myself with excitement. Being

treated like a puppy did not bother me a bit. "What about this hue and cry then? Or maybe they didn't tell you the lion went in the night."

"It didn't."

I blinked. "What do you mean, it didn't?" I asked indignantly. "What is that underneath the caïque? A—a —an elephant?"

"It is not one of the lions from Delos," Nat replied calmly, toweling his face and hair. "Do you want to go in again, because if so, hurry up. I'd like to get—"

"Look here—if that isn't a lion, then I'll—"

"Don't make any wild threats," Nat advised, grinning. "Can't you see? This was the job Bajanis had to do. And a good twenty thousand drachmas' worth it turned out to be. That was what he was doing in the chapel. Remember the clip, clip sounds you heard? He was chipping marble. The box in the yard behind the boutique must have been empty when you saw it. When you come to think of it, four men and a girl would have been hard put to get a boxed-up marble lion aboard that truck in the time you said they spent getting away from the town. They must have brought the empty box to the chapel, fitted the lion into it, then trundled it off down here."

"But what for? Whatever for?" I gasped. "What do they want two lions for?"

"Don't you see?" Nat asked patiently. "I told you they could not take a lion without it being immediately obvious. But they could exchange one, and if it was a very good copy and luck was on their side, they might get well away before one of the guardians noticed."

I gulped. "Whew! You've got to hand it to them!"

"I am almost lost in admiration myself," Nat returned dryly. "I don't suppose the guardians would give the sites more than a cursory look when they come out each morning. And none of the gaping tourists are going to notice anything amiss. If they have got a perfect replica here," he rubbed his forehead, "the mind boggles at the thought of how much time the thieves might have on their side. There are no French archeologists working here at the moment. One of those lecturers coming in on a Hellenic cruise might spot it if he happened to go over, but they don't always do that. I did a tour once and," he grinned in embarrassment, "I have to admit I had had enough of the tourists before we got this far. I usually took myself off for a quiet day on a beach."

"Anyway," I interposed, "if Irene has done her homework properly, she will know the dates of the arrivals of cruise ships, and whether they carry any experts on Greek antiquities. What do we do now?"

"Leave it as we found it. The police have to catch them red-handed, you know. We will alert Athens. Of course, you realize the theft must go on as planned. Now that we know, thanks to you, exactly what is taking place, it's a piece of cake," Nat said confidently. "They will have police behind every stone on the Sacred Way and a helicopter to arrest that yacht, *Fall Tide*. They'll pull out all the stops for this." He rubbed his hands. "They will get the whole gang, of course. There's nothing like an island for trapping people," said Nat happily.

"Napoleon got away from Elba."

"Hey! Whose side are you on?" Nat was looking for all the world as though he had wakened unexpectedly to find it was his birthday. I rushed excitedly back for my clothes. I returned carrying my sandals and sat down on a rock, rummaging in my bag for a comb. It caught in the zipper of my wallet, and as I extricated it, I saw the air letter. "Nat! Oh Lord, it's all here!" I pulled the letter out and flicked it in the air. "I found this in the boutique this morning. It's one of those letters from the U.S. that Kriton is getting in Lee's name. It is from G.—Ghent. Earl Foster Ghent, why not?" I read it out. "*F.T.*—that is, *Fall Tide—will be waiting*—here, you read it yourself while I dry my hair."

He read the letter, then looked at me gravely. "Why didn't you show me that before?"

"It is a fact," I admitted, "that I forgot."

"You thought Lee was involved?" he asked gently.

I heaved a sigh. "Not really. But there was a possibility, wasn't there? I suppose that is why I put it in the back of my mind. I'm sorry. But, really Nat, what would you have made of it without our discovery?"

"Possibly nothing," he conceded. "But it is useful now. It does present the facts in black and white. The police like a bit of solid proof. Are you ready? Let's see if we can get slim you into that chapel without leaving any telltale broken glass. There ought to be marble dust everywhere and chippings. Of course, they may have cleared it up, but my guess is they would not bother. Who cares if the workroom is discovered when it's all over?"

My mind went whirling back to yesterday, scampering over the details. Bajanis examining the lion on Delos. Taking notes for finishing touches perhaps? Picking out the exact areas where the archaic lion would be cut away to be replaced by the new one. Suddenly I remembered the sad and angry expression on Bajanis's face. The look a patriotic Greek might wear when forced to do something against his will? "The Greeks are good family men," I said sadly. "He did it for poor Katerini. And now she has exposed him."

"Life has it in for some people," said Nat.

"That's destiny."

"Yes, I suppose it is."

"You wouldn't think of—" I broke off, knowing he would not. He put an arm around my shoulders, holding me close against him, comforting me because the police were not going to let Bajanis go.

"I banged on the chapel door," I said, my mind still running on yesterday, as we started up the hill again, carrying our wet swimming gear. "Bajanis didn't come out. But he knew someone was there. When I left, he could have looked out of the window and seen it was me."

The appalling explanation came several hours later. I suppose we thought, in our innocence, that the chapel might come up with some answers.

It did. But not that one. Not that one.

"You're right," Nat said, "one of the bars is rusted nearly through. I can do the rest with my hands." He tore it away, opening a gap about twelve inches wide. Ten minutes' work with a pocket knife dislodged the window catch and he pushed it open. There was a curtain which he moved aside so we could look in. "Ha!" said Nat with satisfaction. "There's your proof." In the dim interior marble chippings and marble dust lay everywhere. Bajanis had brushed some of the bigger pieces into a corner, but most of it lay scattered over the floor.

It was a pretty little chapel. There was a blue domed ceiling, and on the walls there were icons set in blue arches. I blinked to accustom myself to the light. There was a gilt and glass candelabra and two brass candle sconces. On the opposite wall beside the window I saw another icon, draped in white net curtains that were bunched together with artificial flowers. A picture of Christ stood on the altar, the head wreathed in pink rose buds set on snow-white leaves. There was a half door at one side of the altar, and on it a picture of the Virgin in prayer. The other half of the door, standing ajar, showed an angel crudely painted in bright colors. A small tin of wilting carnations stood on the floor.

I said, "What is beyond the doors?"

"Nothing much. Do you want to get in and have a proper look? I will bend over and make a footstool."

I found myself backing away. "No. I don't think so."

"Why not? We had better have a proper look around. There might be some useful evidence tucked away." Nat bent over, and reluctantly I kneeled on his back, clutching the recessed sill.

"I would really rather not."

"Come on. What on earth is wrong?"

I could not say it. At this point Zoe was tucked away in the depths of my mind—near where I had stored my thoughts of the air letter from America when I felt Lee might be implicated. "Know thyself," Apollo's Oracle at Delphi had advised. I suppose I knew myself as well as anyone. I did not want to crawl through that opening.

But I did, because I could not talk to Nat about the reason why. I put one leg through the window. There was a small table beneath, incongruously covered with a floral plastic kitchen cloth. Standing on it, I slid myself free of the window, stepped onto a kitchen chair with a yellow plastic seat, then to the floor, where I stood for a moment among the marble chippings. Nat said impatiently, "Go on. Have a look."

I think I had known last night what was in the chapel. And as each hour today had passed, the ghastly consciousness had been there and had grown worse. I said faintly, "I don't think I can."

"Don't think you can what?" Nat's face was silhouetted darkly against the sunlight outside, filling the window. I could not see him clearly.

"I don't think I can look in there," I said, indicating the door beside the altar.

"There's not enough room for me to get through," Nat pointed out sensibly, with a touch of irritation. "Go on. Just give it a kick."

I took a long breath and closed my eyes. Perhaps it was only in my mind, but already there was the smell of death in my nostrils. I went slowly across the chapel floor, imprinting my feet in the white dust. I tentatively pushed the door open. And then I felt myself go numb. Even knowing a bestial act has been committed, on seeing the evidence one can be paralyzed with horror. The sight of Zoe gave me a terrible shock.

It was dark, but I could see her. She was curled up, her painted face thrown back because her neck was broken, her unborn child a sad lump beneath her bright skirt, her shortish legs askew on the marble floor.

Because I tore one of my sandals getting back over the gate where the wild rose grew, I had to hobble all the way back to the town. Even the taxi drivers, it seemed, were taking a siesta this afternoon. We could not go to the Boutique Cleopatra to get another pair of shoes for I did not want to meet Kriton myself, and it was important that he should not know of Nat's return.

"Here," said Nat, handing me a hundred drachma note, "get yourself a new pair of sandals while I go and ring the police. The OTE won't be open yet but my landlord has a phone. Then come to my room. And for heaven's sake don't go near the boutique."

As if I needed such advice! "That's kind of you," I said, trying to thrust the note back into his hands, "but—"

"No buts," he replied authoritatively. "There is a cobbler about a hundred yards up from the road the Cleopatra is in who makes the sort of thing you're wearing. See you."

He went off at an angle down a lane that would lead eventually to his room and I turned directly to the right. Skirting the restaurant where a pelican stood on a chair, head beneath a wing, scratching itself with a long beak while a tourist waited patiently for the right moment to photograph, I turned right, left, then right again and, rather more by luck than good planning, hit the street where the main shops lay.

I hurried along in the direction of the waterfront, dodging among the loiterers, looking rapidly to right and left in the style of a spectator at a tennis match, for the Mykonos shops are tiny and jammed side by side. The

cobbler's shop was one of those holes-in-the-wall that sell
a variety of commodities, but sandals were evidently their
forte, for they stood in neat rows on terraced shelves
across the shop's open façade. I chose a simple pair with
a strong leather sole—no heel, no style, but cool and ideal
for walking. The owner beamed at me when I selected the
pair, and I went inside to try them on.

My head was down, so I did not see Kriton approach.
Not that I could have hidden or even run away. "Thank
you," I said to the Greek. "These will do very well. May
I leave my old pair with you?" He tossed them into a box
in a corner and I straightened, holding out my hundred
drachma note.

"Hello," said that familiar masculine, silk-edged voice.
"Where on earth have you been?"

For a moment I could not speak. I stared at him, the
killer, in dumb amazement. He was smiling, relaxed, casual. Both hands were in his pockets. He looked almost
smug. He rocked a little on his heels, as though he had
the whole afternoon to fill. I moistened my dry lips.
"Swimming," I said. And then, in a voice that sounded
panicky to my ears: "Swimming at Platiyalos Beach."

"Well," Kriton said good-naturedly, "Lee is back."

"Lee!" The fear fled. My head spun with shock and an
almost intolerable relief. The shopkeeper put my change
into my hand and I dropped it into my bag. "Where is
she?" I stepped excitedly out into the street. It was, after
all, only an assumption on the part of the police that Lee
was with Madame Bajanis.

"She went over to thank Irene for helping out. I said
I would wait at the Cleopatra for you, but I got bored, so
I've been walking up and down keeping an eye open for
you." He smiled down at me whimsically. Almost like an
uncle. "I told you she would be back at any time. You
wouldn't believe me, would you? I'll walk back to the boutique with you. She won't be long." His right hand closed
firmly but gently on my upper arm.

Even here in broad daylight surrounded by idlers and shopkeepers, my blood ran cold at his touch. Instinctively I moved just out of reach. "If you will tell me where Irene lives," I said, "I'll go there." I had grown accustomed to using the German pronunciation of Irene's name, as Nat did, and I used it now, saying "Ee-raina." I recognized my hideous mistake immediately, and caught my breath in shock, but when Kriton did not react, I thought it must have passed him by.

He smiled, as though my refusal to go into the boutique with him was rather childish, but was a whim to be tolerated. He looked as though he was thinking indulgently: foolish girl.

"Come with me," he said. "I'll point the house out to you."

I was being silly. It was not a trick, after all. He did not intend to go even the full distance with me. He could be telling the truth, then. Lee must be here. My spirits soared and I exclaimed happily, "Okay, let's go."

It was one of those little places tucked away on the shoreline opposite the area called Little Venice where I had first seen Irene painting. Kriton did not even come within twenty feet of the narrow blue steps. He stood in the street, watching.

The door was flung open. I had already stepped over the threshold when I realized it was indeed a trap, and swung around with one convulsive movement to run.

"Grab her!" ordered Irene harshly. She was sitting on a small, hard chair against the wall, waiting for me as a cat waits for a mouse. One of those big men who had come for the lion box was leaning against the doorpost of an open door leading into a kitchen, and Bajanis was beside me. I flung myself forward just as the Greek shut the front door in my face and lunged.

CHAPTER 25

I was pilloried brutally against a solid chest, a sweating hand against my mouth. I bit viciously, and Bajanis swore, his arm tightening cruelly until my head sang and my ribs seemed about to crack!

Irene said in that cold voice, "Let her go. I think she understands." Bajanis' arms dropped to his sides, and I was free to breathe again—in sobbing gasps. "I am sorry to have to do this to you." Irene's voice was flat, colorless, unfeeling. "But if you cannot keep your nose out of other people's affairs, you're bound to get into trouble."

Bajanis moved and I jerked my head around sharply, but he was only positioning himself by the door. Opposite, in an open doorway, one of those enormous, beefy Americans lounged insolently, watching me from small pig eyes and chewing gum. Irene sat on a flat couch which was covered with a red rug. There was little else in the room: hard chairs, a small, round table on which lay a packet of cigarettes and a half-empty coffee cup.

Anger and terror beat through me. "Where is my sister?" I demanded.

The woman was totally calm, frighteningly self-possessed. Steel glittered behind those cold eyes and in the line of her mouth. "Your sister is not here," she said. "She was sensible and took advice. It is a pity you did not go home when you were advised to."

My heart lurched and the anger gave way to raw fear. "Nat will find me in about three minutes flat." I flung the threat wildly, uselessly, knowing he would never find me.

"Your boy friend? But he has left you and returned to Athens. What else do you expect? He was only a pickup, wasn't he?" Irene asked contemptuously. "If he did happen to return, he would be told you grew tired of waiting, and left for Athens. The *Opollon* has already sailed." She gave me her thin smile.

Somehow I got control of my emotions. I kept my face a blank, made my eyes uncertain, my manner subdued. Then suddenly, when I thought I had caught them all unguarded, I opened my mouth and screamed like a demon.

I never knew what hit me. I suppose it was Bajanis reaching out from behind. Irene had nothing in her hands and she was at least three yards in front of me so it could not have been her. I must have gone out like a light.

I came to lying on the red rug with my hands tied behind my back and my feet strung together. There was a bandage around my mouth and my head was moving in wavy drunken circles, like a hoop slowing down and about to fall. The pain was dreadful. A man's voice said, "She is coming around," and someone else said, "Where is Kriton?" Irene replied, "He has gone to lock up the boutique."

My right arm felt numb. I tried to move my weight from it and in the struggle collapsed onto my front. Someone lifted me up. I saw it was a wiry, fair-haired man with worried blue eyes. He said with a marked American accent, "I think we had better take the scarf off and give her a drink."

"I'd like to be quite sure she isn't going to scream." That was Irene's voice, preoccupied, detached.

The American sat down beside me. He began to undo the scarf. "You won't make a fuss, honey, will you? It would be kinda foolish."

There was not enough strength in me to scream. I nodded, and daggers shot through my head. "Please . . . water," I croaked.

"Christ!" said the American reproachfully. "You didn't have to hit her that hard." Nobody answered. Bajanis went through a door and returned with a glass of water. I pushed myself up on one elbow. He held the drink to my lips and I saw with surprise that his hand was shaking, his face white with fear. In any other circumstances I might have felt sorry for him. He had not meant to hurt me, of that I was certain.

But Irene was evidently not in the least upset that it had happened. "That's enough for her." The total detachment of her voice made my blood run cold. It was as though she were speaking of someone who did not matter at all, and, suddenly stricken, I remembered she had spoken to Zoe in this manner last night. I thought: *Maybe she and Kriton are going to kill me and the others don't know.* The police from Athens might well catch them all red-handed swapping the lions, but by then it could be too late for me.

"Bud!" Irene called peremptorily. Those two big men emerged from the kitchen like robots. Blank expressions, thick lips, small unemotional eyes. Bruisers' faces; hands like hams. I recognized them as the men who had taken the box from the yard last night. The one called Bud said, "Yeah?"

Irene nodded toward me and he came forward, his steps slow now, but no less mechanical. Sick with fear, I closed my eyes. A great pair of hands took me by the waist and lifted me. I was slung like a carcass over the man's shoulder. A pain shot agonizingly through my head. The man's body was rank with stale sweat.

I was only taken into the next room. A bedroom, gloomy because it was shuttered against the sun, was furnished with a bed, a chair and a chest of drawers. I was dropped, but not too roughly, on the bed. Bajanis came with the scarf and tied it around my mouth. "Please—" I began, but his hands jerked the cloth in panicky reaction as though he could not, would not, hear my protest and I was forced into the silence of despair.

> *O friends, come in and help me—*
> *I am here only to ask you this—come in*
> *And help me if you can.*

Sophocles came to life for me in this new weird drama. Playing Tecmessa on a school stage, I would never have had to really guess what my crystal ball had in store for me. But Nat would not come here. He had no idea where Irene lived. All Kriton had to do was shut the boutique and as far as Nat and the police were concerned, the whole party would disappear without trace until the hour was right to leave for Delos. Perhaps they would drop me beside Zoe as they passed the chapel. It would avail me nothing if the chapel was being watched, except that perhaps it might be easier to detect two bodies than one.

I did not hear anyone come into the room. Irene must have been wearing rope-soled shoes. I heard the man Bud say from the doorway, "I can do it now," and Irene's harsh reply, "You know what the plans are." They retreated, shutting the door behind them.

The hours that followed were unbearable. I felt, by the intense quiet in the house, that I was eventually alone. It is said one's life sometimes flashes across one's mind as the axe lifts, as the firing squad raises its rifles. I had more time, of course, to reflect on for I must have lain there alone until near midnight. My past came, frustratingly, in glorious color, too warm, too amusing, too interesting, *too half lived* to be cut off tonight. And what of Lee? How does a girl cope when her identical twin dies? Does something of her die, too? Nat had said, "*You would probably know by some sort of mental telepathy if your sister was dead.*" Does she, then, at this moment, I asked myself, know that I lie here, in a darkening room awaiting death?

At least my head had stopped aching. Through the windows I could hear the muttering of the sea and an occasional cry from a child. The rest was silence, as gloom darkened to twilight, then to night. At last the door of my room opened and the light flicked on. Bajanis entered. He wore a black scowl and his heavily lined face was creased like an old leather coat. He did not speak, but he did pick me up gently in his strong arms, carrying me like a baby. His gentleness did not delude me into thinking he might help me, for his whole mien told me there was something he had to do, and he would do it. Just as he had not wanted to copy the Naxian lion and yet had done it, so he would, for the sake of his beloved daughter, deal as he had to deal with me. He had the intense and relentless seriousness of a Greek tragedian. Whatever end the night was to bring for him, his part was somber and awful, played at a strung pitch, with the heritage of his pagan gods not far from his mind. And I was Antigone.

What law of heaven have I transgressed? What god Can save me now? What help or hope have I . . .?

He lowered me carefully into an enormous basket. "Bend your knees," he said gruffly. There seemed no point in not doing so. He had only to press my shoulders with those great hands and I would go down like a fly. I eased my bottom into the bulbous tube shape of the basket as best I could with my knees beneath my chin. Was this how I was to go into the sea? *Nat! Nat! Nat!* He had to come. The terrifying journey began.

I suppose it was the same little truck they had used to take the box over to the chapel. My basket was set carefully in the back and secured with ropes. Bajanis started the engine and we moved off. The truck lumbered up a hill, then unexpectedly swung around. I caught my breath. Surely we were going along a flat road! And now, down a hill? This was not the road across the island to Platiyalos Beach! When a situation is totally without hope, one leaps with a crazy sort of ectasy toward the unknown. The truck rattled along, now grinding into gear, now running free. My arms, tied behind me, hurt horribly. I had somehow settled against the stiff sides of the basket. Now and then a sharp corner or a bump would throw me forward and several times my face scraped painfully against splinters of cane.

The journey might have lasted ten minutes. We came to a sudden halt and the engine was switched off. I heard Bajanis' footsteps crunching on rough metal. The body of the truck lurched as he clambered up. He lifted the basket and laid it down again as he jumped with a thump of his heavy boots to the road, then he hoisted it onto his back. I tried to cry out but the gag slipped into my open mouth, thick and tasting vilely of sea refuse and unwashed bodies. Now the Greek was feeling his way in the darkness over rough ground, pausing, sliding, clambering across rocks. Time and again, the basket lurched sickeningly.

When he set me down, perhaps five minutes later, my bare right arm, which had taken most of the punishment, was crushed and sore. I was hot, sweating and half choked, with my head throbbing from the blow given me at the house. He lifted the lid of the basket and putting his hands gently beneath my armpits, he lifted me to my feet. "How do you feel?" he asked gruffly, and I'll swear there was concern in that thick Greek voice. He slid the gag out of my mouth and down over my chin to lie round my neck. I gulped deeply of the fresh night air. Ambrosial air, that I might breathe for only a few moments more before drowning, like a cat, in this basket. Below us I could hear the suck and gurgle of the rock-split sea. "How would you feel?" I demanded. On one level I had nothing to lose by insolence, and yet, every unexpected turn brought a small, hysterical, inconclusive ray of hope. He grunted sympathetically and to my astonishment lifted me free. Pressed down as I had been like a concertina, I swayed drunkenly as I unfolded my limbs and tried to stand erect. "Where are we?" He did not answer but I thought despairingly that we must be miles from anywhere, or he would not ungag me. It does not matter if I scream, I reasoned, for there is no one to hear me. And anyway, he may hit me again. I was swaying on the uneven ground. "What about my feet? Couldn't you untie them?"

"No. I must not do that. You are young and would run fast."

"How far would I get on these rocks with my hands tied behind my back?"

"Far enough," he replied, truthfully enough, "in this darkness." He picked me up in his arms. Though he was shorter than I, he was very muscular. The sound of water among rocks increased and my terror returned. "What are you going to do with me?" I asked, my voice high, a little out of control.

"We are to wait here." He set me down on a smooth rock and then he sat down beside me.

"Wait here?" My voice was touched now with crazy

hope. "Wait for whom?" Bajanis did not answer. We must be waiting for Kriton, I thought with a rising sense of fear. Kriton and the lion, and those awful animal-like men who have been brought in because of their terrifying obedience, their insensitivity to death and their enormous strength. It is they who will take the weight of the lion on their giant shoulders. They, undoubtedly, who will kill me. Not Bajanis, for he is not a killer. Maybe Irene will be here too. Or does she prefer to be at home in nightclothes, yawning and looking innocent, if someone should come to the door? "Who are we waiting for?" I asked again, knowing, dreading a reply, yet perversely needing to face it.

"We wait for a caïque."

Of course. And was Delos bristling with police? Was Nat there? Was I to be thrown overboard en route? I could see no intelligent reason why they should burden themselves with me. Tonight was much darker than last night when I had walked across the island in pursuit of the wooden box. Perhaps a bank of clouds had come up to obscure the moon and offer kind cover for the thieves. Only here and there a star twinkled. "Where are we?" I asked again.

"Agios Ioanis," Bajanis said.

Agios Ioanis, I knew, was on the end of the island, facing Delos. Bajanis sat down beside me. He pulled some worry beads out of his pocket and began to rattle them. The noise irritated my nerves but somehow I could not bring myself to ask him to stop. I said, "Why are you doing this to me? You have a daughter, about my age I imagine."

He heaved a terrible sigh. "I have to do it," he said.

"Is your daughter's marriage worth more than my life?"

"Your life?" He spat in that casually unpleasant way Greeks do. "Your life is safe," he said. "My daughter's is finished."

"Neither of which is true," I retorted. "I am to be killed tonight, and your daughter is to get a husband out of this."

He said in a harsh, worried voice, "But you are not to be killed."

"Then why are you taking me, trussed like a chicken, to sea, if not to drown me?"

He put an arm around me, the hand rough as it clasped my upper arm. He held me close to him for a moment, then he said, "You are to be left on Delos. The guardians will find you. Do not worry."

"Come off it." I did not mean to sound scathing, his pathetic innocence astounded me.

He said gently, "Why should we harm you?"

"You harmed me back there in the house," I retorted angrily. "You behaved like a madman."

"I am sorry. I did not mean to hit you so hard. But you must understand, if you had been heard . . . if some-one had come there and found . . ."

I supposed by his faltering words he was trying to convey the fact that he was thinking of his daughter. No theft of the lion meant no money, and therefore no dowry for Katerini, and therefore no husband. His anguish only made me bitter. My life seemed so much more important than a purchased husband. "Why should they have killed Zoe?" I asked.

His arm dropped from my shoulder and he said sharply, "They did not kill Zoe. She is not concerned with this. She does not know. She is with her mother."

"It's a bit late," I told him wearily, "to send you back for proof but—" I stopped dead, my heart leaping into that quick pitter-patter that came so often tonight. *I must not say she is in the chapel, for then he will realize I know about his part in this.* He may not have known it was I who banged on the door of the chapel when he was working on the lion yesterday. I said flatly, "She came to

Mykonos yesterday. And now she is dead. Kriton killed her last night."

"No!" He was shocked, there was no doubt; and unwilling to believe.

"You knew Zoe?" I asked.

"No. I have seen her. Kriton took up with her when—" His total distress silenced him.

"Don't you realize," I asked with a weary patience that was detached from my fear, "I would tell the authorities what you have done?"

"No. It is dark enough tonight. You will not see what the men are doing."

Dear God! There are none so blind . . . "Frankly," I said, "I don't think much of your chances either. If they kill you, too, they save themselves twenty thousand drachmas. It's just good business, isn't it?" He did not answer. "Why don't we both cut and run?" I suggested, confidential, enthusiastic, acting like mad as I had never acted before, pushing him along on a warm tide of my own insistence to live.

"I do not think this will happen," Bajanis said. His face was sheltered by the darkness, but his voice was charged as though, by the sheer strength of his need, he could force the unpalatable truth to be a lie. "I must have the money for my daughter's marriage. You have not seen Katerini. If this man who is willing to take her does not have her now, an offer may not come again."

"Look here," I said gently, "if he only wants her with the money—"

Bajanis cut in: "It is how we do such things in Greece."

Unanswerable. A fact of Hellenic life. I was up against the two things that for a Greek mean more than life itself. Money and the family. I was bound to lose.

What of my family? "Perhaps you would like to tell me what happened to my sister?" I suggested tentatively. "Perhaps you know where Lee is."

"She is safe. She is at my home. She has done something very foolish and had to leave Mykonos. When this is over it will be better that you take her home."

It was true, then. Dear, scatty, foolish Lee was safe, and would go home. I wondered if she would ever know what happened to me. Faintly, I heard the sound of an engine cut across the blackness of the water. A pulse beat in my throat and I began to feel sick. "They're coming," I said, my voice scarcely steady. "Mr. Bajanis, this is our last chance to run. Yours as well as mine."

He stopped rattling his worry beads. In the silence I held my breath, then he said apologetically, "My daughter has suffered enough."

CHAPTER 26

The caïque's engine cut. My eyes had accustomed
themselves sufficiently to see the faint form of the little
vessel as it slid inshore. There was no riding light,
neither port nor starboard. A low voice called, "Bajanis!"
It sounded like Kriton.

"Here!"

"Right! Catch!" There was a dull thud of a thrown
rope and Bajanis went forward. He said something in
Greek and an American voice insisted nervously, "Speak
English! English!"

A hundred years ago, in another world, Nat had said,
"The Greeks don't even trust each other." So the Ameri-
cans weren't taking any chances with incomprehensible
Greek exchanges, it seemed. I heard Bajanis say, "I will

get the girl," and then I could measure his approach by the sound of his feet crunching across the stones.

He bent over me. I turned my head aside to avoid the stale smell of wine upon his breath. He slid his hands around my waist and I said sharply, "Why not untie me and let me climb in with dignity? I cannot run away."

"They would not allow it." His voice was low, but I had a weird feeling that it carried through the silence, as voices do near the water; that those on the caïque heard, and exchanged glances. Perhaps it was only in my mind, but at that moment I felt Bajanis changed sides, endorsing perhaps Kriton's license to kill.

He carried me in his arms as he had held me before and stepped aboard. "Put her down here," said Kriton and Bajanis laid me carefully on what felt like a bundle of nets in the bottom of the caïque. Kriton said sharply, "What happened to her gag?" and I replied, "There's not much point in screaming, is there? Who would hear?"

He ignored me, saying angrily to Bajanis, "You know how sound carries out here," and Bajanis replied, "I will put it back." He knelt down beside me. I jerked my head aside, but he tied the scarf across my mouth, grunting, perhaps apologetically, and whistling through his teeth. The engine burst into life and the caïque moved slowly away from the shore.

Nobody came near me on that slow nightmare journey. Heaven knows how long it took us, with the weight of the marble lion slowing the caïque down. Crumpled low in the vessel, I could not have seen other boats anyway, and there was not more than a sprinkling of stars. I lay there on the nets with the hard cork floats sticking into my back and the acrid smell of fuel oil in my nostrils, listening to the sighing of the wash behind me, and the jug-jug-jug of the engine ahead. My mind, sharp with fear at first, gradually became blanketed in despair, until at last it grew numb. Terror eventually rubs its own jagged edges flat and wears itself away. I waited for death, in the end, with a sort of fortitude.

I do not know how long this state of limbo lasted—this timeless exposure to what was to be, this formal acceptance of my own demise. I had no way of judging where we were or what speed the caïque was making. From time to time I turned my eyes toward the wheelhouse for there was activity there. Men came back from the bow and disappeared inside. They checked the ropes continuously. In the darkness I could not tell which way their faces turned, but I had the feeling that no one was particularly interested in me.

Then a huge figure appeared in my line of vision and made his way toward me. My fortitude went. I stiffened, and froze again with terror, for to judge by his size, he was undoubtedly the American who had offered to kill me in Irene's house. If this was death, then I did not want to die. I struggled against my cords, writhed and twisted, flung myself into a semi-upright position and tried to cry out, uselessly because of the scarf around my mouth, and uselessly, too, because there was no one to hear me. I fell back against the net and the man bent over me, taking me roughly by the shoulder. Then another figure, smaller and more agile, loomed out of the darkness by the wheelhouse and Kriton's voice said peremptorily, "Al!"

The big man let me go. I fell back painfully against the bulwarks. Kriton strode toward us, knelt down beside me, testing my gag, then rising he whispered, "Not now, Al." I strained my ears to hear their voices over the engine noise.

"We're nearly there. You said—"

"I'm telling you," replied Kriton, his voice as hard as iron, "and you'll listen to me. I am giving orders." His voice dropped again so that I could scarcely hear it. "We're going to have trouble with Bajanis if we do it here."

"I'll fix Baj—"

"Listen, you lunatic!" Kriton's words were a steely whisper and a threat. "Without Bajanis we can't get the lion off in one piece. And if we don't keep him sweet, he won't do the job properly. Can't you get anything into that thick head of yours!"

"Whatcha gonna do, then?"

"Afterward. After Bajanis' part is done." Kriton's voice dropped again, confidentially this time, as though wooing the man. "We must not risk upsetting him."

Kriton knelt down and tested my gag once again, pushing at the knot behind my head with rough, careless fingers. "When we have the lion—the old one—on the trolley, and Bajanis up front," he rose, but this time, sadistically, he did not bother to lower his voice, "you can go back and deal with her. Then catch us up. And for Christ's sake, don't disturb Bajanis until the old one is on the trolley. Understand?"

"Yeah."

"Then you can deal with him."

"Okay," said the man called Al, grudgingly. "Okay."

It was sometime before I could think again, and then only that Homer's wine-dark sea would have provided a clean grave. The caïque forged on. Luckily for them, the sea was calm, the night still. Suddenly the moon emerged and with it came a return of that tormenting will to live. Like a mad woman, I sweated against my bounds, jerking them and tearing my already raw wrists. I threw myself about in a nightmare of unthinking panic, then fell back exhausted.

"We're coming in," I heard Kriton's voice say and I could only think: *Twenty minutes to death, or however long it takes a handful of men to haul a marble lion out from beneath a caïque and put it on a trolley.* Sweat pricked out all over my body, and my head spun with an unreasoning insistence that I must live. I had to find a

way. Where were Nat and the police? Were they going
to descend upon us now? Dear heaven, it was my only
chance. I offered up a silent prayer.

The vessel nudged against something hard. A flashlight
blinked in the bow. There was a muted "coo-ee" from the
shore, then the busy pattering sounds of feet on rocks and
a scuffle of stones. But I heard voices—they sounded
like American voices.

Where were the police? Nat knew the caïque would
come here tonight. Why were they not waiting to catch
these men red-handed with their lion? I had had one reprieve. I could not hope for another. *Nat!*

Men were swarming onto the boat, talking rapidly in
low tones. The moon had gone behind a cloud again, but
I could see jumbled forms in the darkness. There might
have been only a handful of men or there might have
been a dozen. Perhaps the entire crew of that great yacht
had come to hasten the job. My own demise came nearer,
agonizing and unacceptable to me. In another wild effort
to jerk myself free, I hurled myself over on my face, but
I only succeeded in imprisoning myself in the nets, breathing the smell of fish in distressed gasps.

"Jesus!" It was Kriton's voice. He put a foot under my
ribs, flipping me over painfully to fall with an agonizing
thump on the planking of the caïque. Bajanis said something indignant in Greek and Kriton hurled an expletive
in return. An American voice, angry and nervous, said,
"You bloody Greeks! If we have any trouble—" and Kriton broke in, "Bajanis, take the girl ashore, then come
back. We need everyone."

Without a word, Bajanis picked me up, slinging me over
his shoulder like a bag of corn. I gasped with pain as my
sore ribs pressed against his back. I choked on the gag,
trying to spit it out of my mouth, chewing on it, not
finding it disgusting anymore, only frustrating, as were
the bonds on my wrists and feet. The Greek carried me
ashore, then stumbling in the dark he made his way up a

slope and put me down gently upon the ground. He was kneeling before me, and I could see his face. It was drawn with anger and distress. I remember thinking: It is nearly all over, you sad fool, for both of us. And then: Since the police are not here at the shore, they will be near the Sacred Way. Bajanis will not have completed his job when he is taken, but Al will already have been back for me. For me it will be too late. I had to get through to Bajanis, to make him understand.

Helplessly, without use of my arms, I flung myself at the Greek. I bashed my head against his shoulder, desperately and mutely trying to make him see he had to loosen the gag. He pushed me roughly down against the stones with one strong hand, and with the other he reached behind him. In the darkness I saw the flash of a blade.

Oh no! Not him! Not Bajanis! I think there must have been a moment when I lost consciousness from shock, and I had a weird feeling of acceptance of the inevitable. Bajanis was taking it upon himself to give me a quick, clean death rather than leave me to an uncertain fate at the hands of the frightening Al. In that moment of eerie, charged silence I heard the quick *grff* of the knife. Emotional nothingness. No pain. Only a feeling of release, as though my feet were floating. Then, with one of those strong, horny hands Bajanis pushed me half over onto my face and there was again that *grff* of the knife, and my hands fell apart.

It happened in a split second, too quickly, it seemed, for real life. Too sudden a reversal for me to take in. Besides, my limbs would not move. Irrationally, not believing what had just happened, I sat there on the rocky ground, quite still. I suppose, after all the terror, my brain simply would not accept the fact that I was free, or perhaps my nerve ends were incapable of relaying it. Without a word, Bajanis shambled off in a scatter and crunch of stones to disappear in the darkness. I must have put my hands up to my face, an automatic movement that slid the gag down over my chin, but I do not remember anything. Only that I was free, and yet I did not move. I could not have been more than thirty feet from the water, for I could hear the men heaving, grunting, muttering together.

"Bajanis!" That was Kriton's voice, and a snarl from Bajanis in return. Perhaps it was the wind that brought me to life. A sudden cool gust that plucked at my hair and clamped my blouse against my sweating back like a sheet of thin, wet paper. Perhaps it was the real-life feeling coming back into my feet as the blood returned. I started to lift myself, then fell back as pain shot through my shoulders like a red-hot knife. Shuddering, I pressed my palms to the ground and tried again.

My legs were stiff and very shaky, but I managed to draw myself onto all fours. Slowly, painfully, I explored the ground around me with my hands. It was rough, covered in sharp stones, small bristling thistles and cutting grass. I began to crawl away carefully and as fast as I dared, the stones bruising me through my thin jeans, scraping my hands. And I was terrified of disturbing a loose stone lest it go flying down into the water and alert the men. I moved carefully uphill for some twenty feet. Then to my relief, I came to a ledge from which the ground began to slope away, gently at first and then growing steep so rapidly I began to slip and slither across small pebbles onto large blocks of stone that obstructed the path and broke my fall. I looked behind. Though it was very dark, I felt I must already be well over head height behind the hill. I hauled myself stiffly and painfully to my feet.

At that moment the clouds moved aside and the moon came out with startling suddenness, shining brightly. I whirled around in panic, but the mound over which I had crawled loomed several feet above my head. I could no longer hear either the voices of the men or the sounds of the sea. Ahead of me, looking ghostly in the moonlight, were the ruins of the ancient city. Mount Cynthos loomed darkly on my right. "*They will have police behind every stone on the Sacred Way*," Nat had said.

The Sacred Way.

I began to run, carelessly, desperately. My raw wrists and ankles did not trouble me, only the shakiness and stiffness of my legs. Within twenty yards I tripped over a slab of stone and fell headlong. I picked myself up, half winded. Mercifully, I had fallen on grass, though the ground was hard and rock-dry. My hands and arms were grazed. I began to run again, shakily and with uncertain steps. Perhaps my circulation was not fully restored for my legs seemed vaguely out of control. I fell again, this time, against a marble block surrounded by tough little thistles, and I uttered a cry of pain. As I squirmed back on my haunches and tried to rise, the clouds slid across the moon. For a while I remained standing, lost in a sea of blackness, knowing with despair that unless the moon showed me the way I would never find the Avenue of Lions.

I do not know how long I stood there. Perhaps only a moment or two. Anxiety and the blackness of the night, together, confused my mind. Some layers of cloud must have slid away from the face of the moon for I found that I could see, faintly and not very far ahead, but enough to make a difference. I set out again, uncertain of my direction. My fall had been headlong, and though I thought I had gotten up facing the way I had been going, I could not be sure. I picked my way carefully across the arid patches between the ruins, climbed over dark low walls, nervously skirting the many black, yawning traps that I thought might be deeply excavated rooms. The night was very still. My soft sandals, making little more noise than the light crunching of loose stones, set my nerves screaming.

Perhaps I walked for ten minutes. Mount Cynthos,

visible on my right, told me that I was at least keeping direction. And then I found the route, flat and leading toward what I figured was the area I wanted. I began to run again, with fear that I might be going astray, but with confidence because there were no stones, and my legs moved easily again.

I fled up a long slope. The last veil of thin cloud must have slid from the moon because all at once tall pillars, half pillars, archways and walls were there before me: gaunt, grotesque, silent as the night itself. Panting, holding a palm to my side which had just begun to ache, I stood a moment trying to recognize the landmarks. They were hauntingly familiar and lay, I felt sure, somewhere south of the Sacred Way. I went tentatively forward, taking the next path. Ah, yes! I recognized the bastions of the Sanctuary of Leto, and with a spurt of new-found energy I fled up the sandy track.

There were the lovely lions, gleaming white in the moonlight, heartbreakingly beautiful. It was silent—too silent. The ruins were eerie and empty. I caught my breath. *A man behind every stone*, Nat had said. The island was death-still. Small hairs began to stand up on the back of my neck. I opened my mouth to try a small "coo-ee," but no sound came. The sweat began pricking in the small of my back. At that moment the wretched cloud slid across the moon and the ruins seemed to close in on me, the lions to blur and shrink.

"Coo-ee!" The sound came, a sickly, hopeless bleat that echoed like a cry from a sacrificial lamb. And then, for answer, there was a shout and the staccato beat of running steps.

What tells us whether a tread is friendly? The steps I heard were purposeful, vengeful, pursuing steps that grew louder even over the thundering of my heart. And they came unquestionably from the direction of the harbor where the caïque had tied up.

I stood paralyzed, unable to think, to accept the shocking fact that I was alone, at the mercy of the owner of those curiously light running feet. I think I knew already it was Kriton. I envisioned his choking fingers, his brutal arms, and once again, in a fuzz of fear, I saw Zoe lying twisted in the chapel with her neck broken and her skirt flung awry across her short legs.

The steps came nearer, hesitated, and suddenly my paralysis left me. Like the wind, I fled up the Avenue of Lions and ducked down behind a broken corner of wall. Silence! Except for the crazy hammering of my heart. Solid and strong as he was, Kriton had that litheness that helped him run so quietly like a jungle animal. He could be upon me or behind me before I knew. With nerveless fingers, I pulled myself up by the rough stones and stood with knees bent looking through a broken piece of limestone. The cloud had moved aside again when suddenly I saw Kriton standing quite still, looking around. Listening.

I held my breath. If he continued up the Way and came abreast of me, he had to see me. I looked around desperately, and with horror I saw that my shelter was less than six feet long. Whichever way I turned to run, I would be exposed, and not only that, but my path would be blocked by marble pillars and lumps of stone. I watched him come, mesmerized now, like a rabbit in the lights of an approaching car. I knew there was no escape, yet I also knew that I was going to run—futilely, crazily—so that my death would be even more violent than I had foreseen.

CHAPTER 27

He advanced toward me, glancing from side to side, knowing his way and knowing, I realized, that I had disappeared close by and must therefore still be near. He came menacingly to the edge of my wall, and I shrank back, waiting, my blood like water in my veins, for him to see me.

He turned. Perhaps my petrified concentration drew him near me. In the bright moonlight we faced each other, my eyes glazed, my face frozen with fear. Then something unlocked in me, and I lunged away. I flew, like a small animal from its shelter, leaping wildly over great blocks of stone, tripping, staggering, half falling. It was my agility against his now, and briefly I held my own. Then I lunged down a narrow passage between two broken walls, turned a corner and pulled up aghast, for my way was blocked by a pile of rubble.

I took a flying leap, but the moment of hesitation had given Kriton an advantage and he lunged, gripping my arm, then losing it, but breaking my flight so that I fell across a marble segment. In a cold sweat I flung myself over into a tortuous roll that took me across sharp stones. My brain registered the searing pain, but there was no time for more than recognition of the fact and I scrambled to my feet, gasping for breath, and threw myself forward again.

All along, I had known there was no escape. He had to win. I had jumped a piece of low wall and was recovering my balance from a poor landing when suddenly the fitful moon showed me with a sickening sense of shock that I had come up against that dark water pit where yesterday I had seen cyclamens growing in the retaining wall.

With no way forward, I moved sideways, tripped and felt Kriton's hands on my shoulder. He spun me around like a top. I don't know whether I screamed. I would have screamed, if there was any breath left in me, to protest against such a nightmarish and sudden death. I remember I was on the ground among the stones, gulping mouthfuls of suffocating dust, skidding to a halt, confined. And then, astonishingly, I was no longer pinned beneath Kriton's vengeful hand. There was a pounding and rattling in my ears. I thought Kriton must already have hit me and my head was broken so that it was full of noise, but numb, and without pain.

I staggered to my feet, and then I saw. Kriton was still there, all right, but someone had jumped on him. There were two bodies locked together on the ground. At that moment the moon went behind cloud. I could only think: there was a pit here, full of water. Then the fitful moonlight shone again. I saw Kriton's arm lift and deliver a wicked blow to the chest of the man half under him. A man with brown hair, high cheekbones, and thick lashes over eyes slitted in anger.

I uttered an involuntary cry, "Nat!"

As though my voice gave him extra impetus, Nat lurched out from under Kriton's body and delivered a staggering blow to his chin. Kriton's head came back in a convulsive movement, but at the same time he reached behind and I screamed, "A knife! He has a knife!" I leaped toward him. I kicked his hand, sending the knife flying so that it bounced, then slithered up against a piece of stone that marked the edge of the water pit. Kriton swung around, his teeth bared, his face wild. He jerked away from Nat with superhuman strength as though his very life depended on that blade. Nat came at him with a punishing rain of blows that would have killed a lesser man.

I stood there, appalled, thinking: *Nat is going to kill him*, and then, inexplicably, for Kriton had been going to kill me, I screamed. I remember that very clearly. It was so morally right, yet rationally wrong, to protest because a killer might lose his life.

A man rasped, "Grab her!" There was a quick babble of indignant, argumentative Greek. Rough, brutal hands grasped me around the waist and tugged me, my feet dragging in the dust, to the shadow of those headless statues just above the water hole. No one seemed to care about Nat and Kriton. I was suddenly aware of movement all around me where the ruins had been empty before. The man who had spoken, a Greek, taller than the rest, slipped an arm through mine. Partly, in some odd way, it seemed to be a gesture of affection, as though he knew me, and partly it was restraint.

"Haven't you caused enough trouble?" The voice was lightly accented, cultured, and very annoyed indeed. "Do you want to spoil everything now?"

"Trouble!" I echoed indignantly, spitting dust out of

my mouth and fingering a painful bruise on my chin.
"Who are you?"

With a mixture of irritation and faint indulgence, the
man laughed. "Come off it," he said lightly and patted
my shoulder. "You must learn to do as you're told. You
have caused us a great deal of trouble and anxiety tonight."

Anxiety for them! Dear God! I nearly said sarcastic-
ally, "Rotten for you!" but stopped because something
terrible was going on by that water hole. "Nat is belting
the life out of Kriton," I gasped. Surely one does not
stand by and see murder done, even to a murderer. Someone stepped forward, and another man materialized silently behind. They pulled Nat, still fighting, off Kriton.
I remember I saw Kriton's great head move and felt a
rush of sick relief.

Nat stood up. He stared down at the Greek, now lying
inert. Kriton opened his eyes and feebly lifted a hand.
Nat said something furious in Greek, and the man who
had talked to me answered soothingly and went over to
put an arm around his shoulders.

I said tentatively, "Nat!" He looked at me with a
closed face, then turned away and began to walk toward
the lions, his shoulders sagging, his head low. I stared
after him in stunned bewilderment.

"My nephew is bound to blame you a little for going, in
the circumstances."

The uncle! The archeologist who had called Nat in to
help the Greek authorities. "Hell's teeth!" I cried, "I
was high—" I had been going to say "highjacked," but
he clamped a hand roughly over my mouth. I shrugged
the hand violently away. I had had enough of that treatment tonight. Someone produced a flashlight. There were
three short flashes in one direction, three in another, and
the Avenue of Lions was immediately swarming with
men. "Stay there," ordered Nat's uncle. "Stay right
there. Right *there!*" he repeated firmly. The moon was

shining brightly now, and I could see right down the
Sacred Way. A little procession of men had appeared,
pulling the trolley with the lion on it.

The men with me went off behind the stones, and I
realized that all the others had gone, too. I stood riveted
to the spot. My head was heavy with pain and some
frightening noises had started up in my ears: *Grrr-rr,
chop, Grrr-rr, chop, chop, chop.* They have broken my
skull, I thought in despair, closing my eyes. Perhaps I
will die after all. The noises grew louder and louder. I
opened my eyes, frightened, and looked around vaguely
for help. With blinding relief I realized then that the
commotion came from above. Looking up, I saw the
bright green and red lights of two helicopters preparing
to land on the low hill that rolled back from the Sacred
Bay where we had landed in the caïque yesterday.

Above the noise of the engines there were shouts from
the Avenue of Lions and dark figures rushing. A shot
rang out, and then another. My heart turned over convulsively. I went over to Kriton and sat down in the dust
beside him, feeling that someone ought to think of him.
He was returning to consciousness. I saw his eyes, remembered Zoe, and the compassion ran out of me. The gag
Bajanis had tied around my mouth was dangling around
my neck and I hastily untied the knot. Kriton lay on his
side. I turned him with difficulty onto his face, pulled
his two arms behind his back and tied them at the wrists
in double and triple knots. Then I removed my blouse
and pushed him over onto his back. He groaned as I
tied his feet together with it, then he opened his eyes.
"Sauce for the gander," I said bleakly, and then, "You
beastly man!" And, because he was staring, I added,
"You've seen a girl in her bra before." The blade of his
knife gleamed in the moonlight. I picked it up and threw
it into the water pit. Kriton went on staring and I
realized he was not looking at me. His eyes looked blankly

into space, and I wondered if he was pondering the inevitability of his future. I looked down at him with intense dislike. This handsome, arrogant brute who moved like a leopard, strutted like a king, looked thoroughly defeated, trussed like a Sunday joint, with blood trickling darkly down his face.

"The police are here," I told him. "Dozens of them. And some pretty important ones, I imagine, in helicopters. You're really going to make the front pages." It occurred to me that this was quite a night for the Athens force. It was not every day someone had a go at stealing a priceless treasure that had been standing for nearly thirteen hundred years.

There was a clatter behind me and I swung around to see the helicopters lift off the hill beyond and make off to the south with lights flashing and blades whirring. To find Mad Midas' yacht? A thrill went through me. It was really exciting to think of a yacht being "arrested" on the high seas. Perhaps dawn would break in time for me to see the yacht coming in. In the faint light I could now make out some uniformed men running up the path from the bay. These were undoubtedly the passengers of the helicopter. They cut into the Avenue of Lions and disappeared in the murky reaches beyond.

I turned back to look at Kriton. Our eyes met, and he spat. "You were going to kill me, weren't you?" I said. He did not answer, and I added, "Just like you killed poor little Zoe." I don't think he was feeling very well at all, but I had little sympathy for him at this point.

Another shot was fired from the direction of the harbor. There were orders and cries of alarm from the Sacred Way. I wondered what was going on but told myself resignedly that I had been forbidden to move and had better stay put. There was an elegant marble column nearby, broken off low by despoiling hands from centuries past. I settled myself carefully on the ground beside it, heaved a deep sigh at my painful bruises, wrapped my arms tightly across my chilly front and began to wonder unhappily about Nat.

An officer stopped himself from staring at me and divesting himself of his jacket, he handed it to me. Then, with continental courtesy, he shook my hand. "My name is Harakopoulos. Stavros Harakopoulos," he said. "We're very grateful to you—and your sister."

Well, someone was grateful, I thought bleakly. "Have you caught all of them?"

"Yes." He puffed his chest out like a pouter pigeon and slapped his sides. "Nobody got away. We had fast boats hidden around the island. They had no chance." He shook his head, musingly. "It was a remarkable thing to do. You have seen the lion Bajanis made?"

"Not really. Only underwater."

"Come with me."

Dawn was beginning to lighten the eastern sky as we walked together down the Avenue of Lions. I could make out the forms of a small gathering of men at the bottom. "By the way," I said as we went past the ghostly, sculptured beasts lined up on their plinths, "where is my sister?"

"She is all right," he assured me. "She was not so badly hurt after all. A broken arm, I believe. She defended herself with great courage, and though she was knocked out—"

"What!"

He stopped when he saw the expression of horror on my face, and taking my hand said gently, "You did not know?"

Dumbly, I shook my head.

He raised both hands and closed his eyes as Greeks will in exasperation. "She is a—what do you call it?—willful girl! She was given explicit orders not to leave Athens, but what does she do? She takes a taxi, rushes to the airport and gets the last plane to Mykonos. She was worried about you," he acceded.

"Of course. But what happened? What happened to her?"

"She went to the boutique looking for you. If she had stayed, she could have been very helpful," the man told me severely. "Your sister knew where the woman Irene lived. But when Mr. Ross rang to say you had disappeared, your sister had gone, and we did not know where. Mr. Ross went to the boutique. Apparently her screams were heard, and people came to the rescue, but there was much excitement and Mr. Ross got the impression your sister was dead." The man smiled, innocently, warmly. "Did you know he is in love with her?"

I felt myself go numb, and it was not from the cold.

"You did not know!" cried Harakopoulos joyfully. "So, there is a romance in your family now." He waved his hands in an expansive Greek manner and then clapped them together. "You will be glad, because he is a very nice boy. His uncle is one of our best-respected public men. He is here tonight. He came here with us."

I heard the news in a sort of stupor. Not again! Oh no! Lee and my men! There was the sound of a police whistle, and then another. A little group of men emerged from the distant shadows. "I did not know he knew her." It was all I could think of to say while I tried to work out the facts and tried to find a line of sense through Nat's diabolical behavior. So that was why he nearly murdered Kriton! Because Kriton had tried to kill Lee!

The police were swarming out of the gloom. There was more lightness in the sky and one could discern forms and shapes now for fifty yards or more. I felt a lump come into my throat. Was it imagination or could that familiar figure, half a head taller than the rest, be Nat walking alone? He came slowly up the Sacred Way, head down, feet dragging. Did we have to face each other? I tried to move away, but could not. The men were gath-

256 The Lion of Delos

ered admiringly around the substitute lion, elegant on its ridiculous trolley. I tried to go and join them but my feet stayed locked on the sandy path.

Nat came and stood within a yard of me, looking at me. He said, "You are very like her, you know." Those dark eyes filled with tears. I could only stare at him. Men swarmed around us, noisy, excited. They patted the new lion, laughing, admiring it, gesticulating in the Hellenic way. I saw them, but my eyes were drawn to Nat's face. I tried to break away, tried to look anywhere but at him. To think of anything but what he was saying. "I was in love with her," he said. "I loved her very dearly."

I cleared my throat, but nonetheless my voice came out rough and trembling. With laughter of a sort, and immense relief and, yes, hurt, I said, "She is not dead. She is in the hospital. Kriton did not manage to kill her. I suppose she was knocked out. The whole affair caused a big stir among a crowd of Greeks. I have been told she is all right."

He did not seem to take it in at first. He stared at me, and then an expression of relief and joy too deep for words came over his face. He turned away, as though he was unable to contain his emotions and went to stand by the real Naxian lion.

I could not just stand there. My footsteps took me to him, though I tried hard to walk away. I should have guessed he had known Lee. That, like all the other men, he liked me because he liked her. Of course he liked us both, but he really cared for her. Lee, the troublesome charmer. He heard my approach and turned. "I was half crazy with shock," he said, his eyes still moist. We stood a yard apart in silence. Then suddenly Nat added violently, "I am sorry to say this, but I must. If you had bloody well stayed in Athens as you were told, you would have been able to help us. This might never have happened."

"Nat!" I exclaimed, my head spinning. "Nat! Look at me, Nat! I am Virginia, the other twin. Not Lee. I am Virginia, Nat! Can't you see?"

I do not remember what happened then. Well, to be honest, I do remember, but there are some moments too private and precious to want to share with anyone, especially after one has already shared them with two helicopter loads of Greek police.

CHAPTER 28

"Thought I was dead?" echoed Lee, fingering a dreadful bruise beneath her right eye. "Well, I thought that myself for a while. It's quite an experience, being bashed up. You didn't exactly get away scot-free yourself, did you? That's a nasty graze on your face."

I sat down gingerly on the hard chair by her bed. "I counted fifteen bruises under the shower this morning. Then I gave up. But the important thing is that you're all right."

"Oh thanks. I say, what's this about Nat and Kriton?"

I smiled. I felt idiotically smug about that. "I told you Nat left me to buy the sandals and I was to go to his room. When I didn't turn up he came to look for me, and there in the boutique was a crowd of hysterical Greeks, and you lying on the floor covered with blood, wearing the same colored blouse I had on that day."

"Oh yes. I didn't tell you, did I? I always liked that red blouse of yours so I bought one just before I left home. Sorry. We did agree not to dress the same anymore, but . . ."

"Don't apologize. Poor you, you got more than your just desserts." Lee did look a mess, swathed in all those bandages and with patches of skin scraped off. "Anyway," I added vindictively, "I like to think Kriton got his— just desserts, I mean—on Delos, for what he did to Zoe." There was silence between us while we thought about her. "Can't you just imagine that scene in the boutique? Greeks at a genuine disaster! It must have been bedlam. No wonder Nat got it wrong."

"I am not certain I've got it right myself yet," said Lee. "Nat came searching for you because you didn't turn up at his room, and found me looking dead?"

"Not only did he assume you were dead—well, all these mad Greeks were shouting murder most foul—but he thought you were me, naturally, since he understood you to be safely in the clutches of the police in Athens. He didn't know your scatty habits, love."

Lee grimaced. "Don't frown at me. Didn't you dash hell-for-leather from England, with scarcely more than your carfare, when you thought I was in trouble?"

"Sure," I agreed warmly.

"Anyway, tell me the rest. They could not have fought it out dramatically as I lay there because you said it was on Delos that Nat beat Kriton up."

"Yes. Someone at the boutique pointed out the door to show Nat which way Kriton had gone, and Nat took off in a crazy chase. Of course, Kriton was bound to win it since he knows the town like the back of his hand. By the time Nat had finally drawn a blank and returned to the boutique, he found it locked and there was no one to tell him you had been pronounced alive and had been whipped off to the airport in great haste by the local police. He had absolutely no lead. He went out to Platis Gialos to meet the plane bringing his uncle and the Athens police, and went with them to Delos where he caught up with me. But thinking *I* was dead, he took me for you and gave me a piece of his mind."

"I'm sorry. I am only surprised he didn't go down to Kriton's caïque and bash him up there while his blood was still boiling."

I laughed. "It takes longer than that for a vengeful Greek, well, half Greek, to cool down. And anyway, they wouldn't let him. The police were determined to catch the thieves red-handed on Delos in the very act of swapping the lions. Nat's uncle took me for you, too, and scolded me for not keeping my—your—promise to stay in Athens like a good girl."

"Damn Greeks!" commented Lee. "They want all the fun for themselves."

"It was a pretty silly thing to do," I said severely.

She tried to draw her knees up under her chin and winced with pain. "Yes, well, I can be silly. You know that."

"If you had been in Athens when I disappeared you could have told the police where Irene's house was, and I would have been found and—"

"Yes. I am truly sorry. Ah, well. As you inferred, I got my just desserts." Lee shuddered. "I'll never forget walking into the boutique. Kriton knew I was me, because he knew you were safely tied up. He went berserk. I suppose it was too much for him, me appearing when he thought he had everything sewn up. Luckily, I was in good voice, and I had time to scream before he grabbed me." She shuddered again. "If those tourists and shop-keepers hadn't rushed in I would be in a morgue instead of this rather nice hospital. Lord, but my throat hurts."

She fingered it tenderly.

"If it is any comfort to you, I think Kriton is in considerably worse shape than you," I told her.

"And they caught everyone?"

"Absolutely everyone," I was happy to report. "Even Irene, pretending to be innocently asleep in her bed. And that mad American, who actually had the nerve to be on his yacht waiting for the lion. They seized the vessel and brought it in to Mykonos." I clapped my hands. "Oh, you never saw such excitement! Every man and woman and dog and cat on the island was there at the harbor," I added, laughing as I recalled the noisy, lively, colorful scene. "Then they brought Mr. Ghent ashore and all the crew, because they had to be flown from Platis Gialos to Athens. And, of course, Kriton and his gang. The noise! The commotion! What is it they say: *Two Greeks together constitute an argument; three, a revolution.* Well, there were thousands! They're marvelous, passionate people!" I exclaimed warmly.

Lee was looking at me critically with her head on one side. "What's all that hand-waving for?"

I laughed. It was true—I seemed to have picked up the Greek habit of using my hands when I became excited.

"I've something to tell you," I said confidentially.

My twin gave me a very cool look. "I'm not sure I want to hear it. He's Greek, isn't he?"

"Half. There is an English half, too," I pointed out defensively.

"Then the Greek half has the upper hand," Lee observed. "If it had not, he would have rushed in and cradled my poor limp form—thinking me was you—" she interjected ungrammatically, "in his arms."

"I don't think Nat would waste time on a lost cause," I murmured, looking mistily into the distance.

"You're dead right. I take it he took one look, saw the

red blouse, accepted what those hysterical people were shouting about Kriton murdering me, and then rushed off to wreak vengeance."

"They're a vengeful race," I explained. "They've been taking bashings, and bashing back, since before Christ. It's in their blood."

"Doesn't it scare you?" She watched me closely.

I thought for a moment. "In a way." But I found myself adding smugly, "It makes me feel safe, too."

We were busy with our own thoughts for a moment. A plump nurse bustled in bringing a carafe of water. Water like wine. I poured out a glass. "A drink for you?"

Lee seemed to be far away. "I was thinking of Taki Bajanis," she said. "Such an unhappy, unfortunate family!" Her eyes filled with tears. "That awful man who wanted to marry Katerini has changed his mind, and perhaps it's just as well."

"Was he awful?" I drank the water myself. It tasted ambrosial. But then, everything was wonderful today.

"Yes. He only wanted the money. She is a sweet girl. When the police get to thinking about what has happened to the family, perhaps they will temper justice with a bit of kindness. The Bajanis were kind to me," Lee said. "They were in a hell of a spot, and it was all Kriton's doing. It doesn't seem fair, somehow."

Gingerly, I touched the lump on my head. But perhaps I should forgive Mr. Bajanis for that, since he had, in the final analysis, saved my life. "He is going to achieve immortality of a kind," I said. "They seem to think his lion will go into a museum. Well, go on show somewhere, anyway."

"What a laugh!" She sobered, the fingers of her right hand playing on the splint of her broken arm. "Do you know, Nat is the first man friend of yours I didn't really care for. I suppose you know they make rotten husbands, the Greeks?"

"Sure." I was thinking indulgently that I might have fought to the last ditch too, if she had married first. We had, after all, been side by side for twenty-two years.

"Do you have to look quite so smug?" she asked irritably.

I tried to appear solemn and could not. "I am afraid so," I said apologetically.

"Oh well . . ." She shrugged. "I behaved badly. Coming here, I mean. It was yours, wasn't it? Greece."

"You found me a husband."

"*Me*! Oh Lord! I suppose I did. Well, if you have to marry him," she said at last, reluctantly, "I am sure I'll get to like him."

"God forbid!" I exclaimed.

Momentarily, Lee looked startled, and then we burst out laughing.

"Oh—well."

"Oh—well."